The People

of the Land

The Story of a Marriage

Bettye D. Grogan

Packaged by Pleasant Word, PO Box 428, Enumclaw, WA 98022. The views expressed or implied in this work do not necessarily reflect those of Pleasant Word. The author(s) is ultimately responsible for the design, content and editorial accuracy of this work.

ISBN 1-4141-0211-9
Library of Congress Catalog Card Number: 2004094013

To my family
Richard, Bruce and Rhonda, Barbara
and Steve

Rodney and Kim—and the "Grands"

Acknowledgements

This book would not have gone to print without the help of friends. Terri Parker spent many hours editing and proofreading, and advising me. Getting to the publisher would have been tough without her guidance. Marcie Blankenship offered many valuable suggestions based on her publishing experience. My fellow crafters at Hoptown Writers listened to my story from beginning to end and gave encouragement and support.

Thanks to my wonderful husband, Richard, who encourages me in whatever I do, and to my son, Bruce Coleson, who is always there for his mom. Gratitude goes to my sister, Mary, a brilliant writer, who for years has urged me on in my writing. And a special thanks to my daughter, Barbara Stoltz, who proudly takes my manuscripts to school for her co-workers to read.

Chapter One

She sat on the concrete bench in the park, shaded by the giant oak. There were bird droppings on one end of the seat, and she carefully arranged her skirts so that the folds of blue checks would not be soiled by the purple splatters. It was her favorite place to sit late in the afternoon.

Just as she breathed a sigh, he was there beside her on the bench.

"Hey, Bethie. What's new with you?"

She groaned inwardly even as she smiled at George Daniel. He was a classmate, a fellow graduate as of last night. They had grown up on the same block, gone to school together for twelve years. He was as familiar to her as her brother, Henry. She focused on the cowlick at the crown of his head that seemed to be always sticking up, even if his sandy-red hair was freshly combed. The sun had brought out the freckles on his ruddy face. It was a nice face with beautiful blue eyes. But George could be such a pest.

Now he was leaning forward, ready to ask the usual question. "Bethie, let's go somewhere tomorrow night, just you and me. We can go to a movie. Or I'll take you over to Nashville to that restaurant that you like so well. Come on."

She turned away slightly. "I don't think so, George."

"Why not?"

"Because I wouldn't be very good company," she said in a softer tone.

As she looked away from George, Brent's face flashed before her mind. She had a crush on Brent Thompson her whole senior year. He asked her out once. They went to the movies with another couple and had a good time. She waited for him to call her again. But he never did. She tried to hang around him at school, but he was always with someone else, someone in the popular crowd of cheerleaders and twirlers. It was obvious that he wasn't interested in her. But she kept the secret hope filed away in her heart that someday he would tire of them and look her way again.

Last night, at Sophie Rich's graduation party, she found out that Brent was moving away and would be going to school in California. That was about as far from Kentucky as you could get. It took the joy out of the gathering for her. And she was furious with herself for letting that get to her. After all, she knew there would never be anything between them. But she came home depressed, and that mood had hung over her all day.

She held up her face to the sun and closed her eyes. Soon it would be stifling hot, even as late as sunset. But this was May, and spring lingered with cooling showers like the one earlier in the day that blew in from the west and sent silver needles of rain that vanished in an hour, leaving the air languid with the aroma of flowers and damp earth. Despite the beauty around her, she felt vaguely uneasy in her own skin. She stretched her arms, needing to feel the tenseness in her shoulders release, and got up to walk to the iris beds where the lightly scented lavender blooms marked the entrance to the park.

Taking her silence as an invitation to stay and talk, George followed, telling her about his day. He proudly pulled a small ruby red jar from behind his back. "I brought you some of Granny's preserves. She had me picking berries all morning and capping them half the afternoon. I'm sick and tired of strawberries."

"Thanks." She took the jar. "Mom will be happy to get this."

He stayed in step beside her as she speeded up, planning to escape across the street to her own house. Twice he asked, "What did you do today?" before she answered.

"Oh, uh . . . nothing. Just rested. I'll be going to work at Bernstein's in a week when the ladies start taking their vacations." Bernstein's was a dress shop on the square. She began to walk a little faster.

The sun was sinking into the pink and mauve clouds like a giant red balloon. The breeze, scented with honeysuckle, ruffled the tree above them where the birds settled into their nests, preparing for the twilight. Folks had deserted their games and strolls for the evening meal. In the stillness she could tell that he had stopped walking.

He called her name softly. "Bethie?"

She hated it when he called her Bethie. Her name was Ellen Elizabeth Warren. Her family called her Beth most of the time. She wanted her friends to start calling her Liz after her ninth grade boyfriend told her that she looked like Elizabeth Taylor. Of course, she knew she didn't. The only resemblance to Elizabeth Taylor was the black hair that she kept long and tied back with a ribbon, refusing to give up her locks even though her friends had the new "poodle" cuts. She had neither the lavender blue eyes nor the delicate white skin of the star. Her eyes were plain brown and her skin a light olive, inherited from her Creole great-grandmother. So the nickname didn't stick; she remained plain Beth.

"Bethie?" He repeated his plea. "Come on. Go out with me."

She stopped. "George, did you know Marie Evans is just dying to date you? Why don't you ask her?"

"I don't want to go out with Marie. I just to go out with you."

She shook her head and took a step, aware that he was still behind her. Looking back, she saw the pleading in his eyes and felt herself weaken. Why not? It would be something to do. She shrugged and smiled a faint smile.

"All right, I'll go. But no fancy restaurant. Let's just have a burger or something and see a movie. Okay? I don't want you to waste a lot of money on me."

"Money is no object for you, Bethie. I'll pick you up about six. Is that okay?"

"Sure, George. Six is fine." She darted across the street, thinking how pleased her mother would be. She had wanted Beth to go out with George for a long time. Her father, before his death, wanted her to go to the community college and on to a state school. Her mother just wanted her to find a nice boy and get married. After all, isn't that what nice girls did in 1957?

Carefully she carried the strawberry jam with both hands as she climbed the stone steps. He watched her until she disappeared into the house, then raised his hands in a victory gesture.

Her mother stood in the cool hall, wiping her hands on a dishtowel. Petite, and tanned, her streaked gray hair stood up in frizzy curls from the dampness, and her dark eyes lit up at the sight of the jar of preserves.

"Where did you get that?"

"George's grandmother made them." She handed her the jar and started up the stairs.

"How lovely. Oh, I could use some help with dinner, Beth," Joan Warren said sternly.

"Okay." Beth followed her into the bright yellow kitchen.

"Peel the potatoes, please. So George found you, huh?"

"What? Oh, yeah. I was in the park."

"He said he was taking you to the movies tomorrow night," Joan Warren said, raising her eyebrows, a teasing expression on her round face.

"He told you that? That creep. He's so sure of himself. I ought to call him and tell him I won't go. Don't really want to anyway." Beth slung the peelings into the garbage can.

"Beth, what is the matter with you? George is nice, and you've known him all your life. He's a good boy with a good future. You know he'll inherit his grandfather's farm. Why are you always mooning after some boy you can't have?"

"That's just it!" Beth turned to face her mother in anger. "I've always known him. He's just like a brother, and he's almost as much of a pest as Henry. Why are you always trying to put us together? I ought to go to the university next fall. At least I'll get away from George and—everybody else."

"Now look here, young lady. You'll watch your mouth."

"I'm sorry," Beth said softly, returning to her potato paring. "I like George, I really do. He just gets on my nerves sometimes."

"Well, you ought to go out with him tomorrow night. If you don't, he'll be so disappointed. And you'll have fun, that is, if you let yourself." Joan sliced the potatoes and put the pan on to boil.

"Okay, I'll go," Beth sighed. Her mother beamed and squeezed her shoulders as she passed. She thought, as she wrestled the ham out of the fridge and began to slice it, that young girls didn't always know what they needed. A nice boy like George would make such a good husband for her daughter someday. Beth was too impressed with strangers. Always looking for someone different. Young girls needed guidance and protection from involvement with the wrong element. She would try and be more subtle in her efforts to bring Beth and George together. She could rest easy when Beth was safety married.

Beth, setting the table with the colorful dinnerware, was a million miles away in her thoughts. She would make her mother—and George—happy by going out with him this once. After that, she would find herself too busy with her job and her girlfriends. This would be the first—and last—real date with George.

Her husband's hand moved from under the sheet, seeking hers as it moved across his body to the edge of the hospital bed. She glanced up from her daydream at the motion and reached over to cover his bruised hand with hers.

"I'm here," she said, smiling.

"Were you napping?"

"No, I was awake, just wool-gathering."

"Thinking about what?" He turned himself painfully so he could see her face more clearly.

"Just looking back, remembering old times."

"We've had some good times, haven't we?"

"Yes," she whispered, as she kissed his hand and rested her cheek against it. "Such good times."

Chapter Two

They were sitting in Perry's Drug Store sipping cokes. It was Saturday night and the only night Perry's was open past six. The black leather booths were in the long passage between the fountain and display area and the pharmacy. Glass doors reached to the ceiling and held bottles and jars, many of which had been there for years. With no windows, it was cave-like and cozy. The only lights were the small lamps casting a yellow glow from the barrier dividing the booths. It was a favorite spot for students to skip class and hide out and smoke. Joe Perry knew them all, but he wouldn't rat on them unless they caused a ruckus.

"What did you think about the movie, Bethie?" George stirred his straw round the sides of the glass.

"I liked it. But I'm a Debbie Reynolds fan. You probably thought it was too sappy with all that singing."

"No. I liked it, too. Although I would have liked a war movie better. You know how us guys are. Are you sure you don't want something to eat?"

"No, thanks. You shouldn't have taken me to the Grill first. It was too expensive. But it sure was good. I'm still full."

"Grandpa pays me well when I help him. Plus I clean out Mr. Nelson's stable three times a week. So I'm doing okay. Don't worry about that." He reached across and took her hand. She let it rest in his. After all, it had been a fun date so far.

"What do you want to be, George? I mean what are your plans? You haven't said much about it at school."

"I'm not sure. I guess I'll take some classes this fall and keep on working for Grandpa. My grandmother would like me to go into law, but that doesn't interest me. You know I really love working on the farm. I love being outdoors, and I like dealing with the animals. Guess that sounds pretty boring, huh?"

Beth smiled. "Not to me. I love your grandparents' farm. And that old house is so pretty. Remember when we had our eighth grade hayride there? Your Grandpa had as much fun as we did. And your grandmother baked all those goodies for us. While we were gone on the wagon, Daddy built that big bonfire. We had so much fun that night."

"You miss your dad, don't you?"

"Yeah, I do. But you know what's so strange? When I dream about him, I can't see his face. Sometimes I wake up and look at the picture by my bed, just to remember what he looked like."

"It's been five years since the accident. You haven't forgotten. It's just that you don't see his face everyday."

"I guess so. I know it's been hard on Mom and Henry. Guess that's why Henry's such a brat sometimes. He needs a firmer hand than Mom's. But I'm glad for that last memory, you know? Who knew he would be killed two days later."

"That's when I fell for you, Bethie."

"Now, George,"

"Well, it was."

She leaned over the table and pulled his head closer. "You just need to go out with more girls, George. There are a half a dozen girls who'd love to go with you."

He pulled back. "I'll have you know that I've dated quite a few. While you were running around with Sophie and that crowd, I went out with lots of girls."

"Name one."

"Well, I dated Sara Jo for about two months. Then she wanted to go steady, and I backed off fast. I took Jenny to the senior banquet, as you know, since you were there with Charlie West. I didn't like Jenny much; she was so loud and crazy. She was fun for awhile, but it soon got on my nerves."

Beth laughed. Jenny was the class loudmouth and biggest gossip. "Well, you've been busier that I thought." She ran her hands down her waist, smoothed down her red skirt as she pulled both legs onto the seat.

They finished their cokes in silence. Joe Perry appeared from the pharmacy and stopped at their table.

"It's nine o'clock, kids. Time to close up." He picked up their glasses in one hand and swiped at the wet rings left on the marble top with his rag.

They went to the front to pay the bill. Joe Perry had been Beth's father's closest friend. He wouldn't let George pay for the cokes. "On the house," he said with a shrug. He never took any money for Beth's treats.

It had begun to sprinkle when they got outside. Lights were dimming up and down Main Street, and 'open' signs were being flipped over to read 'closed.' Clerks were hurrying to their cars, calling good-byes, happy to have a Sunday to look forward too. The neon signs made rainbow-like reflections in the wet street under their feet.

"You should have let me bring my car," he said, looking up.

"Oh, I love to walk in the rain. Anyway, it's barely sprinkling, and I sure won't melt."

"I like walking in the rain, too. But I just hate for you to go home all wet. What will your mother say?"

"Nothing. She knows me. I used to play in the rain all the time. I liked to walk down Sixth Street to the library. All those big trees made the street so gloomy and dark. I imagined that I was Nancy Drew, and there was something mysterious going on in some on those old houses."

He pulled her arm through his and they matched steps. "There probably was. Remember when Mrs. Fincher ran off with the car salesman? She was back as soon as he weaseled her out of her money."

"Yeah, I remember that. Mr. Fincher took her back. Nobody could figure that out. Must have been true love on his part."

"There is such a thing as true love, Bethie. Or do you believe that?"

"I'm not sure. So many people are getting divorced these days. It makes you wonder. Oh, I'm sorry, George. I forgot about your parents."

"It's okay. Mom's been gone so long. Dad and I never hear from her, except for the annual Christmas gift. She has called a time or two when she visits a friend here, but I've never been home at the time. Dad tells her what I've been doing, and she thanks him and hangs up. Strange, huh? But I would never want to live with her again, never. My dad and I are too close."

"Yeah, your dad's a great guy."

They walked along quietly with the mist falling on their faces, inhaling the aroma of the rain on warm blacktop. They looked in windows as they passed noting the flickering blue glares of the TV sets and guessing what programs were being watched in darkened living rooms. Too soon they rounded the corner and up the sidewalk to Beth's house.

"Well, Nancy Drew, here we are at your house. It looks mysterious, do you think we should investigate?"

"The only thing mysterious around here is where Henry manages to hide my things, and why Mother lets him get away with it." She rolled her eyes as they ran up the steps to the shelter of the porch.

She opened the screen and called, "I'm home." Then she turned to George. "It was a nice evening, George. Thanks. I had a real good time."

"Mind if we sit in the swing for a little while?" He quickly deposited himself there and was patting the other cushion for her. She sat down beside him, and they drifted back and forth listening to the rain gently falling.

Joan came out on the porch, pinning up stray bits of hair back into her bun.

"Umm! I had to come out and smell this rain. Nothing smells quite like spring rain. Hello, George. How are you?"

He stood until she sat down in the peeling brown wicker chair. "Fine, thank you, Mrs. Warren."

"And your folks, how are they?"

"All fit as a fiddle. Grandpa has arthritis, but doesn't let it slow him down much. Granny is doing fine, bossy as ever."

Joan smiled. "How about some cake? I just finished icing a German chocolate. It's still warm."

He started to say 'yes', but caught Beth's glare and answered, "No, Ma'am. We had a big supper and just had a coke. I'm fine."

"Well, I'll leave you then. Don't forget to lock up when you come in, Beth. Henry's over at Jimmy's house for the night, so it's just the two of us."

"Good night, Mom."

Joan closed the screen slowly, smiling. She was glad that Beth had gone on this date. She felt in her heart that there would be more dates to come. And maybe there would be a wedding someday.

As soon as Joan went in, George scooted closer and put his arm around Beth. She didn't argue. It was getting chilly, and his closeness felt warm. They talked for a few more minutes, but gradually the conversation began to die. The swinging made Beth sleepy, and she stifled a yawn. When the wind began to blow, they got up to take down the hanging baskets of geraniums.

"You'd better go, George. It's getting late, and it looks like we're going to have a storm."

"Must be that cold front Grandpa was predicting. I had a good time, Bethie. Thanks for going with me."

"I enjoyed it, too. Good night."

"Just one more thing. I need to do something that I've wanted to do for years." He pulled her to him and kissed her. She started to push away, but it was such a sweet tender kiss. She found herself returning it with fervor. When they broke apart, he kissed her lightly on the nose and was gone into the rain and wind. She watched him run to the end of the block and turn up his own sidewalk.

She locked the door and climbed the stairs to her room. Kicking off her shoes, she pulled down the window and put her forehead to the pane before closing the curtains. The wind was whistling around the eaves and the maple by her window was brushing against the screen.

Sitting down at her dressing table, she looked at herself in the mirror. Her curly hair had turned to frizz from the rain, and she was flushed and smiling. There was a sparkle in her brown eyes. On her date with Brent, she hadn't felt as relaxed nor had so much fun. She remembered that Brent never let her talk; he was so busy talking about himself. She touched her lips, feeling the kiss again in her mind. And who would have thought that George could kiss like that?

He was snoring, his cheeks slightly puffing as he exhaled; his face relaxed and turned away toward the wall. She moved stiffly from his bed where she had been sitting to the hard chair and tried to adjust the cushion so she could lay back. She didn't expect to sleep, anyway. In the morning they would know if the cancer was back and, if so, how much it had spread.

She wished she had asked their doctor to give her something to help her sleep. Her mind was churning in so many different directions. If the report was bad, she would need to call the girls. They would have to go back to Houston, and the endless tests and treatments that had left him so weak before. But the torture had been worth it. It had bought them five years. Five good years.

He was always upbeat, even when he was so sick. And he was optimistic now. She wanted to have the same faith that he had and fought against thinking the worst.

She settled herself as comfortably as possible in the chair, put her head back, and ran her hands through her salt and pepper hair. Pushing her worries and questions to the back of her consciousness, she took deep breaths. She would wash her mind with memories, memories of a lifetime together, the good times and the bad. She touched her lips, chapped from the dry hospital air, remembering, as she traced the outline of her mouth, the sweetness of that first kiss.

Chapter Three

She pulled on her heavy jacket, flipped the hood up around her curly hair, and braced herself to face the cold wind. The unexpected snow had begun to fall at the start of English class, and it blew in with such ferocity that the ground was covered in mere minutes. Classes were hurriedly called off and teachers and students were wrestling with books and briefcases, each in a rush to get home before the roads got treacherous.

As she opened the door, a blast of arctic air and stinging snow hit her in the face. She had on leather soled loafers, and she soon found out they were hazardous. As she ran down the steps, her feet slid out from under her, and she sat with a thud on the bottom step. A classmate gave her a hand up as he went by, so she carefully made the short walk to her car, taking baby steps and feeling the pain in her tailbone with every move.

Driving slowly and carefully, she inched out of the school parking lot and through town. Stores were closing up; only Perry's would stay open. Unlike the northern part of the United States, southerners are not prepared for heavy snows, and a few inches could paralyze a small town. The streets of Hartonville would be totally deserted by nightfall.

Her mind drifted back to class. She was disappointed that there wasn't time for her to read her paper before class broke up. Having written an essay on the disappearance of small country churches that were once so prevalent, she had researched and written what she hoped would earn her an A. Most of her writings did. She had always loved to write and was enjoying every minute of English 101.

She frowned as she skidded slightly and took her foot off the brake. The car righted itself, and she accelerated up the slight hill before turning in her driveway. She gave a sigh of relief as she turned off the motor, gathered her things, and plowed carefully up the steps. Stomping her feet, she pushed open the leaded glass door and dropped her books on the bench in the hall.

"Beth, I'm so glad you're home," Joan called over the upstairs banister. "I've been worried that you might have an accident coming home. The radio said classes were called off."

"Oh, I had an accident, all right." Beth rubbed her tailbone, which was still throbbing. "I slipped down the steps going to my car."

Joan came down the stairs with a worried face. "Are you really hurt? Do you think we need to have it checked?"

Beth laughed. "No, Mom. It'll be okay. My pride hurts worse than my rear. I am worried about George though. He wasn't in class, and when I talked to him last night, he was through with his paper. I wonder if he got sick or something. I think I'll put on my boots and walk down."

"Come and sit down, Honey," her mother pulled her into the living room to the flowered slip covered couch.

"What is it, Mom?" She began to feel nervous.

"Honey, George's grandfather died this morning. Bill called me about an hour and a half ago. He and George are at the farm with his grandmother."

"Oh, no." Beth jumped up and ran out into the hall. "I must go out there now. George loved his grandfather so much. He was such a good man and so good to everyone. I can't believe he's gone. How did he die?"

"Heart attack. He was going to check on the animals. Mrs. Daniel saw him fall, and she ran right out. She knew he was gone, but she called the ambulance. They got there at the same time Bill and George did, but it was too late."

Beth felt tears sting her eyes. She reached for her coat, releasing wet snow that splattered her shoes.

"No, Beth." Joan took the coat away and hung it back on the hall tree. "Look out there. It's coming down even harder now. I don't want you taking the risk of driving down that crooked road in this weather. The radio was warning folks to stay off the roads unless it's an emergency."

"This is an emergency," Beth argued. At the same time she saw the foolishness of going out in the storm. Opening the door a crack, she could see that the wind had calmed, but the huge wet flakes were falling so fast there was practically no visibility.

"I'll call. At least I can talk to him."

"Yes, call, Honey. I'll fix you a bite of lunch while you're talking. How about a cup of coffee now? I just made some. No, sit down, and I'll bring it to you." Joan turned her daughter back toward the living room and set her down.

Beth looked up the number of the farm and dialed. George answered on the third ring.

"George, Mom just told me. I'm so sorry. I wanted to drive out, but it's so bad I'm afraid of getting stuck. How are you? And how are your grandmother and your dad?"

"In shock, really. Granny just can't sit still. She's packing a few things now. It'll hit her soon enough, and when it does, it'll be hard for her. Dad's taking it badly. Oh, it's so good to hear your voice. You're right about not getting out. I don't want you on this road; it's really slick."

"Was he already gone when you got to the hospital?" She took the mug of coffee from Joan and touched it to her cheek, needing its warmth.

"Yeah. I think he was gone when he hit the ground. When we left the hospital, the snow started coming down, and by the time we got back here, we could hardly get up the drive. As soon as we check the cattle, we're going to bring Granny to our house. She doesn't want to leave, but it will be closer to the—the funeral home and all the places we'll have to go. Besides, you know the electricity will probably go out here. I'm surprised it hasn't gone out already."

"I wish I was there to help you."

"Come down when we get back to our house. We should be home in a couple of hours if we can make it back in."

"Well, I'll let you go. I'll see you all when you get home. Please drive carefully."

"Thanks for calling. I'm sorry that I couldn't have been the one to tell you, but you left early this morning."

"I wish I'd been home. But you go and help your grandmother now, and I'll see you later. I love you, George."

There was a moment of surprise for both of them. In the nine months they had dated, she had not said those words though George had said them often.

"Thanks, Sweetheart. I love you, too."

As she replaced the receiver, a flush of warmth rose to the roots of her hair. She did love George. The sadness of loss was quickly replaced with the joy of that realization. She was still smiling when her mother called her to lunch.

They were just sitting down to a bowl of soup when Henry came crashing through the back door, slinging snow across the floor as he threw his coat over a chair.

"Hang that up, Henry," his mother said sternly. Beth blinked. She usually talked so gently to Henry. He obediently picked it up and took it to the hall tree without argument. Passing Beth's chair, he put his hand on her shoulder.

"I heard about George's grandfather." He gave her a comforting pat as his mother poured his bowl of soup. "I'm sorry, Beth."

She smiled back. 'Sometimes,' she thought, 'he's not so bad.' She watched him inhale his lunch with all the vigor of a thirteen year old, his red head practically in his bowl.

"I've never seen snow like this," he said excitedly, as he wiped his mouth. "I'm getting the sled out of the garage. Boy, will we have fun on Crider's Hill. It should be good and slick."

"Well, wait until it slows down before you go out," Joan said. "You couldn't find your way home right now as hard as it's snowing."

Beth cleaned up lunch things while her mother prepared casseroles to take to George's house. Time seemed to drag. Finally, the snow lightened up and became finer and icy. Standing at the front window, she saw Bill Daniel's car as it made its way to the house on the corner.

"They're home," she called to her mother. Joan put the dishes into a picnic basket, and they donned their coats and gloves. Henry was already shoveling the sidewalk along with his buddy, Jimmy, stopping occasionally to have a snowball fight. They respectfully stopped their war while Beth and Joan crept slowly down the steps and into the street, carefully clutching their dishes against their coats.

George opened the door as they came up the steps. His grandmother's suitcases were still in the hall, and Bill had gone to the basement to stoke up the furnace. Joan took the food into the kitchen and unloaded it while George took Beth into the living room where his grandmother sat in front of the fire.

"Beth. It's so good to see you. Thank you for coming." Her usually sharp blue eyes looked cloudy with grief and confusion as she took Beth's hand and pulled her down beside her.

"Mrs. Daniel, I'm so sorry. It's so hard to believe he's gone." She took the work-worn hand into hers and touched it to her face. Mrs. Daniel sighed, and a tear made its way down the tracks in her cheeks.

"We had almost fifty years together, Beth. He went the way he would want to go. He never was very sick in his whole life. He always did just what he wanted, ate what he wanted, and worked hard. So he had a good life. God has been very good to us." The tears came faster, and Beth got up to let her mother give comfort.

She walked to where George stood with his father. Bill gave Beth a hug and went to sit with Joan and his mother leaving Beth and George alone.

"Let's take Granny's things into the bedroom." They each picked up a bag and went down the hall to the cavernous bedroom off the kitchen. The room was plain, lacking a woman's touch, but neat. They put the bags on the bed and opened them.

"Granny will want to put her things away," George said, as he put his arms around Beth. She clung to him, feeling his shoulders shake with sobs, murmuring softly to him until he gained control. She pulled him to the end of the bed and they sat, hand in hand.

"Have the arrangements been made?"

"Yeah. Mr. Combs has the body. He's done our funerals for years. Services will be Thursday at ten at the church. Visitation Wednesday night, of course. Gosh, I still can't believe we're here talking about Grandpa's funeral. He always seemed indestructible."

"I know. And this weather makes it doubly difficult to deal with." She rubbed her hand across the pebbly chenille spread. "Do you think your grandmother will move in here with you and your dad?"

"Probably. Unless we move in with her. I know Dad doesn't want to give up his job with the post office to farm. That leaves me, I guess. I had really gotten into history and thought that I just might like to teach it someday. But someone has to work the farm."

"There are plenty of men who can do that, George. Don't give up any of your plans."

"I know. But I love that farm, and I want to be the one to run it, at least, as best I can. Grandpa had such good help in Charlie and Wade. I know they will help me just like they helped him. No, I'm not giving up anything. I'll be getting what I've always wanted."

"Do you think you'll still go to school?"

"I'll finish out the semester and see how it goes. I had this idea coming home. It's not a new idea, I just didn't think about bringing it up this soon. Marry me. Marry me and we'll live on the farm. We'll make it into a money-making venture and raise lots of little farmers."

Beth laughed, but became solemn as she saw the sincerity in his face. "We're too young, George," she said, smoothing back his ruffled hair. "I have school to finish. This is just our first year at college. We have so much time to think about that."

He looked so disappointed that she regretted her blunt refusal. She took his hand. "This isn't the time to talk about this. You're feeling too many emotions now to think ahead. But I promise to think about it, and later, when your family gets back to normal—at least as normal as it can be without Grandpa—we'll talk more about it. Okay?"

He pulled her to him and kissed her hard. "Okay. But I don't want to wait, Bethie. I've loved you all my life. Being young doesn't matter if you've always loved a person." They held each other until Bill came in with Granny, and they broke apart.

The weather cleared in time for the funeral. The snow had begun to melt under a bright January sun, making puddles of water among the dirty piles of snow. The small church was filled to overflowing with friends. Beth had always thought of Bill and George as being rather reclusive. But the outpouring of the community was overwhelming, showing just how many friends the Daniels had. The minister joked about Grandpa's great sense of humor, read from Romans 8, and later, in the cold clear morning air, they laid George Wilford Daniel to rest with kind words, as befitting a good and honest man.

The house was full after the funeral. So many friends came and were asked to stay for lunch. There was laughter amid the tears. Beth was accepted as one of the family, and it made her feel a special bond that pulled her more closely into the Daniels' circle. She and Joan and even Henry stayed to serve friends and family from the dozens of dishes that had been brought in. As people began to leave, they began the clean up. Henry washed dishes, as Beth and Joan emptied the remains of the dishes into smaller containers. There was enough food left to last for days.

"I'm impressed, Henry," Beth teased her brother. "I didn't know you could wash dishes. Haven't seen you doing much of it at home."

He flicked suds at her. "Don't get used to it. That's your job since you're a girl. I'm just doing this for George, since he'll be my brother-in-law one of these days. Have to stay on his good side." He winked wickedly, his dark eyes sparkling.

Beth blushed under her mother's sharp gaze. When the kitchen was clean, they said good-bye to Granny and Bill Daniel. Granny had insisted that they take a dish home for their supper since there was so much food. Joan went ahead, Henry followed carrying a chicken casserole, and George and Beth walked behind.

"Thanks for everything, Bethie. You've been such a help. Granny really loves you, you know."

"And I've loved her since eighth grade. Now you all need to get a good nap this afternoon and rest up."

"Dad insisted Granny go rest, but chances are she won't stay down long. She doesn't feel at home at our house yet. It'll take time for that. We'll take her back and forth until she decides if she really wants to move in with us or stay on the farm."

"By herself? It'll be lonely for her, especially during the cold weather with not so much to do. But that's home to her."

"That could be our home, too, Bethie. I can't think of anything else except marrying you and moving out there. I stayed awake half the night thinking about Grandpa—and you. He would be so happy if he knew that you and I were carrying on the Daniel tradition, keeping the farm in the family."

They climbed the steps to her house in silence. The warmth of the ties of friends and family had touched Beth deeply. Could they really make a go of it? She had come to care for him so much. Living on the farm together, making a success of it, and raising children—could that really be her life's work? Today it seemed like the right thing to do. She turned to George as he opened the door for her.

"Yes, George."

"Yes?" his eyes opened wide as he grabbed her hands.

"Yes, I'll marry you. But let's don't say anything for awhile until things settle down. Then we'll tell our folks."

He enveloped her, holding her so tightly she could hardly breathe. Pulling away to catch her breath, she added, "on one condition."

"Anything," he said softly.

"You will break this habit of calling me "Bethie." You know I never did like it."

"It's always been my pet name for you. I didn't realize it bothered you. Tell you what; I'll only call you that during our most—ah—intimate moments. How's that?" He grinned and nuzzled her ear.

"Deal," she said, shakily, not wanting to pull away now.

"When? When will you marry me, my darling Beth?"

"In May, George. In May."

From the living room window, Joan watched them as she pulled off her scarf and gloves. She knew there would soon be a wedding for Beth and George. She was pleased; pleased that Beth hadn't insisted on going to the university; pleased that she was dating George steadily. To see her daughter in a happy marriage would be a dream come true. But why was it that she felt lonely already?

Chapter Four

*H*enry banged on her bedroom door like a madman.

"Get up! Get up! George has called off the wedding so we're going to eat wedding cake for breakfast." He cackled at his little joke until Joan yelled from her bedroom.

"Henry! You stop that right now! I wanted your sister to sleep late this morning. What are you doing up this early?"

"I'm excited, Mom," he said as she came stomping from her room, tying her robe around her. "I've never been in a wedding before. So far it's been pretty dull. Thought I'd add a little excitement."

"Henry," Beth called groggily through her closed door. "Go spread your excitement somewhere else." The thump of a shoe flung against her door punctuated her displeasure.

"You need something to do," Joan told Henry, grabbing his arm. "Come with me. I'll find you a job."

"Oh, crap. I don't want a job."

"Watch your mouth!"

Beth lay still, listening to their argument fade. She hadn't really been asleep, just dozing and waking up every few minutes as she had all night. Pre-wedding jitters, she told herself.

Rising, she put on her seersucker robe. It was worn thin at the elbows and frayed at the hem. From now on she would wear her nice new ones. But today she would revel in the comfort of the familiar.

She kneeled on the window seat and opened her curtains. A perfect May morning sent sunrays dancing into her pink painted room. The grass was glistening, and she could see tracks in the dew where Mr. Gary had crossed the yard when he brought the milk. She traced her soon-to-be new name, Beth Daniel, on the windowpane as she listened to the morning sounds of her waking street. A dog barked to be let back inside, and she heard the familiar squeak of Henry's bicycle as he rode down the street. She breathed in the aroma of bacon frying and coffee perking. Pulling in her head, she realized the coffee aroma was from their kitchen.

She turned to the closet. Hanging from the door facing was her dress. It was not her dream dress, but her mother's wedding dress. She had found THE dress at Bernstein's. With her discount as part time help, she could have gotten it at a very reasonable price. But the expression on her mother's face kept her from insisting on buying it. Joan wanted her to wear her own dress so badly, even though she never said anything. She just got the dress from the attic and hung it up for Beth to look at. Not wanting to hurt her mother's feelings, Beth had told her that she preferred that dress to the new one. Joan was so excited about passing the dress down, she was glad that she had swallowed her own disappointment.

They had to make it over somewhat. It had aged to a warm ivory, and they couldn't change that. But they had remodeled the too puffy sleeves and let out the darts to fit Beth's more ample figure. Ivory lace had been applied to soften the starkness of the plain satin, and Joan had hand-sewed pearls in the lace. The result was a lovely tea length dress, simple, but elegant. Beth chose to marry in a quiet ceremony in her home, so she dispensed with the veil and instead chose a picture hat with long lace and ribbon streamers.

As she viewed it with a critical eye, she felt a cold wave of fear sweep over her from head to foot. Shakily, she sat back on the bed. She felt the same rush of terror at the rehearsal the night before, but she tried to ignore it and carry on with her brightest smile. She couldn't let George know that she was having doubts. Her heart was pounding so fast she was afraid she might faint.

Flinging herself back against the pillows, she willed herself to shape up. "It's my wedding day, and brides get these scary feelings—it's normal," she told the inner Beth, who was breathing deeply to avoid sheer panic. "Food," she said aloud. "I need food."

The knock on the door made her jump.

"Good morning. Sorry Henry woke you up. It's a glorious day out there—a perfect day for your wedding." Joan smiled as she shooed her daughter off the bed to make it up. Beth helped her spread the blue and pink quilt and plump up the matching pillows.

"Now, let's go down and have coffee and donuts. I sent Henry to the bakery, and he should be back in a minute. Since that's your favorite breakfast and your last one at home, I figured we'll have our own little celebration." Joan beamed as she laid the suitcase on the bed and opened it. "Then we'll pack your things."

Beth stared into the bag as tears began to flow down her face. She turned to hide them, wiping at them furiously with her hands.

"Why, Beth, what's wrong?" Joan turned her daughter to face her. "Are you having the jitters? Don't worry, Honey. That's normal." She hugged Beth who stood stiffly, hands to her sides.

"No, Mom. That's not it. I don't think I'm ready. I'm not even sure if I really love George."

"Of course, you do. You know you do. Now dry your eyes and let's go down and put something in your stomach. You haven't eaten much lately. How about if I fix eggs? Maybe you need more than donuts." She reached for the tissues and handed one to Beth.

She blew her nose and let herself be led down the stairs to the kitchen. Pouring two cups of coffee, Joan placed them on the table just as Henry came in with a bag of donuts in one hand and a huge pastry, half eaten, in the other.

"Boy, these are good," he sat the sack on the table and disappeared before his mother could think of something else for him to do.

They drank in silence at first, nibbling at the sweet treats and Beth began to feel better. Then they talked about old times, and managed to laugh, even though they both hid heavy hearts that felt the passing of those years of innocence. The phone broke their interlude of remembrance.

"Good morning, my beautiful bride."

"Good morning. And goodbye. I don't have time to talk to you until about four this afternoon."

He laughed. "Okay. I just wanted to say I love you."

"I love you, too. Now hang up so I can be about my business." She blew a kiss into the phone and hung up, feeling a little of the fear creep back into her head. But Joan took her hand and led her up the stairs where they spent an hour packing her trousseau.

The day went by in a blur. Mrs. Nickols and her husband came at two and wrestled her harp into place in the living room. Joan had wanted Beth's cousin, Mary Nell to play the piano, but Beth had put her foot down. Mary Nell was fifteen and not a good pianist, and she had her heart set on Mrs. Nickols playing the harp. She had asked Mary Nell to help serve the cake and punch instead. Sophie would be her maid of honor.

The living room had garden flowers on every table, and the altar in front of the fireplace was banked with borrowed ferns. The mantel held tiers of candles sitting on folds of tulle that draped into wide bows. Henry had placed candles in the windows after Joan had carefully pinned back the drapes. Joan and Beth had tacked up swags of tulle around the beautiful front door and the stairs and placed baskets of flowers on each side of the last step. The effect was homey and lovely.

In the dining room the cake stood on a crystal pedestal that had been in the family for years, a simple three tiered cake with an accompanying sheet cake iced in chocolate. The heirloom lace cloth draped the table, and Joan had laid out the best china and polished up her own mother's silver. At the last minute, Henry brought in straight chairs borrowed from the funeral home for the guests. The stage was set.

Sophie came flying into Beth's room around three.

"Sorry I'm late," she said, hanging her yellow dress beside Beth's. She grabbed her friend's hands and danced her around the room. "This is the day, Beth. Your wedding day. Are you as excited as I am?'"

Beth returned her hug. "I'm so happy that you're my maid of honor. I love you, you crazy girl. Just promise me that you'll come out to the farm to see me. Don't let me die on the vine out there missing my best friend."

"Oh, silly, I'll be out there so much George will be running me off." She tossed her blond curly bob. "Now, help me dress, and then we'll concentrate on you."

As Sophie buttoned up the many tiny buttons on the back of her dress, Beth could hear Mrs. Nickols warming up on her harp. She could hear Joan greeting Aunt Mary and Uncle Paul, Bill, Granny, and, finally, George. The melodious voice of the minister greeting the neighbors, who had known both George and Beth since they were babies, rose above the music.

Slipping into her shoes, she let Sophie position the hat on her dark hair. Not liking the beauty parlor set her mother had insisted on that morning, she removed the hat and Sophie brushed furiously to get it back into her own style. Satisfied, she again put on the hat and pulled her curls toward her face.

"Now, that looks more like you," Sophie remarked just as Joan rushed in to tell them it was time. They both looked approvingly at the reflection of the bride in the long mirror.

She looked beautiful. Even she realized it through the haze of nerves that made her hands so shaky. The hat framed her oval face. The sweetheart neckline of the ivory dress brought out the olive in her skin, and the princess lines complimented her small waist. The pearls that lay at her throat were old, like the dress, and they shone with their own luster.

"You are beautiful." Joan brushed away a tear as she hugged her daughter. "Smile, honey—that's better. Now do you feel ready? Henry is here to take you down."

Beth nodded numbly, taking Henry's arm and giving her maid-of-honor a quick kiss on the cheek before Sophie preceded her to the stairs. Joan waited for her brother, Uncle Paul, to seat Granny first, then her. A smiling Sophie floated down the steps and took her place at the altar. Then the strains of The Wedding March rang through the house.

"This is it, Sis," Henry said, feeling very important in his dark suit. "Are you ready?"

Beth nodded and gave his arm a little squeeze. As they descended the steps, she looked at the small presence as they turned to watch her arrival. Granny was lovely in her pale blue dress. The smiling faces of friends and neighbors looked up at her with admiration. Her eyes took in each one: the minister, Bill, his son's best man, and a nervous looking George. Her George was nervous, too. She felt calmness pass over her, and she smiled radiantly at him. He broke out in a grin from ear to ear. Suddenly, happiness flowed over her very being. This was the right thing to do, to marry this wonderful young man.

As she passed from Henry's hands to George's, they looked at each other with such adoration that sniffles were heard before the timeless words were even uttered. They stumbled through their vows, and by the time the traditional ceremony was over, they were trying to hold back their giggles. Then when George kissed his bride, he grabbed her so fiercely that her hat fell off, sending Sophie into unsuppressed laughter and the audience into happy applause.

The reception went by like a dream, in which they moved and greeted and smiled—and too soon it was over. With a parting hug from Granny, her mother, and Bill, in a shower of rice, they were off.

Later, in their hotel room, prior to leaving on their honeymoon in the mountains the next day, they lay side by side on the big bed, reliving the ceremony and reception. Beth still wore her going away dress and George was still in his suit.

"Henry did good," George observed. "I kept expecting him to pull out a rubber snake or something to liven things up."

She laughed. "I would have killed him if he had. Did you see Cousin Mary Nell spill punch all over the minister's suit? I could have died. I'm glad I didn't ask her to play the piano. She would have hit so many sour notes that everyone would have left holding their ears."

"The harp was beautiful, just perfect. In fact, everything was beautiful." He rolled over and took her in his arms. "But you know what? You were gorgeous, in fact, the loveliest bride in the whole world."

"Really?' She looked at him happily. "Did you like the dress? I mean, it was a little old fashioned, but it meant so much to Mother that I wear it."

"It was perfect for you. You couldn't have been lovelier if you had on a designer dress from New York."

She buried her face in his collar and, to her horror, she burst into tears.

"What's wrong, Honey?"

"I don't know," she sobbed. She tried to stop, but found she had no control, so the tears flowed along with a maddening case of the hiccups. He held her until she became quiet and pulled away from his tear sodden suit.

"Are you okay?" he asked in concern.

"I'm sorry. I don't know what's the matter with me." She accepted his handkerchief, mopped her face, and blew her nose.

"Look, Honey," he said, slowly choosing his words. "If it's our wedding night that's bothering you, I can wait. Hey, I can wait as long as you need me to. I am so happy that you're finally my wife. That's all that matters, really. We can just go to sleep if you're worn out. There will be years and years to make love. Don't let that scare you."

"I'm not scared of that. Are you?"

"A little. I'm not experienced, Beth. I want to make you happy, that's all."

She stood up and pulled him to his feet, ashamed of her crying jag. She was a wife now, and a lucky one at that.

"Husband, you always make me happy. And I definitely don't want to go sleep. I have a gorgeous new white nightie that I want you to see. Since we have so much to learn about each other, I'd like to start right now, if you don't mind. It could take us all night, possibly longer."

He grinned a slow grin, "Oh, Bethie. I love you more than you'll ever know."

Joan hung up her dress and pulled her hair down from atop her head, dropping the pins on the edge of the sink. She was satisfied that she had looked good in her pale gray dress with her hair done up in curls. Also she was satisfied that it had been a beautiful, if small, wedding, one that Beth would always remember. The music was lovely, the house looked beautiful, everything went smoothly.

Henry was in his room; she could hear his radio playing. He was a mess sometimes, but he was easier to raise than her daughter had been with her teen-age moods. She would miss Beth, though. But at least she was close by.

She looked up toward the ceiling with a sigh. "I wish you could have seen your lovely daughter, Carl. She looked so beautiful in my dress. But maybe you did see her. Do you see me now? Do you know how much I miss you tonight?" Sighing, she reached for her robe and crept down to the porch. She sat in the swing looking at the stars blinking in the inky sky, remembering her own wedding and the handsome man who had been taken from her too soon.

Chapter Five

Granny swiped at the sweat running down her brow with the back of her hand and sighed as she set the burnt cake on a trivet.

"That child," she murmured. "She went right out and left this cake baking and forgot about it. Now look at all that sugar and butter wasted." She shook her head in disgust. She turned from the charred mess and lifted the lid of the large pot containing roast and vegetables. "Well, she hasn't messed that up," she said to herself as she gave the pot a stir. Taking her iced tea in one hand, she opened the back door to let in fresh air and let out the burned odor, in spite of the window air conditioner rumbling in the window.

George and Beth had been married three months. They had been so sweet in insisting that she stay in her home, even though the farm was really George's now.

"It's your home, Granny," George had said. "We thank you for letting us live here. We both want you here with us, if you can put up with us, that is. We'll try not to be nuisances. You can do just like you always did, except that Beth can help you with the cooking, canning, and all."

She loved Beth but was skeptical about how much help she would be with the cooking and the canning. Granny pulled up a chair on the back porch, set her tea on the wide arm, and put her feet up on the rail. Pushing back her damp hair that escaped from its pins, she took in the familiar view. The farm spread out like a fan, with the barn and equipment sheds in the middle, fields on the side. Behind it lay the rocky hills that shimmered like a blue haze in the early autumn heat and humidity.

Beth came running from the barn, arms flying, dark hair streaming behind her. She hit the porch step with her toe and yelped, grabbed her foot, and dropped to the step with a moan.

"I took the cake out," Granny said softly.

"Oh, is it burned?" Beth pulled her foot from her sandals and rubbed the throbbing toe. Granny nodded, looking off in the distance, and Beth slapped her bare tanned leg with her palm.

"I'm so sorry. I went out to the barn for just a minute to play with the kittens and forgot about the time. I'll go in and clean it up."

"Beth, sit and talk to me."

"Oh—er—okay." Beth pulled up another chair and put her feet by Granny's on the rail.

"Honey, wouldn't you do better if you were on your own? I think I get on your nerves sometimes, especially in the kitchen. I know you are a pretty good cook, but lately you've burned dinner twice. I try to stay out of your way, but I find myself going behind you and turning things off and on for you. Am I bothering you? You know you can tell me the truth and it won't hurt my feelings."

Beth stared at her feet for a minute before she answered. "Granny, I'm sorry. I guess I have a lot to learn. I always helped Mom cook, but she got it all to the table at the same time. Guess I just can't get the hang of it. Be patient with me?"

Granny smiled and patted her hand. "You'll get the hang of it, Honey. Just keep trying."

George parked the tractor under the big shed and strode up to the porch.

"Well, here are my two ladies just loafing when they should be cooking for a hungry man." He took off his sweaty cap and ran his fingers through his sandy hair. "I thought I'd never get that hole in the fence fixed. That cow really tore it up when she got hung. I'm glad Wade took care of the milking for me so I could get that chore done." He gave Beth a quick kiss and she followed him into the kitchen. Washing his hands at the sink, he sniffed.

"What's that smell?"

"I burned the cake," Beth answered, biting her lip as she picked at the remains of the spice cake.

"Beth. That's the second cake you've burned, Honey. What did you do, forget you put it in the oven?"

"Yep." She handed him a towel, feeling regret at the sight of George's soulful gaze at the remains of his favorite dessert. "Sorry. I got carried away with the new kittens. They're so cute and cuddly. But the roast is okay. I fixed it the way you like it, with gravy and potatoes and carrots."

"Yum. I could eat a horse. We'll have jelly and biscuits for dessert. That'll be okay."

"Biscuits!" she exclaimed. "I forgot to make the biscuits. It won't take me but a jiffy. You pour yourself some tea and keep Granny company on the porch. I'll have it all ready in a snap."

He pulled her in his arms. "Are you okay? Is it Granny? Does she bother you? She's so used to doing the cooking, and it's hard for her not to help."

"No," she said quickly. "It's okay, it's just me. I've got a lot to learn about being a farm wife." She just couldn't say that indeed Granny got in her way sometimes, that two women in the same kitchen was one too many.

"And you're doing a fantastic job," he said, kissing her on the tip of her nose. "On the wife part anyway." He dodged as she swatted him with the towel.

Getting his glass of tea, he walked out on the porch and sat in the chair opposite Granny.

"Everything okay?"

Granny took a deep breath and blinked unexpected tears. "No, George. I think Beth would do better if I weren't around."

"Now, Granny. I don't think that's so."

"You newlyweds need to start life by yourselves, not with an old lady around who's set in her ways. I think I make her nervous sometimes."

"We want you here," George protested. "And you'll have to remember that Beth and I both are swimming in strange water. She's never managed a household, and I've never been a full time farmer before. We'll grow into our jobs," he said, wisely.

"Oh, George. You're so grown up. Your grandfather would be so proud of you. And that's another thing. I'm afraid that I'm moody sometimes, missing him like I do. I still don't feel like myself. I may never . . ."

"Yes, you will. You're tough, remember? You lived through the Depression. You lost two babies before you had Dad. And you helped raise me—that was some job. And you never once got down so far you didn't bounce back."

"How do you know all this, Mr. Wise Man?" she eyed him over the rim of her glasses.

"Dad told me when I was just a little guy. Now enough of this nonsense. Let's go in and help Beth get this food on the table before I starve right here on this porch." He gave his grandmother a kiss on her leathery cheek and tasted her tears.

Later that evening, undressing for bed, Beth was quiet. Sensing her disappointment over the dinner, he pulled her down on the bed and nuzzled her neck.

"You're doing great, Beth. Now, don't get upset over every little thing."

"I'm not, George. It's just that I can't seem to do anything right. I keep trying to be like Granny, but I'm clumsy, forgetful . . ."

"That's the trouble. You're trying to be just like Granny, and she's been at it a lot longer than you have. She had to learn sometime, too. Look at me. Wade and Charlie have to remind me about things that I should be doing all the time. I don't take it personally. In fact, I'm glad they do."

"I don't take it personally, George. I just feel inadequate, that's all. I'm a fair housekeeper, but a terrible cook."

"You are not a terrible cook! You'll get better at it with time. Meanwhile . . ." He kissed her gently.

"Oh, there's something else, George, I wanted to tell you last night, but Wade came in and you all talked until late." She pulled up, leaning on her elbow, and added shakily, "I may be pregnant."

"What?" he sat up quickly.

"I'm running late."

"It's too soon," he said as he rose from the bed. "We agreed we'd wait at least a year before we even thought about starting a family."

"I know, Honey. But you remember . . ."

"Yes, I remember," he finished. "That was my fault."

"Maybe I'm not. It's just had me kinda worried."

He could see her eyes were glittering with unshed tears.

"Oh, Sweetheart. If you are, that's great. We'll just have a baby sooner, that's all. Me, a father. I just didn't expect it to happen so quick."

She tried to smile, pushing back the giant wave of resentment that rose from the pit of her stomach. In the movies, the happy husband took the wife in his arms and covered her face with kisses. She suddenly felt let down and tired.

"Well, we'll wait a couple of weeks and then I'll go to the doctor. Right now, I just want to close my eyes and sleep."

"Whatever happens, Beth, it'll be okay. I love you, Sweetie."

"Yeah, I know. I love you, too, George." She turned out the light and cuddled up next to him. In less than a minute, George was snoring. Beth lay quietly for awhile, feeling sad and lonely. Throwing back the sheet, she got up and slipped out to the living room. Turning on the light, she stretched out on the couch and picked up a magazine.

She couldn't concentrate, so she turned out the light and stared out the window. The moon was full, leaving long shadows of the big oaks on the lawn. The Irish setter moved like a specter up the walk and settled on the front porch. A barn owl called "whooo" from the top of the pine tree. The light from Granny's upstairs window went out taking its warmth and leaving a lonely landscape. Not many cars cast their headlights down the country road this late. She missed the streetlights of her old neighborhood. Suddenly, she felt homesick for her house, her comfortable room, and her mother, even Henry.

She hadn't wanted to be pregnant yet, but she knew she probably was. Something felt vaguely different about her body. She patted her flat stomach and imagined it full and round. Tucking her chin down, she closed her eyes and rubbed her fingers across her gown.

"Are you in there, Baby? If you are, it's okay. I'll love you and take care of you. Your daddy will, too. He's just in shock, and he's tired from trying to be like his grandfather and running this farm. But we want you; we do. You'll like it here. And you'll love Granny. She'll be so happy. You'll give her something to look forward to. Maybe that's why God is sending you to us right now."

She smiled at herself. "I guess I need you, too. I like talking to you already. I promise to talk to you every day so you'll know what to expect when you get here. But I'd better get you into bed now. We need our sleep, don't we?"

"Who are you talking to?" George appeared in the shadows, yawning and rubbing his tousled hair.

"My . . . our baby. I just wanted him—or her—to know we love him, even if he is a surprise."

"Come here." He opened his arms, and she fell into them, holding on to him with all her might.

Chapter Six

Felicia Joan Daniel arrived on the scene on April Fool's Day, 1959, just as twilight settled into a moonlit night. She came into a world of excited parents, grandparents, and a delighted great-grandmother. But the biggest surprise of all was Henry's devotion to the tiny baby. No one expected the fourteen-year-old with the embarrassing soprano to bass voice to be enthralled with every move she made. He was at the farm every time anyone else was going there, leaving behind his baseball buddies to practice without him.

His devotion began the day she was born. He was helping George on a Thursday afternoon after school, and they were working the back field, getting ready to plant corn. He had become adept at farm work and delighted in helping George, who was fast becoming his hero.

Inside the house, Granny was taking a late nap and Beth and Sophie were having a cup of hot tea in the living room.

"I'm a little jealous of you," Beth told Sophie, as she pulled her swollen feet under her, resting her stomach on the throw pillow.

"Why, for goodness sake? You have it all, nice house, baby on the way, adoring husband. What more could you want?" Sophie reached for one of Granny's oatmeal cookies. "Me, I'm only half through with college, and if I do decide to go into law school, I'll have more years after that."

"But it's so exciting. You'll be entertaining big-time clients in your lovely mansion—that you can certainly afford by then—and I'll be raising babies out here on the farm."

"I'll leave my kids out here for you to take care of when I'm busy with all my wealthy clients." She jumped, squealing, as Beth tossed a balled up napkin that neatly landed in her teacup, splashing her carefully pressed cotton skirt.

"I'm not complaining," Beth said, as she watched her friend wipe up the tea and pour them both more from Granny's blue checked teapot. "I just can't wait for the baby to get here. Guess I was supposed to be a mommy and not a great writer."

"You can go back to school later, Beth. People are doing it all the time now."

"Yeah, I may just do that, someday. For now, I have the best job in the world right here." She patted her girth, then gave a breathless grunt. Sophie popped up from her chair like lightning, blond curls bouncing.

"What is it? A pain?"

"No, more like a sudden shift. The pain is in my back."

"Here, you lay back and put your feet up. You may be starting your labor." Sophie propped her up with pillows and put the chair cushion under her feet. Beth giggled at her friend's serious face.

"Relax, Soph. I've had this backache for days. Besides, I've read all the books, and they say the first baby takes forever. Comforting thought, isn't it?"

"Well, I'm going to call George in, just in case."

"You are not!" Beth rose on her elbow and patted the couch. "Just sit and talk to me. We don't get the chance very often. You'll be back to school next week, and I won't see you for months."

"Yes, you will, I'll be home this summer. I have to work, can't go to summer school this year. Maybe next. Can I do anything for you?" Sophie's blue eyes showed concern.

"No." Beth slumped against her pillows, but the pain in her back made it impossible to be comfortable. A fine haze of sweat was forming on her upper lip. Feeling the urge to stand, she reached out to her friend. "Help me up, Soph, I think I need to walk."

Sophie grasped her under her arms and helped her to her feet.

"Lean on me," she said, as they walked slowly toward the kitchen. At the kitchen door, Beth stopped and looked at her feet.

"Soph, watch out," she said nervously, as she felt the warm liquid run down into her shoes. "I think my water just broke."

"Oh, my goodness," Sophie let go of her arm and ran to the back door. "I'm going for George. Hang on, Beth." She flew out the door, banging the screen, yelling at the top of her lungs, and leaving Beth alone clinging to the door facing.

"Don't leave me," Beth called to her, weakly. "Silly goose," she muttered as she waddled to the laundry basket to get a dirty towel and leaned over to wipe up the floor. She was instantly assaulted with a pain so fierce that she couldn't straighten up. "Granny!" she screamed just as Granny appeared from her room.

"Oh, Honey, here let me help you." A knowing expression crossed her face as she saw Beth's wet legs. "Looks like we may be getting us a baby tonight, huh?" She set Beth in a kitchen chair and wet a cloth to wipe her face.

"Now you just sit still and I'll get George."

"No, Sophie's gone to get him," Beth grunted as she tried to straighten her back. "Get the bag, Granny. It's by the closet door. And put in my house shoes, will you, please? And the baby blanket that you made, it's on the chest." She sat perfectly still, feeling another ripple of pain seize her back and press toward her stomach.

Sophie, George, and Henry came running through the door, panting and gasping for breath.

"Beth. Are you OK? Is it really time?" George turned helplessly around; hands lifted palms up as though he didn't know what to do next.

"Yeah, I think so. George, Honey, you forgot to take off your muddy boots. And you, too, Henry. What a mess."

"I'll clean it up later," Sophie said, wringing her hands. "Now don't you worry about a thing. Where's your bag?" She and George bumped into each other like an old Keystone Cops comedy as they ran toward the hall.

"Granny's going after it . . . oh, here she is. Did you get the blanket, Granny?"

"Yes. Now everybody just be calm and let's get Beth in the car. George, you call Dr. Williams and tell him we're on the way."

"But I'm going, too," he protested.

"I know, Dear," Granny said, patiently. "We'll be in the car waiting for you. We won't leave without you, Daddy."

"I'll meet you all at the hospital." Sophie kissed Beth on the cheek. "You're going to have a baby!" She squealed, excitedly clapping her hands.

"That's the idea, all right," Beth moaned as they helped her down the steps. "Oh, Soph, call Mom. This happened so fast, I forgot to call."

Somehow they all got to the hospital at the same time, and only three hours later, Beth delivered a nine-pound girl.

George was in shock. He moved around like a zombie in the waiting room, pacing from one end to the other. Joan watched him in amusement, her own anxiety calmed after the announcement that both mother and daughter were doing well.

"Nine pounds! That's a big girl, huh?" he sat by Joan and tried to relax. "I can't wait to see her, just can't wait."

Joan threw her arms around him, laughing. "Me either!"

After what seemed an eternity, a sour-faced nurse finally strutted into the waiting room. "Mr. Daniel?"

He jumped. "Yes?"

"You can go in now. Your wife is resting comfortably. She's back in her room—205."

"Can we all see her?" Joan asked.

"Are you all family?" The nurse looked at them over her glasses, doubting.

"Yes, we're all family. And we're all going in," Granny said firmly, and led the way down the hall with the nurse glaring at her back.

They opened the door, and George rushed to gather a tired Beth into his arms.

"Oh, Honey. I'm so glad you came through this okay. I was so scared something might happen to you." He held her and tenderly stroked her damp, dark curls from her forehead.

She smiled, groggily, as she caressed his cheek. "I'm fine, Sweetheart. It wasn't bad at all. Have you seen our girl? She's beautiful." She held her hand out to Joan who stood with tears glittering in her eyes. "Her name is Felicia Joan, after you and Granny. We wanted to surprise you," Beth said, proudly. Joan's tears turned to happy sobs, and she clutched Beth in her arms. Granny beamed with delight as she leaned against her grandson, briefly touching her head to his shoulder.

Henry twisted in the hard plastic chair. "Well, when can we see . . ." he began, just as a tiny blond nurse, looking nervously over her shoulder, came in bearing the pink bundle.

"Shhh," she whispered. "I'm not supposed to be doing this." With a big smile, she laid the bundle in George's arms, and they all crowded around, pulling at the blanket, oohing and cooing.

"Oh, sweet baby girl," was all George could say, over and over. He looked at Beth with so much love in his eyes that Sophie had to dash from the room to cry. After allowing the new father to meet his daughter, Granny took the baby from George.

"Here, Henry, don't you want to hold her?"

Henry held out his arms and walked around the room with her as though he had held many babies in his lifetime, completely ignoring George who followed him ready to catch the baby at any moment. He pulled the blanket from her head and grinned. "She's got your kinky hair, Sis."

"Thanks, Henry," Beth laughed, supremely happy to lie quietly and let her family get acquainted with the new little girl.

"I'm an uncle," Henry said in wide-eyed amazement as he returned the baby to Beth. "I've never been an uncle before."

"That's a big job, Henry," Beth said softly. "We'll have to count on you to baby-sit for her once in a while. Think you can do that?"

"Sure. Anytime," he beamed.

"It's a shame Dad missed this," George said, regretfully. "But he'll sure be excited when he gets home from his trip tomorrow morning."

"Quick, give her back," the nurse said, "before old Hatchet . . . I mean Mrs. Dobbins comes in." She whisked the baby away just minutes before Mrs. Dobbins opened the door.

"Everyone out except the father. This new mother needs rest. You may all view the baby from the nursery window," she said primly, nose in the air.

"Thank you, Mrs. Dobbins." Granny smiled sweetly, and they all snickered behind the stiffly starched back that marched in front of them leading the parade to the nursery window.

Chapter Seven

$\mathscr{B}$eth heard the sleet hitting the windows, drumming erratically against the panes with the sudden gusts of the November wind. There was snow in the forecast, but no one believed it because it was just November. In the mid-south snow hardly ever came before January. As the temperature dropped steadily all day, George was forced to come to the house in the middle of the afternoon looking for his heavy winter work coat and pile lined cap. Later, after dinner, Granny had prevailed upon George to light a fire in the fireplace to ward off the chill in the large living room, and they had enjoyed its heat.

She moved away from the warmth of George's back. It seemed foolish to brave the chill when the bed was so cozy, but she had tossed restlessly for an hour and was tired of fighting for sleep. Slowly, she crept from the bed, wrapped her warm flannel robe around her, and slipped out into the hall, flipping on the light. She opened the nursery door and crossed to Felicia's bed. The baby's breathing was soft, her chest rose and fell, and her mouth made sucking noises. Beth gently touched the rosy cheek, her finger moving up to the soft down of dark curls that lay tucked behind her ear. She was a beautiful baby, the best of George and herself. Beth hadn't expected such a good baby, but was delightfully surprised when she began to sleep all night after the first month. In spite of that, Beth found herself getting up to check on her at least once every night. Sometimes George did, too, though he hardly remembered getting up the next morning.

A love so deep welled up in Beth's throat that she had to blink away a tear as she whispered, "How blessed I am." She bent over and kissed the tiny fist curled up next to the chubby face, then tiptoed from the room.

The embers in the fireplace were still glowing so she opened the glass doors and added another log and a piece of kindling. It blazed up instantly, casting flickering shadows in the darkened room. Satisfied with her fire making skill, she moved to the desk and turned on the lamp. Bills were neatly stacked, ready to be paid. But she was in no mood to work with figures.

She took a piece of paper and paused, pencil to her tongue, as she gathered words that were circulating around in her brain to describe her precious daughter. Her eyes closed as she pictured Felicia nursing, Felicia crawling and pulling up on her skirt with shaky legs, Felicia as she just saw her by the glow of the hall light. Her words began to flow . . . my babe lies sleeping . . .

lashes flutter light as fairy kisses . . . lips as sweet as dewy buds . . . does she dream, my babe, of warm breast milk . . . of her mother's eyes, the touch of her father's hands? On and on she wrote, pausing to close her eyes and ponder the right word. When she was finished, she read it over, changed a word or two, and then lay the paper under the farm journal. Her feet were cold, and the fire was down to coals again. Turning out the lamp, she again checked on Felicia. All was well there so she crept back to bed and snuggled close to her husband, careful not to touch him with her cold feet.

The next morning, they awoke to a light snow, an icy film of snow that made the roads hazardous. They spent the day inside while flurries blew the remaining autumn leaves in dizzy swirls from the trees. In the afternoon, George paid bills and Granny sat knitting a sweater for Felicia.

"We had an early winter like this back in '39," Granny murmured as she looked out at the snowy landscape. Beth paused in her letter to Sophie to watch Granny as she rocked, mouth set in concentration, fingers flying with the pale yellow yarn looping around and over. Putting the letter aside, she began another poem about Granny. She glanced up frequently as she wrote and finally Granny noticed.

"What are you doing, Honey? You keep looking at me. Are you drawing my picture?"

"Not exactly. Just making some notes for something I want to write."

"Oh." Granny smiled, her face drawing up into fine wrinkles, and continued with her work.

"What a lovely face," thought Beth, "a face that has known great love and great sorrow. A face that that has felt sun and wind, has looked up to pray and down to weep." New thoughts rushed in, and she was so engrossed in her poem that she failed to hear Felicia waking up from her nap.

"Daddy's coming, Baby," George rose from the desk and went to his daughter. Beth slipped the pages away with the others and followed.

As the days drifted into the holidays, she often found herself pausing to write down some new thought, a phrase that came to her while doing dishes or wrapping presents. Some mornings she was up before daylight, awakened by the urge to write. Soon she had a folder of poems and notes for more.

Felicia's first Christmas was the best ever for Beth and George. She was pulling up and walking around tables now, and they had to keep a close eye when she was around the brightly decorated tree. Everything went into her mouth; tinsel was her favorite. But at night, when the tree lights gleamed and sparkled in the darkened living room, her little eyes were wide with wonder, and she sat still in Granny's arms until her heavy eyelids drooped and she could gaze no more.

Christmas Day, Joan and Henry came with Bill before noon to help Felicia open her gifts. She crawled among the wrappings, enjoying the papers and ribbons more than the gifts, until Henry helped her open his present. He had picked out a yellow felt duck, and she took to it immediately, carrying it around all day.

"I knew she'd like it. I bought it myself," he said proudly, as they cleared up paper and ribbon. Beth gave him a hug that embarrassed him and noticed how much taller he had gotten. He was growing more handsome every day, looking more and more like their father, green eyes and deep auburn hair. Beth choked up for a moment, remembering Christmases past when her father was alive. Quickly she ruffled her brother's hair and hurried to the kitchen to help Granny and Joan.

The dinner was steaming on the long harvest table in the dining room as they gathered around, holding hands as Bill said grace, a beautifully worded prayer of thanks for his new granddaughter and the blended family. Out of the corner of his eye, George noticed that his father held Joan's hand a little longer after the Amen.

"This is the best turkey and dressing ever," Bill told Granny as he helped himself to a third helping.

"Beth and Joan had a hand in it, too. And Beth made the sweet potato casserole herself," Granny said proudly.

Everyone agreed that it was the best Christmas dinner they had ever tasted, right down to Joan's famous coconut cake and ambrosia. Sated, they all collapsed in various chairs and sofas napping or talking softly until it was time for George to milk. Bill and Henry helped. Then all prepared to leave, gathering up gifts, and heaping kisses on a tired, cranky Felicia.

Beth had to rock her daughter to get her settled down after the exciting day. As she pulled the door almost closed, she groaned with fatigue and fell into George's arms.

"It was a wonderful day, but I'm worn out. How about you?"

"Umm, me, too. I love my new jacket. How did you know what I wanted?" He kissed her dark hair.

"I saw you eyeing it in Penney's window when we went in for groceries one Saturday. But I just love this bracelet. Thank you so much," she pulled back and turned the delicate silver marcasite on her wrist.

"I know you like old-fashioned jewelry and it really is old. I got it at the antique shop, the one on the corner. Now, what do you say, Mrs. Daniel, that we turn out the Christmas tree and snuggle up in our nice warm bed?"

"Excellent idea, Mr. Daniel," she grinned. Shoving boxes under the tree, she unplugged the lights, and was about to turn out the floor lamp when George stopped her.

"Beth, I meant to ask you, what's this in the blue folder?"

"Oh, just some poetry and stuff I've been writing."

"Can I read it?" He sat at the desk and began to read while she puttered in the kitchen, putting up the clean dishes.

"Hey, Beth," he called. "Come in here."

"What?"

"These are good, Honey. I love the one about the baby. And 'The Matriarch' is just such a beautiful description of Granny. You should do something with these; send them in to a magazine or something. I know, you ought to take these to the paper. Mrs. Whitford's column has some pretty awful poetry in it. Yours is so much better than anything she puts in her articles."

"Do you really think so?" Beth was beaming.

"I sure do. I didn't know you had so much talent, Beth."

She took the folder from him and pulled one sheet from the back pocket. "I wrote this one for you. Come to bed and you can read it out loud."

Snuggled together under the blue plaid blanket, he read the love poem aloud, stumbling a little with the emotions that caught in his throat.

"Wow!" He rolled his eyes. "You'd better not send this one to Mrs. Whitford. It would steam up her glasses. Do you really mean all this, about us?"

"You know, George," she said, after a long pause. "I didn't really love you when we got married—I mean, not the way I do now. It just grows and grows every day. I never knew I could . . ."

"Shhh," he murmured as he turned out the light, whispering his own words of love as he pulled her down into the warmth of the blanket.

Later, contentedly wrapped in his arms, her mind went back to the blue folder. She found herself rehearsing what she would say when she took her poetry to the newspaper. It would be so nice to see her words in print. If she hadn't been so tired, she would have been too excited to sleep, just thinking about it. But the day, though a happy one, took its toll, and she buried her face in her husband's shoulder and slept.

"It was a wonderful day, Joan," Bill said as he walked her to her door. "Good night, Henry, Merry Christmas."

"Merry Christmas, Mr. Daniel," Henry called as he shouldered his way in the door, burdened with the heavy box of gifts.

"Would you like to come in for a moment, Bill? I can fix us a cup of tea—or coffee."

"Oh, I'm still too full from all the food we've eaten today. But I'd like to sit and talk a minute, if it's not too cold for you."

"Oh, no," she pulled her scarf tighter around her neck. They sat in the swing, silent at first, listening to the sounds of Christmas day ending in the neighborhood: good-byes and Merry Christmases hung in the still air.

"Joan, you know what good friends we've always been, you, Carl, and me. Then when Carl died, we didn't see as much of each other. I was afraid of being misunderstood, I guess, and you seemed so distant. I know you were grieving." Bill shifted in the swing to face her in the moonlight.

"I was. It took me a long time to get over it, and I still miss him. But I certainly didn't mean to lose my friendship with you. I guess I stayed in my own little world too long."

"Well, you've been busy raising your children, and I was working and helping part-time on the farm and raising George. Now our children are grown—even Henry will soon be out of the nest and off to college. Do you think we could start to think of ourselves for a change?"

"I'd say it's about time we did," she smiled at his handsome profile, outlined against the Christmas lights in the window.

"Would you like to go to dinner Friday night? We could drive into the city and eat at that Italian restaurant where the three of us went right before Carl passed away."

She felt a warmth surge through her body. Suddenly her coat felt too heavy, and she nervously unwrapped the scarf.

"I liked that place. Yes, Bill, I'd love to go to dinner with you." She felt the quiver in her voice.

"Great! I'll pick you up about six."

"Six is fine."

He rose. "I'll not keep you out in the cold any longer. Again, it was a wonderful day. Aren't we fortunate to share the same grandchild?"

Joan walked to the door, laughing. "She is something, isn't she? We're definitely blessed to have her in our lives." Turning to him she said, softly, "Good night, Bill."

His lips brushed her cheek like he always had before, but tonight it sent a current through her. "Friday night at six." He grinned and was gone.

She waved as the car moved away from the curb and closed the door behind her. Leaning against the glass, she felt the pounding of her heart as she unbuttoned her coat. She felt like a giddy schoolgirl. "What a wonderful Christmas," she murmured as she turned off the porch light and went to help Henry put away the gifts.

Chapter Eight

One sunny day in January, Beth paused before the door of the Weekly Clarion, drew a deep breath, and walked into the din and clatter of the newspaper office. Crossing over to the cluttered receptionist's desk, she asked if she could see Mrs. Whitford.

"Honey, she works from her home," the blond receptionist told her, snapping her gum. "She just brings her column in every week, and goes over it with the editor, Mr. Winters. Do you know where she lives?"

"No," Beth's face clouded with disappointment as she hitched Felicia, bundled up like a little Eskimo, higher on her hip. Just then a tall thin woman breezed through the door wearing a ratty fur coat and a big smile.

"How are you this beautiful day, Eugenia?" she asked as she removed the bulky coat revealing an out-dated but expensive gray suit.

"Well, speak of the devil," Miss Gum Popper exclaimed as the cheerful woman walked over to the reception desk. Turning to Beth, she waved her hand and went back to her clutter. "Here she is, Honey. Uh, Mrs. Whitford, this lady wants to see you."

Mrs. Whitford hung her coat on the already loaded coat rack and turned to Beth. Her face lit up at the sight of Felicia.

"What a cute baby," she cooed. With a proud smile, Beth pushed Felicia's hood back to better show off her daughter, and Mrs. Whitford wiggled the baby's chin with a long carefully manicured finger. She was rewarded with a big grin from Felicia that showed off her new shiny bottom teeth.

"She is gorgeous. You must be so proud of her. Come on back here, my dear, it's a bit quieter in the back office." She led the way past presses clattering and workers laughing and talking around the Coke machine. The acrid smell of ink and paper was intoxicating to Beth as she looked about in awe.

"This is Mr. Winter's office, but he's out to a club luncheon, goes every Tuesday." Mrs. Whitford closed the door against the noise. "Now what can I help you with?" She pointed to the opposite chair, and Beth sank into it gratefully. As soon as she sat down, Felicia began to squirm.

"I—I wondered if you would be interested in putting any of my poetry in your Poetry Corner column," Beth stammered as she struggled with the wiggling baby and wondered why on earth she had let herself be talked into coming here.

"Here, let me have her," Mrs. Whitford stood and reached for Felicia. Balancing her on her knee, she unzipped the bunting from the burdened child. Immediately Felicia was mesmerized by the watch pinned to her suit jacket, and her little fingers reached for it.

"Now, where were we? Oh, yes, you have some poetry? You could have just mailed it to me, dear. But since you came in, I'd be glad to read one or two while you're here."

Beth quickly pulled her blue folder from the diaper bag and reached for the baby.

"No, she's happy. Just put one in front of me and I'll read it while she investigates my watch. Don't worry, she can't pull it off."

Beth sat quietly while Mrs. Whitford read one poem, changing pages when she nodded until she had read four of the poems. The watch was old stuff, and Felicia was now discovering her dark horned rimmed glasses. Mrs. Whitford laughed as she pulled back from the chubby hands.

"What is your name, Dear?"

"Beth Daniel."

"Well, Beth Daniel, these are very good. I'd be delighted to put them in my column, not all at once, of course, but some every week. My column is very popular with teachers, and is used a lot in the schools. I was an English teacher for years, you know. And sometimes our contributors' work is a good example of how NOT to write. But yes, you have a lot of talent, and I'm glad you showed these to me. Mr. Winters will be delighted with these, I'm sure. We don't often have work of this quality."

"Oh, thank you so much," Beth said, relief showing in her face. "I was afraid you wouldn't like them. It would be a thrill for me to see my work in print."

"Well, you shall. And I've enjoyed this visit with this lovely creature. Will you bring her back to see me sometime? Maybe you could come to my home for lunch one day when it gets a little warmer."

Beth left the paper walking on air. She was going to be a published author, even if it was just in the local paper.

At home, George and Granny were just as excited when she told them the news. Every week her family waited anxiously for the paper to come so they could see their up and coming author's work. Mrs. Whitford was as good as her word and had something of Beth's in every column. At church and on the street, friends would stop Beth and compliment her on her writing, and it fueled the fire in Beth. She was churning out poems and essays just about every day.

"Thank you, Granny, for getting supper on the table," Beth said one evening as she hurried into the kitchen. "I had an idea and the time got away from me. Do you get tired of looking after Felicia for me? I get so carried away sometimes. I'll give you a break tomorrow and let you rest." She began to spoon baby food into her daughter's mouth only to have it spewed back at her.

"Whoa, Beth. She's been fed already. And, no, you know I don't mind helping you while you work. But I will take you up on tomorrow. Bill is coming to take me to the doctor, and we're going to go over some business."

"You aren't feeling well?" Beth looked at her in alarm.

"Just a check up. I'm fine." Granny turned her back and stirred the stew pot.

Beth decided then to do most of her writing at night after chores were done and Felicia was put to bed. She had imposed enough on Granny. So while George read his farm journals, Beth spent the winter evenings writing.

Spring came early and daffodils and forsythia glowed like molten rivers of gold over the front yard. One day the sun was warm, the air filled with the fragrance of wild onions. By night a late snow had covered the yellow carpet and bent the tender limbs of the blooming bushes. This was fodder for Beth's pen, as were the new calves being born, and the spring flood that devastated their neighbors on lower ground. Anything that had to do with rural life, its joys and its uncertainties, were examined and written about with both humor and pathos.

On April Fool's Day, the family gathered for Felicia's first birthday. Even Sophie made it in for the occasion. It was a beautiful warm day and they had a late afternoon picnic on the front lawn. The birthday girl was bombarded with gifts, mostly clothes that were oohed and aahed over by the female assembly. They were sitting around the picnic table after a feast of grilled hot dogs, baked beans, and potato salad when the phone rang. Henry ran to get it, first thinking it might be one of his buddies with plans for the prank night they had conjured up.

"Beth, it's for you—Mr. Winters."

She took the phone from Henry, bewildered. She had never talked with Mr. Winters himself.

"Hello, Beth. I'm afraid I have some sad news for you. Mrs. Whitford passed away this morning at the hospital."

"Oh, no. Was she in an accident?"

"No, Beth. She had been ill for some time. She just kept it pretty much to herself. She only told me a few weeks ago."

"I didn't know. Oh, I'm really sorry. She was such a sweet person, and she's been so good to me, showing me how she puts her column together and everything. Are the arrangements for the funeral made yet?"

"Yes, it will be Wednesday at 10:00 at the funeral home in Greenville. Beth, she thought a lot of you and really thought you had talent. She told me a few days ago that you would be ideal to take over her column. And I agreed with her. I don't want to discontinue the column because it is a favorite with our readers. We may have to revamp it a bit. But the job doesn't pay much. Would you be interested?"

"Yes. Yes, I would love to try although I know I can't fill her shoes."

"Come in as soon after the funeral as you can, and we'll talk about it."

She hung up feeling both saddened and elated at the same time. Returning to the family gathering, she told them the sad news first. Granny was especially moved, as she had been a faithful reader of Mrs. Whitford's column for many years. But the mood changed when Beth told them that she would be taking over the column.

"Honey, that's wonderful." George picked her up and whirled here around. "My wife, the newspaper columnist." Then he added soberly, "She must have thought a lot of you to recommend you for the job."

"She was a gracious lady." Beth began picking up paper plates and glasses. "I just hope I can justify her faith in me."

"You can, Sweetie," Joan helped her load up the tray with the remaining food. "I'll help you any way I can."

Joan's help became necessary sooner that she planned. Beth's new column was expanded from poems and recipes to local news of interest, and she found herself away from home more than she liked with appointments to keep and people to interview. She also discovered that she was expecting their second child.

It was not a smooth pregnancy like the first one. Beth had morning sickness well into her fourth month, and she grew much bigger than with Felicia. At the end, she did most of her column from her bed since the doctor was concerned about her legs swelling. She felt like a big blimp, propped in bed with a lap desk balanced on her raised knees trying to hand write over the mound of her stomach. Felicia spent time in the bed with her mother, joyously climbing over her, loving the game of shredding paper and falling back into the pillows as Beth wrestled her down and tickled the pudgy little body. When they tired, Beth would read from the stacks of books kept in a basket by the bed.

"I could never make it without you both," she told Joan as she took away the limp child who had been read to sleep, and Granny cleaned up the mess around the bed. "Just one more week, one more." She rubbed her tummy as she threatened, "And you'd better not be late."

"Just give us another healthy baby," Granny grunted from the floor as she picked up giblets of paper.

Angelea Wilford Daniel wasn't late. Beth went into labor early the next morning, but, unlike the first child, this baby girl wasn't born until after twenty-four hours of grueling labor and finally, a C-section. She weighed ten pounds four ounces. The doctor suggested that two would be a nice family for Beth, and a worried George agreed.

He sat on the hospital bed by Beth as they held their second daughter. She was a carbon copy of Felicia with dark hair and eyes.

"No more babies," George said, as he kissed the bottom of one tiny foot.

"Right now, I agree." Beth was exhausted. Her hair fell in stringy clumps around her shoulders, and her face was red and swollen after the long ordeal. But she smiled happily at George as he cuddled their new baby.

"Two little girls is enough, Honey. And this one looks like she's half grown already."

Beth laughed. "But she's beautiful, just like her sister."

As the nurse took the baby back to the nursery, George left Beth to get some much-needed sleep, leaving her in Joan's care. Her mother plumped her pillows and tucked her in before she went for yet another cup of coffee to fortify her for the hours ahead at the hospital. But Beth was too wide-awake and uncomfortable to rest. She sat up carefully, still woozy from the medication, and stared out at the rainy March day. Soon George would be too busy planting to be of much help with the babies. Granny couldn't handle everything; she was slowing down more and more, even though she would never admit to being tired.

"I'll just have to find a way to do it all," Beth thought. "Other women do it, and I can, too. I want to be a writer; I've always wanted to be a writer." But at that moment, as tired as she was, she couldn't figure out just how she could continue with her newfound career. The pain pill took effect and she closed her eyes, hoping that somehow she would find that way.

Chapter Nine

George sat in the swing in the back yard, Angelea on his shoulder sleeping like the angel she was. He pushed the swing with his foot while he patted the sturdy little back; his face tucked into the curve of her neck, inhaling the sweet odor of baby powder.

Felicia played in the sandbox in the late September sun, pouring more sand in the grass than in her pail. Red, the Irish setter, lay next to the sandbox, guarding his charge. He was never far from the babies when they were outside. George smiled as he watched his firstborn, so much a clone of her mother.

"I'm twenty-three years old and already have two little girls," he thought with a smile. "But I wouldn't trade places with anybody." His countenance sobered when he thought of the farm. It hadn't been a good year. The summer was dry, and the late corn burned up. Thank goodness the winter wheat crop was good and the price was okay, not as high as he would have liked. After three bumper years, an off year was probably to be expected. But it sure put a hurt on the finances. With a wife and two children to consider, finances were constantly on his mind.

For the first time since his grandfather died, he had thoughts about going back to school and getting out of the farming business altogether. He hadn't mentioned it to Beth, nor to Granny, but the bad year had brought him down to the reality of being a farmer. Sometimes he wondered if he had the endurance, the patience that his grandfather had all those years. He knew he could find a buyer for the land, but of course, he would never sell the house. It was Granny's home as well as his family's. In quiet moments, he wondered how it would have been if he had finished his education and become a teacher. He would be in his first year of teaching by now.

Beth was taking classes in addition to her newspaper column. She tried to work it all in, but he could tell it was taking a toll on her nerves. Joan and Granny did more and more to help her out. He took up the slack whenever he could. She was so determined to get her degree and to improve her writing skills that he didn't have the heart to make her slow down. And the money from her job would help out this year.

It was almost time for her to get home from her class so he rose with the sleeping Angelea still on his shoulder.

"Felicia, I'm going inside now and put Angel in her bed. You be a good girl and stay in the sandbox. I'll be out to get you in a few minutes." She looked up, gave him a big smile, and continued dumping sand, this time on the patient Red, singing her own version of JESUS LOVES ME with great flourish.

He put the limp child in her crib, and then went to the kitchen to see what he could do about supper. Granny was at Cousin Lillian's; he would pick her up whenever she called. He opened the refrigerator and pulled out several bowls. With just the two of them, plus Felicia, the leftover spaghetti would be just fine.

"Hello. I'm home," Beth called from the front door.

"In the kitchen."

She barreled into the room, eyes sparkling, tossed her books on the table, and grabbed him in a bear hug.

"What's all this," he laughed as he returned her hug and gave her a kiss. "You must have had a really good day."

"I have. I have. Oh, George, you'll never believe what Mr. Dobbs hit me with today." She followed him as he poured the pasta in a pan and put it on the stove without replying, his mind on putting together a fast supper.

"You're not listening." She took his face in her hands. "George, he wants me to write a book."

"A book?"

"Yeah, he said my poetry and essays are so good, he thinks I should put them in book form. He has a friend in the publishing business, and he says that those kinds of books are selling well right now. He thinks his friend will want to publish it, and he wants me to get one together and send to him. What do you think about that!"

"That's great, Honey. I'm really proud of you, you know that." He paused. "But how on earth are you going to put together a book with school and everything else?"

She dropped her arms. The disappointment on her face made him feel a heel for being so negative.

"I didn't mean it couldn't be done. Honey, of course, you've got to give it a try."

"I know it's been hard on you and Granny with my being gone so much. But I can do this at home. And I've got so much material already written. This is such an opportunity for me, for us. I have to take advantage of it. Do you know how many real writers would give their eye teeth to get a book published?"

"What do you mean 'real writers'? What do you think you are? Now, move your books, so I can get us something on the table to eat."

"I'm sorry." She moved her books and started putting out silverware, telling him every word of her talk with her English teacher about the proposed book. Her dark eyes glowed with excitement, and he put aside his doubts and tried to catch her enthusiasm.

"Mommy, Mommy," came from the yard, and Beth went out on the porch.

"Hey, Baby. How's Mommy's big girl?" The dusty little girl ran to the porch and up the stairs, flinging her arms around Beth's legs.

"Oh, you're so dirty, Sweetie. We'll need to wash you up before you can eat a bite. Have you had fun today?"

She picked Felicia up and set her on the counter, reaching for the bar of soap. Felicia twisted her head in protest as her mother scrubbed her dirty mouth and hands. Setting her in her booster chair and pacifying the child with a cracker, she started to get glasses out when there was a knock on the door.

"Who could that be? Get her milk and I'll answer it." She opened the door to a thin, pale woman wearing a dark coat, in spite of the warm evening. "Yes?"

"You—you must be Beth," the woman stammered.

"Yes, I'm Beth. And you are . . . ?"

"I knew you when you were little. I haven't seen you since then."

Just then, George came to the door. He stared at the woman, and then gasped, "Mother?"

"Hello, George. I know you're surprised to see me. Can I come in?"

George stepped aside and Hilda Daniel walked slowly into the living room. Beth saw George's face grow chalky white, as his teeth clenched in anger.

"Well, Mother, I don't know what to say. I haven't seen you in years. To what do we owe the pleasure of your company?" The words were crisp and tinged with sarcasm.

"I know it's been too long, George. I can't apologize enough for my long absence. And I don't blame you for being sharp with me. I deserve it." Beth saw tears forming in the dark gray eyes, and she moved quickly to offer her mother-in-law a chair. Hilda almost fell into the chair, and she looked as though she might faint.

"Can I get you something?" Beth asked, but George held up his hand.

"Wait, Beth. Let's find out what's going on. Mother, why are you here? You haven't seen fit to come around for years and suddenly here you are on my doorstep," he said, anger rising in his voice from a throat that had gone dry.

"I heard you married Beth and that you have children. I was just in town for a short time and thought I would like to see my grandchildren. But I can see it was a bad idea." She started to rise, but Beth motioned her to sit still.

"Excuse us, please. Just for a moment." She took George's cold hand and pulled him into the kitchen. His voice was shaky.

"I don't want her here, Beth. She has no right to be here. She left us years ago, and that's the way I want it to stay."

"George, I know you have no reason to trust her or even like her, but she is your mother, no matter what she's done. She looks like she's just as scared as you must be. Why not be civil? Show her the children. Talk to her; tell her what you've been doing. Then maybe she'll leave and go her way."

"Oh, I'm sure she'll do that, just like she did before. She's good at leaving. The point is, Beth, I don't want her to see the babies. She doesn't deserve that courtesy, any courtesy from me. I just want her out of here." He turned back toward the living room, but Beth grabbed his arm.

"Wait. You're a good person, Honey. Maybe most of that goodness came from Bill, I don't know. But she brought you into this world, and I'm thinking that she

90

must have some good traits, too. I think that if you send her away in anger, it will eat away at you. Now, I'm going to put on some coffee. Go talk to her. Maybe you can have some of the questions answered that have been bothering you all your life." She released his arm, and for a moment he just stood there. Then he nodded and went back in the living room.

Beth took her time in putting on the coffee. She took a puzzled but delighted Felicia back to the sandbox to get dirty again. When she went back into the room, the silence was deafening. Hilda looked ready to flee at any moment, and George sat slumped on the sofa staring out of the window.

"Coffee's perking," Beth said, lightly, as she pulled a chair up a little closer to Hilda. The weary looking woman took that as a sign of encouragement and began to speak, slowly and carefully.

"I know I haven't been a good mother, George. Right now, I can't remember a good reason for leaving you and your father. I guess there wasn't one. I was young and bored. Your dad was working and helping on the farm, and I felt alone. I shouldn't have; I should have pitched in and helped him and toughed it out. But I was craving excitement."

"And the other man gave you plenty of that, huh?" George said dully.

"I thought he would. Instead he put me through hell, drinking and moving around from place to place. He could never hold a job long."

"What happened to him?" George asked in a bored voice.

"He died four years ago. Liver cancer."

"Where have you been living since then?" Beth leaned forward in her chair.

"We had an apartment in Nashville, and I stayed on and worked at a department store. That is, until a month ago. I got sick and had to quit. I've been at my friend Lou's for a week."

"So, what do you want from us?" George rose and stood in front of his mother. She looked up at him and smiled.

"I just wanted to see you. And your children, and Beth, here. Just wanted to see how you were doing. Lou wrote me every time she heard anything about you, so I've kept up that way. I've wanted to come and see you for years, but I was—ashamed."

George pulled the curtain back at the sound of a car in the driveway. "It's Wade, and Granny's with him. Great! I'm sure you're dying to see your former mother-in-law, too. By the way, is that your brown car?"

"No, it's Lou's old car. She lets me drive it, she has a new one."

He stared for a moment at the rusty faded old vehicle. "I've seen that car around. In fact, it was parked next to my truck when I went to the feed store yesterday."

Hilda hung her head. "Yeah, I came out yesterday and was going to stop. But I saw you in your truck, and I followed you. I just wanted to get a glimpse of my grown up son. I was still trying to work up my courage to talk to you." George shook his head in disbelief.

Wade and Granny appeared on the porch, and Granny thanked him for bringing her home as she opened the door and stopped short. For a moment, a heavy, uncomfortable moment, not a sound was heard.

Wade broke the silence. "I was delivering Miz Lillian some catalogs my wife had saved for her, and Miz Daniel said she was ready to leave so I just brought her on. Wanted to talk to you, George, about some things, but I see you have company, so I'll just run on. See you folks tomorrow."

"Thanks, Wade," George called to the retreating back and put his arm around Granny, still standing in the doorway with her mouth agape.

"Hello, Felicia." Hilda rose shakily from the chair.

"Hilda." Granny nodded as she looked questioningly at George.

"Mother just stopped by to see us and the kids, Granny. Isn't that just great?" He rolled his eyes.

Granny took Beth's vacant chair. Looking at her former daughter-in law, she saw nothing of the lovely carefree girl her son had married many years ago. This woman looked aged and tired. There were deep creases around her mouth, a sad defeated look on her thin face. Her clothes were old and worn and the wary look in her eyes caused Granny to force a more pleasant voice than she felt. "Well, Hilda, suppose you tell us why you've chosen now to visit with us after all this time?"

"Felicia, you and Bill did such a wonderful job raising George. I just wanted to see him and the children— and Beth, too—before . . ." her voice broke and she paused . . . "Felicia, I'm dying. My doctor tells me I

93

don't have very long." She dropped her head, bleached blond hair falling over her face, and sobbed.

The only sound in the room was the constant tick-tock of the grandfather clock. In the middle of the stunned silence, little Felicia bounced into the room, sand sifting from her clothes, and flung herself at Granny's knees.

"Hewoo, Gammy," she lifted her face for Granny's kiss.

Granny stroked the dark curly head that stretched toward her face and lifted her eyes to Hilda's. "This is your older granddaughter. Her name is Felicia, too," she said softly.

Hilda clutched her chest and covered her mouth to keep from crying out. Recovering, she smiled at the baby, "Hello, Felicia. What a pretty girl you are."

Felicia smiled shyly and ran to George, running on her toes. Thinking that he was playing peek-a-boo with her, she tried to lift her father's head, which was buried in his hands.

Chapter Ten

The grandfather clock in the darkened living room chimed ten o'clock. Usually Granny was in bed asleep by this hour, and Beth and George were busy picking up toys or winding up the typing, doing all the late night chores before turning in. This night, they were gathered around the old oak kitchen table.

As soon as Hilda left, George called Bill, and he came right out. He put on tea while Beth got Felicia down. Angelea was fed and wide awake after her late nap, so she had no intention of being put back in her crib and let it be known with all the sweet cooing and gurgling she could muster.

Bill filled Beth's cup, took the baby from her, and sat next to George. He was concerned about his son, who had not said a word since he arrived at the house. Granny had repeated the visit from Hilda practically word by word to Bill on the porch before he ever went inside, but he was unprepared for his son's dark demeanor.

George got up and filled a glass with water from the tap. Leaning back against the sink, he broke his silence.

"Well, what do you think, Dad? Do you think she came back to be taken care of now that she's ill?"

"That's exactly what I think, Son. I think she realizes after all this time that she's lost everything, and she wants to settle her affairs, so to speak. She doesn't want to die without making peace with you, and maybe with me, too."

"She doesn't want to die alone," Granny said, softly. "None of us do. And she has no family left and only one good friend, at least here, and that's Lou Harris."

"Yeah, Lou wasn't the best influence on Hilda back then. She's the one who introduced her to that guy," Bill said. There was a trace of bitterness is his voice.

"So she's back home because she's going to die, and she wants peace and comfort. Well, I'm sorry. I can't give it to her. I still remember wishing I had a mother like the other kids, somebody to tuck me in at night, to be at my ball games, to do all those things." He saw Granny's eyes fill with tears and quickly added, "Not that you didn't do those things for me, Granny. You were more of a mother than she ever was." He walked behind her and gently massaged her shoulders.

"You can't remember, Son," Bill interjected, "how happy your mother was when she was pregnant with you. And after you were born, she was just enthralled with motherhood. Then things changed when you were about three. She just did an about face and left before we could even attempt to work things out. Maybe she had been depressed, and I just didn't recognize it, I don't know. But I still remember the girl she was once. I hope I didn't poison you with my own bitterness, Son." He patted the chair next to him, but George continued to pace.

"No, you didn't, Dad. "You always said she just made a big mistake and let me know it had nothing to do with me. I always appreciated that. But the truth is that I grew up with kids who had two parents, and I resented what she did to our family. She could have at least remembered my birthdays. A present every Christmas just wasn't enough. And now I'm finding it hard to let her into my life again just because she's lonely . . . and dying."

"Honey, sit down," Granny commanded. "Your mother was once family. I loved her then. My feelings are much like yours, but yet, I can't just stand by and watch her face this thing alone. I couldn't do that to anyone that I could help."

George sighed and looked at Beth. Poor Beth who had such exciting news about her book and hadn't even had a chance to tell anyone. She smiled at him across the table, reaching her hand across to meet his. "What do you think, Beth?"

"I agree, Sweetheart. She needs our help, despite what she's done. But I just don't understand what we can do. Should we bring her here or find a place where she will be taken care of? You all know more about what we need to do to help her. I'll go along with whatever you decide."

"There isn't a place close by except the small nursing home in Greenville. I don't think it's much. I've been there and it's pretty depressing," Granny said thoughtfully.

"So then all we can do is let her live here until the end. I don't know if I can handle that." George squeezed Beth's hand.

"First, I'll go by Lou's and talk to Hilda." Bill rose and put his teacup in the sink. "I'll get the name of her doctor and go see him, talk to him about the time frame, and what she needs in the way of medicine. She probably hasn't the money for the drugs she'll need. Then we can decide. Let's all pray about it and sleep on it." Then he added as they followed him to the door. "You know, this puts a kink in my plans. I guess you all have figured out that Joan and I have become pretty close."

George and Beth smiled at one another. They had figured that out weeks ago.

"Dad, tell us what kind of plans you're talking about. Would there be a wedding in the works?"

"We're talking about it," Bill nodded with a smile a mile wide.

"I knew it," Granny hugged Bill. "Talk about a family. We'll be all kinds of in-laws. I think it's the best thing I've heard all day."

"Well, Beth got cheated out of telling us some pretty important news tonight. Go on, Honey. Tell them your news." George gave Beth a nudge.

"Mr. Dobbs wants me to gather my essays and poems and put them into a book. He's already talked to a publisher friend about me."

They all excitedly hugged Beth. "My daughter-in-law, the writer," said Bill. "I'm so proud of you, Beth. And listen, you can't let this stop your writing, you hear? You've worked too hard." Beth kissed her father-in-law on the cheek.

"You're the best," she whispered. "And I'd love to have you for a stepfather and a father-in-law."

Granny put cups in the sink wondering if she really had the energy to care for her errant daughter-in-law who had caused so much pain. Calling goodnight, she slowly climbed the stairs to her room. Offering to care for Hilda was easy. Pushing aside all the years of resentment and doing it was something else. She dropped to her knees when she reached her large four-poster bed. Usually she prayed with her head on her pillow, but this called for some serious praying.

Beth put Angelea in her crib and patted her until she drifted off with a small sigh, having found her pink thumb for comfort. She pulled the door partly closed and sought George. She knew she would find him on the back porch. Pulling two pillows and a blanket from the hall closet, she went to join him. He was stretched out on the squeaky old glider staring out into the dark where a cool drizzle had begun to blow against the screen. Red had taken refuge at his feet.

"Move over," she said as she tossed him the pillows and crawled in next to him, pulling the blanket over them. They lay in silence listening to the rain and inhaling the fresh fragrance that cleared and cooled the night air.

"What are you thinking, Honey?"

"I'm thinking that I'm not happy about this, but, as Granny says, all things happen for a reason. If we bring her here, it will be a lot of work for you. And you have so much on your plate already. We'll need to hire a nurse when it gets to the point where she needs more care, that's all there is to it. And we don't have the extra money, Beth."

"Bill will help there, and so will Mom. And I'll keep on working for the paper, which brings in a little. As for the book, it may have to wait."

"No. No. No. I want you to put together that book. The market may not be receptive to that kind of book later. You work with Mr. Dobbs and follow his advice. I want you to have this chance, whether my mother ends up here or not. You should not have to pay for something you had no part in."

She turned on the narrow glider and snuggled her face in his neck. "We'll make it, Honey. We'll just take it one day at a time. And you'll be glad when it's all over. I know you will. You're a good man, George Daniel, and I love you very much."

He pulled the clip from her long hair and ran his hands through the curly strands as he held her close. She smelled like baby shampoo and breast milk. The ache in his heart, the anger in his very bones seemed to melt in the comforting warmth of her embrace. Exhaustion overtook them both, and they slept there until Red woke them whining to be let out, and they crept like two sleepwalkers into their own bed.

A week later, Hilda was ensconced in the household. Beth and George gave up their bedroom and took the spare room next to Granny's room upstairs, moving the babies up with them so they could hear them at night. The room was wall to wall beds. But that was the least of their inconveniences.

Hilda felt as though she should cook and wait on everyone to pay her way. Granny became testy having another woman in her kitchen. Beth worked among them joking and trying to keep the tension down. But finally Granny had her say.

"Hilda! Please go sit down and let me fix this meal."

Hilda looked stricken as she turned away, so Granny softened her tone. "I know you feel like you're beholden to us for taking you in, and you want to make up for it. But you can't. We wouldn't do this if we didn't want to. Now you just try to relax, okay? We know you don't have much energy, and we want you to save what you have."

Hilda smiled and went to the living room. The first night's dinner was stiff and uncomfortable. But the two babies broke the ice when it came to bath and bedtime. Beth allowed Hilda to bathe the girls and help her put them to bed.

"What's your name?" Felicia asked Hilda as she dressed her in her pajamas.

"My name is Hilda."

"Hilly?"

"That's close enough," Hilda laughed and held her soft wiggly body close, inhaling the fragrance of a clean baby. Both she and George relaxed more as they talked about the children later that night.

As the days passed, Hilda spent more and more time in her bedroom, resting. Bill had learned from her doctor that her time was indeed short. But she never complained and was continually thanking them for allowing her to stay with them. She had a deep-seated fear of hospitals, and Granny determined that she would only go there as a last resort.

Beth meanwhile found it difficult to concentrate on her writing with so much going on and spent more time at the paper doing her column there as well as the work on her book, worrying at the same time about Granny having so much more to do. But George refused to let her give up her classes.

One Sunday as they were all getting ready for church, Hilda came downstairs in her best dress. "I would like to go with you, if that's okay," she said softly, looking at George who was trying to buckle a shoe on Angelea's swinging foot.

"Sure," he said, with a surprised look on his face.

"I know I have a lot of people to face, and I may not be strong enough to do it if I don't do it now," Hilda said in a whisper.

They arrived at the church a few minutes early and took their usual places down front. Hilda proudly carried Angelea back to the nursery, and Beth took Felicia to the children's class. Hilda could feel the congregation's eyes on her, probably wondering what she was doing there, but she held her head up high.

At the end of the service, the minister asked if anyone needed help or prayers, and Hilda went to the front and whispered to him. He listened, then put his arm around her shoulders, and said to the audience, "Hilda Daniel has come forward. She has something she would like to say to the congregation." He sat down and motioned for Hilda to speak. She looked thin and nervous, but her voice was strong and calm.

"Many of you know me from a long time ago. And many of you know that I have made some pretty bad mistakes in my life, mistakes that hurt my family deeply. I wish I could go back and make up for those mistakes, but I can't. What's done is done. I just want you all to know how sorry I am, and beg the forgiveness of you and of my family. They have been kind enough, in spite of everything, to take me in and care for me through my illness." She glanced at Bill, who sat with Joan holding his hand. "I want to thank Bill for his kindness in making sure that I have everything I need. And my son, George, who spent most of his life without a mother, for letting me back into his family. And Granny for her forgiveness and goodness, Beth for trying so hard to make me feel at home.

"Now I ask for the prayers of all of you that I will be forgiven for the past."

She sat down, trembling, and the minister led them in a prayer for her and the family. When he concluded, there wasn't a dry eye in the house, including George's. After the last song, the whole congregation gathered around her hugging and crying with her.

George stood back and watched, Felicia in his arms.

"Why is Hilly crying, Daddy?" Felicia pulled her daddy's face around to hers with her chubby hands.

"She's crying because she's happy, Felicia. She's happier than she's been in a long time. And we have to help keep her happy, because she's sick now, and she needs our love."

"I wuv her," Felicia said seriously, nodding her head.

"We all do, Honey." He kissed her and motioned for Beth and Granny, and they followed Hilda and the well wishers out of the door of the church. Outside, Hilda turned and came to George, and he gently held her frail body in his arms, Felicia squeezed between their grasp.

"It'll be okay now, Mother. Everything will be okay now." He felt as though a load had been lifted from his soul.

"Thank you, Joan, for being so patient," Bill said as he reached across the table and took her hand. They were having lunch at the grill before going home from church.

"What else could you do, Bill? You're a good man to see her through this; not many men would. Makes me glad because I know you'll take good care of me when we do marry."

"And I promise that will be soon, Love. I don't see how I can wait."

"We've waited all these years, Honey. No sense getting in a rush now. We'll have the rest of our lives." She leaned across the table and gave him a quick peck on the lips, ignoring the elderly ladies at the next table who immediately put their heads together and began to whisper.

Chapter Eleven

Hilda was with them for four months, forced to spend the last two in bed. They brought the children in to her as often as she felt like it, and it seemed to brighten her spirits. But the time came when she was in so much discomfort that she only wanted her painkillers and the grown-ups around her.

One bad day she pulled George close to her. "When I'm gone, I want you to look in my purse. There's something that I want you to have, but only after I'm gone. Okay?" She groaned from the effort of speaking. George held her hand and nodded.

The last week she was in a lot of pain and not always conscious, so they had no choice but to take her to the hospital. George stayed with her almost around the clock. She died early one morning, just as the sun was coming up over the distant hills.

They buried her in the family burial ground in the lower meadow, walled off by an ornate Victorian fence and guarded by two tall oaks that still held their brown leaves. It was an unusually warm, sunny day for November as they laid her to rest, the sadness tempered with the knowledge that they had done the right thing in caring for her. George was especially grateful he had overcome his anger and was at peace with himself.

After the burial, remembering his mother's request, George opened her purse and went through the contents. In her billfold, there were pictures of George as a baby, and a newspaper clipping from when he won the science fair in the sixth grade. There was the usual clutter of lipsticks, tissues and loose change, but in a side pocket of the worn black bag, he found a brown envelope with a check for five thousand dollars and a note that read:

Dear George,

This money wasn't mine. What little money I made, I used to live on. It belonged to my husband who won it gambling. He died before he could spend it, and I saved it for you as a small way of thanking you for all you've done for me. Use it for whatever you need. And try to remember me fondly. I always loved you.

Mother.

With tears running down his face, George sat in stunned silence as he fingered the worn pictures and the yellowed note. Beth put her arms around him as they sat on the bed where his mother had so recently laid in pain. Granny smiled at the two of them. The money would come in handy in this bad year at the farm. "Save most of it for the children's education. Hilda would like that," she whispered as she closed the door and left them alone.

They followed Granny's advice. But some was spent to relieve bills that had gone begging. It was a weight lifted from George's shoulders to be able to pay on his loan from the bank for this year's seed. As he left the bank that day, he silently thanked his mother for her special gift. And he was able to put his heart back into farming.

"How's the book coming?" He asked Beth at supper one night.

"I have it all ready to take to Mr. Dobbs for his critique. I'm sure he won't want it all in the book. I had over seven hundred typed pages." She spooned baby food into Angelea with one hand and with the other, grabbed Felicia's milk glass that was about to get hit by her waving spoon.

"Wow. How on earth did you manage to do that much with all that's been going on around here?"

She pointed to her eyes. "See these bags? I've been up late almost every night."

The next morning the carefully packed and typed manuscript was taken to her teacher; she waited anxiously for his comments. After a week, he asked her to stay after class one afternoon.

"Beth, these poems and essays are just wonderful. I've marked the ones that I think you should leave out. Some don't really fit into the general context, but hang on to them because you can use them in the next book."

She smiled. "Next book?"

"I think the publisher will like this. With the environmental emphasis that's so prominent these days, it's a good time for a book like this. And I like your title, THIS TENDER LAND. Take it home, make my suggested corrections and adjustments, and I'll go over it one more time before you send it to the publisher." He stroked his gray beard and grinned at his protégé.

"Oh, Mr. Dobbs. How can I ever thank you for all the help?"

"No need for thanks. I know talent when I see it, and I'm just happy to be a part of it."

Beth floated home on a cloud of happiness.

In four months the publisher called Beth and told her the book was accepted, and he wished to see her to discuss the arrangements.

"George! George!" She ran breathlessly to the barn where he was trying to milk Gerty, who was getting rambunctious.

"Not so loud. This cow is going nuts as it is. What is it anyway?" His voice was testy.

"They accepted my book, George. They want me to come to Atlanta to talk about the arrangements."

George jumped up, and Gerty kicked over the bucket of milk. But he didn't care; he was too busy hugging Beth.

"When are you going?" He asked, excitedly.

"WE are going. I'm not going all by myself. Do you think I need an agent?"

He laughed. "Go call Mr. Dobbs right now."

She rushed in and called. Mr. Dobbs was almost as excited as they were. He volunteered to go along, since he was a friend of the publisher.

Granny was more down to earth about the news. "You need to go shopping, Missy. You want to go in to that publisher's office looking elegant and sharp, like an experienced author, not a poor little farm girl!"

"I agree," George said. "You haven't had any new clothes in ages. I could use a new suit myself, being as I'm the husband of an almost famous author."

So they spent a day shopping. George bought a dark suit, and Beth brought a tailored gray suit and an elegant black dress with new shoes. She had never felt so frivolous in her life.

Everyone in Bernstein's was excited about outfitting Beth for her day at her publishers.

When the day came, dressed to the hilt, they set off before dawn with Mr. Dobbs and drove to Atlanta. Neither George nor Beth had ever been there before, and found themselves rubber-necking at all the buildings. Mr. Dobbs smiled as he showed them some of his favorite parts of the city.

"You can tell we're hayseeds," Beth laughed, as they walked from the parking lot to the publisher's office.

Mr. Dobbs introduced them to Charles Lang when they were ushered into his office. The soft gray walls were covered with book jackets highlighted with indirect lighting. Beth lightly touched glossy covers with awe. "Yours will be up there soon," Mr. Lang smiled. Beth instantly liked this plump balding man with the soft voice.

"We're just a small publisher, Beth," he explained. "I think we can get your book out there with an attractive cover that will compliment your writing. However, it needs pictures. We have an excellent photographer that we'll send down to get the local color. We need to discuss contracts; of course we'll need one for the photographer as well. So, shall we gather around the conference table and work out details that will be mutually satisfactory?"

He called his secretary for coffee, and they followed him into the light airy room. Beth's heart was pounding so hard she thought it might just jump out of her chest. Only George's hand clutching hers kept her feet anchored to the floor.

Hours later they were sitting in a restaurant that Professor Dobbs had recommended. Beth gazed at the elegant furnishings and felt a little ill at ease.

"We don't have restaurants like this at home," she laughed.

"No, Mary's diner doesn't quite match up to this," George grinned. "But you need to get used to it. Published authors can live in higher style than farmer's wives."

"No, thank you. I'm happy to be a farmer's wife."

"I don't want to put a damper on your enthusiasm, but all will depend on the success of the book," the professor reminded them. "But I do feel it will be a good seller in our part of the country. Beth, you will probably be called on to do a promotion tour, bookstore signings and such."

"I can handle it!"

John Dobbs had to return that night, so they made the long drive home, arriving around midnight. As they dropped him off at his home, Beth promised, "I'm dedicating this book to you, Mr. Dobbs, you and my family."

"I'm honored, Beth, to be in such company. Good night."

The living room lights were burning, and Granny was at the door to greet them. Too excited to sleep anyway, they sat down and gave her the details of their day in Atlanta.

"Young lady, you are going to be one busy girl," Granny hugged her. "I'm so proud of you. And your mom and I will help with the girls all we can, especially if you have to be gone some."

"Oh, Granny, what would I do without you? But we'd better wait and see if this book sells."

"It will," Granny assured her. "I know it will."

The book came out in the spring. The beautiful cover showed a sweep of their own land with their farmhouse in the distance. The photographer had captured the local flavor of the farms and small towns, and Beth was pleased with what it added to her prose. Even though sales were slow at first, Beth delighted in seeing it in the bookstores. As Christmas drew closer, sales began to pick up. Coffee table books were in, and bookstores were soon reordering THE TENDER LAND. Beth was suddenly busy arranging book signings as well as finishing up her degree.

As she went about her hectic schedule, she couldn't know that her life would take turns that she never imagined.

Chapter Twelve

Beth stood at the bottom of the stairs, tapping her watch. "Felicia! You're going to be late for school. Angelea smiled up from the bottom step where she sat, tying her shoes.

"She's going to miss the bus," she said with a smirk.

"No, she isn't," Felicia yelled as she ran down the steps, jumping over her sister.

Beth glared at her older daughter. She was her twin in everything but size, while Angelea's dark hair had lightened to the auburn shade of her father's. At eleven Felicia showed a rebellious streak that surprised Beth and George. She had been such a compliant child until the past year.

"Well, when will you be home this time?" she asked her mother curtly, as she gathered her books from the hall tree.

Beth cringed at her tone. It made her feel guilty that she was going on yet another trip. Her books, THE TENDER LAND, and the second, HARVESTIME, had been successful, and Beth had followed them with her first novel THE PEOPLE OF THE LAND about the Depression years which made the bestseller list. So she suddenly was a celebrity with interviews and writer's conferences to attend. At first, she was shy and unable to take any trips without George, but as time went on, she learned to travel alone. As her confidence grew, she learned to say no to some of the things that would keep her from her family and her writing. But Felicia seemed to resent every trip she took.

"Honey, I'll just be gone four days. And you get to go straight from school to Grandma's and Grandpa's. You love staying in town with them, don't you?"

Felicia sighed. "Not really. Oh, I guess. I don't have my bag packed though, I had so much homework, I forgot."

"That's okay. They will bring you out and get your things. Now, both of you be on your best behavior for Grandma, you hear? Uh oh, here's the bus. Don't forget to tell Mr. Brown that he needn't stop for you the rest of the week. Quick, give me kisses." Beth grabbed Angelea in a bear hug.

"Bye, Mommy. Have a good time. Love you." Angelea was out the door in a mad dash.

"Bye." Felicia said sullenly, breezing by her mother with her mouth in a pout.

"Hey!" Beth took her arm. "Don't I get more than that?"

116

Felicia managed a tight smile. "Sorry, Mom. I love you." She threw one arm around her mother's neck and was gone.

Beth watched them board the bus, saw Angelea climb back off to pick up papers that had fallen from her notebook. She smiled, shaking her head, as she stepped out on the porch and waved until the bus pulled away. The spring air was still chilly, and she hugged herself as she inhaled the tangy earthy air. She was glad that she chose to wear the long skirt and boots with the rust sweater; it was still a winter clothes day.

For a moment, she wished that she didn't have to go to this conference. It seemed like she and George hadn't had any time together lately. He was so good about her fame and travels, but she felt like she had neglected him, especially the last year.

She sighed and turned back into the house. Joan would be here to pick her up and drive her to the airport shortly. Joan was so happy since she and Bill married. They went quietly to a justice of the peace and married shortly after Hilda's death and settled into Joan's house. Beth loved it that her girls spent time in her old home, her old room when she had to be gone.

"Shouldn't you be getting ready?" Granny handed her a second cup of coffee as she entered the kitchen.

"Thanks, Granny. I'm almost ready. Sit with me a moment."

Granny eased into the chair opposite her. She had really begun to slow down the past two years. Her health was good, but arthritis had taken its toll of her energy, and she was secretly glad that Joan and Bill could keep the girls. Their pre-teen moods sometimes got the best of her. That just left George to keep an eye on, and sometimes she enjoyed having her handsome grandson to herself.

"How long will you be gone?"

"Just four days. Then there won't be any more trips for a while. I love what I do, Granny, and feel so honored that my books are selling, but I cherish my time at home. It's the best place to be."

"I know you get a little tired, Honey, but you wouldn't have it any other way. And George is so proud of you."

"You don't think it bothers him that I'm making so much money right now? I mean it won't last forever, and most of it has gone towards the girls' college and fixing up the house a little."

"No, Beth. You know things like that don't bother George. His ego is intact."

They heard Joan's rap on the door and yelled together, "In the kitchen."

Joan floated into the kitchen like a spring breeze, eyes sparkling, and her salt and pepper hair perfectly groomed.

"Wow, you smell wonderful," Beth told her mother as she hugged her.

"Bill bought this for me yesterday. Like it? He's so good to me, just buys me gifts all the time. Granny, you sure raised a wonderful man." She glowed as she helped herself to coffee.

"Two of them," added Beth. "Relax, Mom, and I'll finish my packing. Be ready in a jif."

She went back to their bedroom where an assortment of clothes was spread on the bed. Quickly, she folded and arranged them in her suitcase. Her packed briefcase stood ready to go by the foot of the bed. She set the luggage by the door and went to the hall closet for her raincoat. She turned and walked unexpectedly into George's arms.

"I don't want you to go," he said as he held her.

"Then I won't," she said, pulling back to look into his eyes. "I'll call and say I'm sick if you really want me to."

He laughed. "You'd never lie and you know it. I'll just miss you, that's all."

She kissed him hard, breathing in the manly smell of earth and animals. "I'll be home in three days, actually four since I won't get in until night. You'll pick me up at the airport at nine?"

"Yes, Ma'am. I'll be there with bells on."

Arm in arm they joined Granny and Joan, who rose, taking her last sip of coffee.

"We'd better go." She kissed her son-in-law and Granny on the cheeks.

George loaded the car and gave Beth a long kiss. "See you Friday night?"

"Bye, Darling." She turned and climbed into the car to hide the sudden tears that welled up.

"What's with the tears?" her mother asked as they pulled onto the highway.

"I just don't want to go," Beth wiped her tears with her fingers.

"Oh, you'll be okay once you get there and get to meet all those other authors. It'll be so exciting to read your work and encourage the new writers."

"I know. I'll be fine once I get on the plane."

And she was. As the plane lifted off into the bright sunshine, she was already thinking about the busy days ahead.

George worked the lower field for planting and came in chilled, tired, and hungry. Granny had fried chicken with all the trimmings, and he fell into it with gusto. Later, they sat quietly reading, occasionally making small talk. Both were thinking how quiet the house was without the girls and Beth.

Alone in his bed, he thought about the changes in Beth that her fame had brought. The shy little farmwife had become a coast to coast traveler, sure of herself and her talents. How proud he was of her. He pushed down his loneliness with the thoughts of her homecoming with delightful stories of her new associations. As he drifted off to sleep, he promised himself that he would arrange to go with her on the next writer's conference that came up.

The next day brought rain, so George went in for supplies and to the grocery for Granny. He was rounding the aisle in a hurry and crashed right into Sara Jo Mackey's cart.

"Hey! George. You're a really bad driver!" his old school chum laughed. "How've you been?"

"Sara Jo! I haven't seen you since high school. I thought you married Elton Bailey and moved away. Back for a visit?"

"No, back to stay. Elton and I came to a parting of the ways." She dropped her head and George noticed how lines had formed in her round face. She brushed her unruly hair back and laughed a little too loudly.

"I'm sorry. Was it recent?"

"I just came home last week. We—I have a little boy, Terry. We've been staying at Mother's."

"That's too bad. You should come out to the farm and see us. Beth would be so happy to see you."

"I've read Beth's books. She's really done great. I know you must be so proud of her. Say, have you got a few minutes? I'll buy you a cup of coffee."

George looked at his old classmate's face and felt sorry for her. "Sure. How about we finish shopping and meet at Perry's?'

Later, they settled into a booth in the familiar dark area in the back of the drugstore.

"This brings back memories," Sara Jo remarked wistfully. "Nothing has changed, has it?"

"Not here," George said looking around. "But we've changed a little." He touched the beginnings of gray that lightened his temples. They chatted easily about their high school days for awhile.

"Tell me about Beth. Do you have children?" She stirred her coffee, looking intently into his face.

"We have two girls, eleven and nine, Felicia and Angelea. They're our pride and joy. We live on the farm, of course."

"Your grandmother? Is she still living?"

"My, yes. She keeps us all in line. She's getting a little feeble with her arthritis, but she keeps on going."

"And Beth?"

"Well, you've read her books so you know what she's been doing. She surprised us with her talent. And it amazed her when the books became top sellers. The down side is that she's gone a lot more and neither of us likes that part. Enough about us. So tell me what you've been doing."

"Well, I guess we'll be getting divorced, seems to be the only way out. We got along so well at first. Then he lost his job and things got rough. He hates the job he has now and takes it out on Terry and me. I just couldn't take it anymore. But I can tell already that we're not going to be happy at Mother's for very long. She's so angry with me for leaving Elton."

George smiled in sympathy. Then he remembered his Dad's empty house, having been vacated by the last renters.

"Sara Jo, would you like to rent Dad's old house? He married Beth's mom, by the way."

"You don't mean it? What a hoot! That's really keeping things in the family. But the house—how much does it rent for?"

George shook his head. "I'm not sure, I'll ask Dad. It needs some repairs. The last renter left it in quite a mess. But a few days work and it could be livable again. What do you think?"

She reached for his hand. "Thank you, George. I appreciate it. Let me talk to Mother and Daddy and see if they can help me until I get a job. I would love for Terry and me to be out on our own. He's getting so spoiled at home."

"Well, just give us a call. Dad won't be renting it until he fixes it up again. So think it over. Now I must get these groceries back to Granny before she sends out a posse for me." He rose and patted her hand. "It was good to see you, Sara. Don't be a stranger, and let me know about the house."

"Thanks, George." She watched him as he strolled toward the front, stopping to chat with Mr. Perry before going out into the street. She sipped the rest of her coffee slowly, thinking. "George is more handsome than when he was in school. I really liked him then, but he always cared for Beth. Beth, the famous writer. Oh, well, maybe he'll lower the rent for an old girlfriend, and I'll have a place to call my own for awhile. It might be nice to see him now and then though."

She left the drug store and drove to her parents. Terry was playing on the old swing in the side yard, his blond hair glinting as he swung from shade into sunlight. He had become quiet with her since they left Elton, like he was angry with her, too. She pulled into the drive and began to unload groceries. He ran to help her, and she gave him the lightest bags.

"I can carry another bag, Mom," he said. "I can help you with that big one."

"No, Son, I can carry the heavy one. You go open the door for me." As he walked ahead of her, she decided that she would find a way to take care of Terry with no help from his father. She would show him that she didn't need him after all, for anything. With George's help, she could make it on her own.

Chapter Thirteen

Felicia's face drew into a frown as she whined. "But you said you weren't going to be gone for awhile. I wanted to have a sleep-over Friday night, and the mothers won't let my friends come when you aren't here."

"Why not? Granny and Daddy are here, and you could probably talk Grandma and Grandpa into coming out, too."

"But, Mom. They expect you to be here."

"Felicia, I'm sorry. My editor wants to go over the new book with me, and I really need to be there. If you'll wait until next week to have your slumber party, I'll be here."

"Jennie is having one that week," Felicia moaned. "The girls think I don't ever have company at my house because you're always gone."

"Now, Honey, you have girls out all the time." Beth began setting the table for dinner. "Get the napkins out of the cupboard, please."

Felicia sighed and put the napkins around with a mistreated look on her face. She brushed back long bangs with the back of her hand, glaring at her mother as she plopped down, making as much noise as she could muster.

Beth poured herself a glass of iced tea, and sat down with a heavy heart. She hated fussing with her daughter; it took the energy right out of her body. She had been gone a lot, and she hated that, but it was necessary. As soon as she conferred with her editor, there would be no need for trips until the book actually came out, and that would be months. If she could just get her family through one more absence.

"Why is this week so important anyway?" She asked her pouting daughter.

"Mom! My birthday is Saturday, remember?"

A rush of guilt poured over Beth like a bucket of ice water. Felicia's birthday. She had forgotten for a moment. She bought her gift two weeks ago, but after that her mind had been on her writing.

"Yes—I know," she stammered, twisting her wedding ring around with her thumb, hoping her daughter couldn't see the guilt on her face. "But you don't have to have your party on that day. After all, you're almost sixteen now, not a little kid," she offered lamely.

"So I should wait a week, a month—how long, Mother? Until YOU have nothing else YOU want to do?"

George entered the kitchen just as the angry girl whirled to face her mother. "I don't like the tone of your voice, young lady." He frowned at the two of them. "Just what's going on here?"

"Mom is going to be gone all weekend, and I can't have my sleep-over. I've been planning on it for a month, not that I matter!" she huffed.

"Well, your mom doesn't have to be here, does she?"

"Yes, I guess I do," Beth admitted. "Granny doesn't need to stay up half the night listening to giggly girls. That's my job. Look, Felicia, I'll call Horton books and ask Jim Evans if we could wait until next week to go over the book. Would that please you?"

"Forget it! Just go on to your old meeting, it doesn't matter if I have a birthday or not! You care more about your old books than you do us anyway." She flounced out of the room leaving George and Beth with their mouths open.

"You just let her get away with that!" Beth accused, knocking over her iced tea.

"Me? Why didn't you stop her? Besides, Beth, I can hardly blame her. You promised her that you would be here next weekend, remember? She asked you about the party last week."

"She did?" Beth scooped up ice back into her glass and swiped the spill with vicious swipes. "I remember now. Guess I had my mind on my book. I've been working so hard." She sat back down, put her head on her arms and murmured, "I feel like such a wretch."

George didn't move to comfort her. Instead he sat opposite her and pulled her face up by her chin.

"Listen, Beth. We're all proud of what you do, but sometimes I think you forget you have a family. You go in so many directions and at such a pace. Now I know that you could do this another time, so why don't you do that? Call Jim; tell him that you have a family emergency. One week won't matter with the book."

"So Felicia throws a temper fit, and you come to her rescue. You always take her side." Beth rose and paced the kitchen. "You don't know how hard I work, and you really don't understand how this book publishing business works. Do you think I'm the only writer Jim deals with? I could easily be cast aside for the next copycat writer that mimics my style, and my books would be back in local bookstores again. If I work too hard to please my publisher, it's because I have to maintain a place with him, a good relationship."

"And this has nothing to do with your ego? Beth, stop it. You're set in the literary world enough that you could take some time off for your family. And not just Felicia, but the rest of us. How much time have you spent with me lately? When did we last go out for dinner or even to a movie? You work every night until I'm asleep, so there's no sex life anymore . . ."

"George! That's not true," she said in horror. "I don't neglect you that way, I don't."

"When was the last time, Beth? You don't remember? Well, I do, and it's been too long. But back to these girls, they need a mother around. Angelea is independent and no trouble, but Felicia is going through a bad time. Have you noticed what she wears lately? She looks like a hippie, and I'm not too sure about that boy that comes around here. She spends most of her time sitting in the car with him instead of asking him in."

"What boy? You mean Charlie? He's harmless. And as for dress, all the kids are dressing that way now. You're blowing everything out of proportion, George."

He sighed, got up and went to the door. "Well, you do what you want to. That's what you'll do anyway." He opened the door and went out, giving it a slam.

"Where are you going?" she shouted through the glass.

"To fix the door over at Dad's house, it won't shut good, and she can't lock it," he yelled over his shoulder.

"She, meaning Sara Jo," Beth murmured as she watched him climb into his truck. Jealousy did a dance with the anger inside her brain. "He's always working on that house—making it cozy for Sara Jo. And he walks out and goes to her leaving me to fix the mess with Felicia. Coward!" She wanted to bawl like a baby, but instead she swallowed back the tears as Angelea came in to get a cold drink.

"What's with Filly?" she asked, using her nickname for her sister.

"Filly is mad at her mother, as usual, because I have a meeting Friday in New York and won't be here for her slumber party."

"But you promised her, Mom," Angelea took a big swig of cola. She shook back her long silky auburn mane and leaned against the refrigerator.

"That's what your dad said. Oh, Angel, I didn't forget her birthday, I bought her gift two weeks ago, but I did forget about this party thing. I'm going to call Jim and cancel the trip."

"Good. That should shut her up for awhile," Angelea rolled her eyes as she returned to her room.

Beth went to her office and picked up the phone. After waiting for four minutes, Jim finally came on the line.

"Hey, Beth. How's the book coming? Do you have it ready for our meeting Friday? I have several covers I want to go over with you."

"Jim, something has come up here at home, and I won't be able to make it. Could we please reschedule? It's really important or I wouldn't ask you to do this for me."

"Well, Beth, I'm sorry. We're behind on this as it is. But if you can't come, you can't come. Let me get back to you about another time. I'll have to check my own schedule. Things have really been crazy here," he said in a displeased tone of voice.

"Thank you, Jim. As I said, I wouldn't ask for more time if it wasn't important."

"Yeah. I'll get back to you, Beth."

She hung up, knowing that she had angered the only person that she had any difficulty with since Horton bought the rights to her books. Jim was a hard man to please, and she was just a little intimidated by him.

Feeling exhausted, she climbed the stairs and knocked on Felicia's door. "May I come in?"

The door unlocked with a snap. She pushed it open, revealing a messy room and a red eyed girl with curly hair; hands on hips, glaring back at her.

"I changed my meeting. So get on the phone and call your friends, and we'll plan a big wing-ding."

"Well, you shouldn't have done that just for little ole me," she said, sarcastically, plopping on the bed.

"Hey, I can change my mind," Beth said, angrily.

"I'm sorry, Mom." A long pause, then, "Thank you."

Beth sat down with her on the disheveled bed, and they hugged for a long time. Felicia broke away with a smile and a sheepish look on her beautiful face. "You're the greatest, Mom. I'm sorry that I've been such a brat."

"I'm sorry, too, Honey. Sometimes I get too busy and forget about everyone but myself. I certainly will watch it from now on. Just as long as you understand that I do have to do whatever it takes to keep my books on the market. They're your future, too, your and Angelea's."

"Daddy makes a living for us, too, Mom," she reminded Beth.

Beth started to reply, but thought better of it, and closed the door, leaving Felicia dialing a friend. Feeling better but suddenly dry, she went down to get the glass of tea she hadn't gotten to drink.

"All settled?' Granny asked, as she cut a tiny sliver of warm apple pie, nodding with satisfaction when the flavor pleased her taste buds.

"You heard?"

"Couldn't help it. Voices carry. Do you think George will be home for supper?" She eyed Beth, warily.

"I don't know. He's pretty mad at me. But he never misses a meal, so I expect he'll be home," she said, hopefully.

"Why don't you wait for him and go out for dinner? I'll feed the girls. You need the time together."

Beth mulled the idea over for about two seconds before answering. "Great idea. Granny, I don't know what I'd do without you."

"And Beth?"

"Huh?"

"Dress up a little. You've had on those ragged jeans all day. Go put on a little make-up, make yourself pretty."

She hugged Granny. "You're right. I'll go take a long shower and get dolled up. Thanks." With a twinkle in her eye, Granny waved her hand in dismissal as Beth kissed her wrinkled cheek.

After her bath, Beth used her favorite perfume and put on the navy pantsuit that George especially liked, and waited.

At nine o'clock, she got up from the sofa, went to her bedroom, and undressed. Pulling on her robe, she went to the kitchen for something to quiet her angry stomach and ease her aching heart.

George and Sara Jo sat at her table with the remains of pizza congealing on their plates. Tools lay by his chair that had repaired the back door.

"Thanks for the pizza, Sara. I should be getting on home. I was so upset with Beth when I left. Now I feel bad that I didn't go straight home after I fixed your door. But I did enjoy the pizza. Granny's cooking is great, but it was a welcome change." He rose and picked up his tools, putting them into a carrier on the sink.

"George, thank you for fixing the door. And thanks for listening to all my troubles. There really isn't anyone I can talk to about my situation. Mom is still ticked off at me and keeps harping about my getting back with Elton."

"Maybe you could try counseling, Sara. It wouldn't hurt to give it a try. And if he's been calling you everyday, it sounds like he would do anything you wanted."

Sara Jo rose from her chair and stretched like a cat, pulling her sweater even tighter across her small breasts. "Thanks for all your advice. I'll think on it. I just don't know if I want him back. He gave me such a hard time. That does something to a woman," she purred, softly.

"Yeah, I guess so," George said, thinking of his own retreat from his house earlier. "Okay, I'm gone. Remember to lock the door after me." He stepped out on the back stoop, and she followed him.

"Thanks again, George." She reached up and pulled his head down and kissed him on the cheek, quickly sliding her lips over to his in a soft wet kiss.

"Sara . . ." he pulled his face back with a start.

"George, I'm lonely. What's wrong with a little kiss?" She moved up against him, pressing her body to his. He wanted to back away in protest, but his feet seemed glued to the concrete. As she slipped her arms around his neck, he kissed her lightly until her lips opened under his. Then hastily pushing her away, he stammered a 'goodnight' and stumbled his way to the truck. Once inside, he laid his head on the steering wheel, feeling shock waves running through his body. So that's how easy it would be to be a cheating husband. Just one more minute and he could have betrayed Beth and their marriage.

He cranked the truck and drove slowly home, hoping Beth wouldn't be able to sense the guilt that swelled in his still pounding chest.

Chapter Fourteen

The melody of the laughter of a dozen girls rang through the house as the clock struck eleven. They were gathered in the kitchen in their pajamas. Felicia and Angelea handed out cold drinks from the refrigerator and, grabbing two plates of chocolate chip cookies and brownies, they ran back up the stairs with much squealing and giggling.

George ran his fingers through his rust colored hair that was beginning to gray around the edges and wondered if there would be any sleep in the household at all this night. Beth had gone up to join the girls for a cookie and a little conversation before leaving them for the evening.

He pulled on his own pajamas and lay on top of the sheet, listening to the chatter filtering through the ceiling. He was glad that Granny was at Cousin Lillian's house for the night, she was a real bear when she lost sleep. Matter of fact, he was, too, but he was glad that his girls were having a good time and that their friends felt at home here. Beth was good at making them feel easy, she could join right in with them, and although his daughters would never think to put it into words, they loved that about their mother.

Beth. She was such a puzzle these days. She had been so distant this week, even though he had tried so hard to be loving and considerate. Maybe it was the guilt that he felt every time he thought of Sara and their kiss that fueled his desire to please her. Did she feel that? Could she forgive him if he told her or would that just create more distance between them?

He sighed and turned the lamp off. The breeze coming in the open window was welcome as it blew the sheer curtains in ripples. The smells of the farm were soft, earthy, and comforting. They usually induced sleep, but there wasn't that accompanying silence that soothed his mind—not what with all the commotion upstairs.

He was proud of Felicia for sharing her night with her younger sister. And Angelea was so delighted to be included in the junior class set. He must remember to tell his girls how proud he was of them tomorrow. He needed to do that more often.

He felt Beth slide in quietly under the sheet, and pull it up carefully so she wouldn't wake him. He debated about letting her go on thinking that he was dozing, but he knew it would be obvious as he tossed and turned.

"I'm not asleep."

"I doubted that you were with all this giggling. They are having such a good time, but I do hope sometime around dawn they will give it up," she laughed.

"We'll catch up tomorrow night. They are leaving before tomorrow night, aren't they?"

"We'll drive them home, if we have to," she yawned.

"So we might as well talk, we haven't had much time for that lately. Got anything on your mind?" He turned the lamp back on.

"No. I have to go to New York Tuesday. This time I have to go or Jim will have a fit. Besides I want to get this book ready for the market. I think I need to take some time off. My creative juices need regenerating."

He reached for her hand, but it felt stiff and cold in his. "I'm glad. You need a break. It will be refreshing to have you in the house with us and not holed up in your office."

She withdrew her hand and rose up to fluff and adjust her pillow. "What about you? What's on your mind?"

"Getting everything in the ground on time. Buying another bull for the herd. The usual stuff. Having my wife back . ."

"Don't start," she warned. "You've been a million miles away since you went to the rental to fix the door and stayed half the night. So let's don't go down that path again."

"I apologized for that," he snapped. "I told you she enticed me with the pizza," he added in a more jovial tone.

"Just pizza? Well, how is she doing with her divorce and all?"

"Okay, I guess. She said he calls her every day. I think she's the one who wants the divorce, not him."

"Too bad," Beth flopped over on her side. "Maybe she wants to start over with someone else."

He almost told her right then about the kiss. Why shouldn't he? After all, he hadn't been the aggressor. But then he hadn't exactly fought it either in his moment of weakness.

"Who knows. From now on, I'll ask Wade if he'll go over and do the repairs as they come up. Would that make you feel better?"

"Why should it?" she snapped. "But do you think it's necessary for you to go every time she calls? After all, your dad is only a few houses down. Call him."

"She's jealous," he thought to himself with a silent chuckle before he answered. "Yeah, I just hate to bother Dad when I told him I would take care of it. But it is handier for him. Believe me, Beth, I have better things to do."

She closed her eyes and murmured a goodnight, and soon he could hear her regular deep breathing. Turning out the light, he wondered how she could sleep with all the rustling and giggling from upstairs. There would be no sleep for him until this crew settled down.

The next morning, she was as fresh as if she had slept eight hours. The girls were all still asleep, having given in to it around three o'clock. The smell of sausage frying caused George to hurry his early morning chores and head for the kitchen.

"How can you be so perky this morning?" He asked as he washed his hands.

"I feel great. Sit down, your breakfast is almost ready." She poured his coffee and stirred the scrambled eggs, emptying them into two plates. They ate in silence for a few minutes.

"George, go with me," she said suddenly. "Go with me Tuesday to New York. Let's take a couple of days and tour the city. I checked the girls' calendars and they don't have anything special going on." She looked at him hopefully.

"I would love to go away with you," he reached for her hand, and then drew it back with a snap. "Oh, Beth. I forgot the co-op meeting Tuesday night."

"Do you have to go?"

"I am the chairman of the committee to appear before our congressman to push the new farm bill. I'm sorry. You know I would love to go, but if I don't attend this, nothing will get done. Everybody waits for me to do everything."

"I'm sure someone else could chair the committee this one time," she protested.

"I'll call James Harris and see if he'll take my place just as soon as we're finished. I really do want to go with you, Beth." Their eyes met across the table, and she knew he meant it.

But, as it turned out, James Harris was in the hospital with pneumonia, and Beth sadly went on her trip alone.

"Phone for you," Granny called loudly from the porch. George jogged from the equipment shed, washed his hands hurriedly, and answered.

"George?" the familiar purring voice of Sara Jo came over the line.

"Hello, Sara. What can I do for you?" He said, crisply.

"George, I hate to bother you, but the kitchen sink is stopped up. I can't imagine why; I promise I didn't put anything down the drain that would have caused it. Could you come over and fix it?"

"I'll call my dad, Sara. He's just down the street and he's a better plumber that I am."

"But I had hoped you'd come so we could talk. I need your advice. Elton has refused to sign the divorce papers, and I don't know what to do." He could hear the breaking in her voice.

"I'm all tied up today, Sara. But I'll see that it gets fixed."

"Then you'll come tomorrow? I can wait one day, I guess."

He frowned as he asked, "Will you be there in about an hour?"

"Yes. I'll be waiting," she said, huskily.

He hung up and quickly called his dad, but there was no answer. Slamming down the phone, he walked out on the porch and sat down with a sigh. He didn't want to see her. There was no temptation now from her all too willing closeness, and he was tired of her dependence on him to solve her problems. The thought crossed his mind that she probably did clog the drain on purpose just to get him over.

"What's wrong with your hearing?" Granny asked as she came up the steps. "I've been talking to you, but you don't seem to hear me."

"Oh, sorry. Sara called and wanted me to come right away and fix her sink. I called Dad, but there was no answer, so I guess I might as well go and get it over with." He paused, then added with a smile. "Hey, Granny, why don't you go with me? You can talk to Sara while I fix the sink."

"Now why would I want to do that?" Then her blue eyes took on that all knowing look and began to twinkle. "But if you want me to, sure, I'll go. Just let me wash my hands, I've been digging in the flower beds."

They pulled up in Sara's driveway, and she was out the door in a flash, grinning from ear to ear. But she stopped short when Granny stepped out of the truck.

"Oh,—I—hello, Mrs. Daniel. I didn't expect to see you. How've you been?" She gave George a hard look as she spoke.

"Just fine, Sara. I just rode along with George to get out for awhile. He tells me you've fixed up the house real cute. I hope you don't mind my coming by. I thought we could chat while he works on the plumbing." Granny's pat on Sara's hand and her too bright smile was all innocence.

"Of course," Sara said, unclenching her teeth.

The sink wasn't clogged badly, and George had it cleaned out quickly. He couldn't hear much chatter from the living room as he worked, and he felt sorry that he had put Granny in such an uncomfortable position.

Wiping his hands on an old towel, he went in where the two of them sat smiling, looking around the room.

"Well, all fixed. Anything else need doing while I'm here?"

"No. Thank you very much," she said coldly, tossing her blond mane and rising from her chair. "It was good to see you, Mrs. Daniel. Please give my best to Beth." She managed a phony smile.

"I will," Granny opened the front door and went on out to the truck.

Lingering for a moment, George politely asked, "Have you heard from Elton today?"

"Yeah, he called this morning. I may be moving out soon, George. He's coming down this weekend, and we'll probably give it one more try. I've been doing some thinking. Terry really needs his father." He felt sure in his bones that she had just made that up, that Elton had no idea about these plans but would probably be most agreeable to them.

He felt relieved anyway. "That's great! Well, I wish you the best, Sara, you and Elton. Just let us know for sure when you're moving. You can leave the key with Dad." George headed for the car.

"George," she said, just barely loud enough for him to hear. "It could have been so different."

He turned around and smiled. "No, it couldn't, Sara." He opened the truck door and called, "Good luck."

The front door slammed with a bang as he cranked up the engine.

"Well?" Granny questioned him with her sharp blue eyes.

142

"Well, what?"

"Did I help by coming with you?"

He laughed and grabbed her hand. "Thank you, Granny. You always come through for me. Yes, you helped tremendously."

She grinned and asked no more questions.

When Beth got home, George didn't let her unpack. He had made reservations at the Hilton in Nashville, and arranged for them to have a long weekend together. When they arrived, Beth was amazed that he had reserved the bridal suite, and there were two dozen yellow roses on the bedside table.

"George. I can't believe all this. Why are you being so good to me?"

"Because you are the love of my life, and I wanted to do something special for you."

They only left the suite long enough to eat.

Chapter Fifteen

Felicia twirled the phone line around her fingers as she walked back and forth across her room. Her heart was beating like a drum. Ben Utley was on the other end of the line; Ben Utley, the most popular boy in her class. She could hardly believe that he called her, that she was actually talking to him. She could envision him, his tall wiry body slung across a chair; his almost shoulder length dark hair falling over his gray eyes.

He had flirted with her in the hall several times, but he did that with all the girls, so she hadn't thought much about it. Now he was on the phone, telling her that he loved her hair, the way it curled around her face, even after she had Angelea iron it straight every morning. She shook her long hair when he said he had always wanted to touch it.

"I thought you were going with Junie Wages," she teased. "That's been the word around school."

He laughed softly. "That didn't even get off the ground. Junie is . . . okay, I guess, but not for me. I can't seem to keep my eyes off you, Filly. You aren't going with anyone, are you?"

"No, not lately. I've been too busy trying to keep my grades up. Mom and Dad have really been on me about grades. You know, college next year, and all."

"Yeah, I get the same drill."

"But you always make A's. It's easy for you."

"Hey, I have to study, too. But enough of that. I wondered if you'd want to go to the movies tonight. We could eat at Corny's first."

"Yeah, I'd like that. What time?"

"I'll pick you up about six?'

"Okay, see you then."

She hung up and squealed, flinging herself on the bed and punching her pillow wildly with her fists. Angelea came running in the room.

"Was it HIM?"

"Were you listening?" Felicia jumped up.

"No, I wasn't listening, but I couldn't help hearing you scream your head off!"

Felicia grabbed her sister's arms. "Yes. Yes. It was him, and he asked me out tonight."

They jumped up and down arms entwined, squealing together.

"What are you going to wear? You can borrow my yellow sweater and long skirt, if you want."

"No, I think he'll wear jeans, so I'll wear my new bell bottoms and the plaid shirt with the fringe on the bottom. What do you think?"

"That's okay, you look good in that."

"Now I'd better clear it with Mom," Felicia said, rolling her eyes as she and Angelea ran down the stairs.

Beth was sitting on the porch with a fresh cup of coffee, looking out at the beautiful trees. This autumn had been so lovely and warm; the trees at their peak were breathtaking. She had enjoyed her hiatus from writing, enjoyed messing around the farm with George and spending more time with the girls. But now she was feeling the itch to get back to it. She had a notebook full of ideas and notes that held some promise for a new book. She closed her eyes as pieces of a plot ran through her mind.

The girls were upon her before she heard the door slam.

"Mom. Guess what? Ben just called and asked me out tonight."

"Really? Do we know Ben?"

Felicia frowned. "No, I don't think so. But Mom, he's just the most popular boy in my class, that's all. I can't believe he called me. ME!"

"Why not you, Sweetie?"

"Is it okay?"

"I guess so. Just be home by eleven. Where are you going?"

"Just to Corny's for something to eat and then to a movie."

"Is your fella coming out to see you tonight?" She turned her head toward Angelea who perched on the arm of her chair.

"I don't know. He hasn't called," she said wistfully. Angelea wasn't allowed to date yet, but Billy Prentice had been spending Saturday nights at their house for weeks.

"He probably will." She patted her daughter's knee.

By six o'clock that night, Felicia was a wreck. She was ready thirty minutes early and paced the floor, giving a sigh of relief when she saw his Mustang coming up the drive. Beth saw the red Mustang and gave the sigh of a worried mother.

Felicia introduced Ben to Beth and to George, who had just come in from the barn. George gave him the usual once over, asking whom his father was, where he lived, while Felicia wiggled uncomfortably. But Ben smiled and answered his questions politely and soon they were off.

"I hope he's a careful driver," Beth said as she watched the car wheel out onto the highway with a squeal. As the red car left, Billy's old pick-up turned in. Thankful that one daughter was safely at home that night, she went to the kitchen and checked the chicken casserole. She knew from experience that Billy liked her chicken casserole.

Ben and Felicia ate hamburgers among a crowd of young people they both knew. In fact, they all ended up at one table, and Felicia was delighted that everyone saw them together. Now she wouldn't have to brag to all her friends Monday morning.

At the movie, he held her hand. She could hardly concentrate on the movie for wondering if he would kiss her goodnight. A delicious shiver ran through her at the thought.

When they got out, it had turned chilly and Felicia wished for Angelea's yellow sweater. They drove around the square several times and around the drive-in where they pulled in for a coke. As they sat, sipping their drinks, Ben's friend, Jim "Red" Jolly came up to the car. He leaned in Ben's window and, after first looking around, handed him a reefer. Ben inhaled deeply.

"Thanks, Buddy," he said with a grin.

Felicia bit her lip. She knew a lot of kids were into pot, but none of her crowd was. The smoke made the car smell like burning rope. She felt uneasy, but managed to smile and chat with Red until he handed Ben another one and they finished it off between them. She grew quiet watching them. Suddenly she wished that she were home, eating popcorn with Angelea and Billy, her mom and dad. She looked at her watch; it was almost ten-thirty. She interrupted Ben and Red's conversation about the upcoming game.

"I'd better get home, Ben."

"It's only ten-thirty," he protested.

"Yeah, but by the time we get to my house . . . I'm supposed to be home by eleven."

"Little girls can't stay out late," Red teased.

"Hey, buzz off. I want to make a good impression on her dad." He winked at Felicia who was blushing at Red's teasing.

They left the drive-in and headed toward the highway.

"Are you high?' she asked.

"No, Sweetie, just feeling good. You should try it sometime."

"No, thanks."

"Don't be such a prude. I don't smoke it much, just whenever I want. It's not really addictive, Filly."

"Oh, come on, Ben. You know it leads to the harder stuff. They say everybody starts with marijuana."

"Who is 'they'? Just adults trying to tell us what to do. You need to relax, Filly. Move over here closer to me and let's stop talking about that."

Like a robot, she moved next to him. It did feel good to put her head on his shoulder and feel his arm around her. She didn't even realize that they had passed her driveway until she noticed the mailbox as they sped past. She jerked away from Ben, feeling suddenly frightened and angry.

"Hey, Ben. You just passed my house. And you're driving too fast. You're scaring me!"

"Relax, Filly. I'll turn around in a minute. I need to blow my engine out a little," he laughed as he pushed his foot to the floor.

Beth put her book down and looked at the clock as it struck eleven. She glanced over at George who was dozing on the couch, oblivious to the TV blaring. She rose and turned it off. As she straightened up, she caught a glimpse of the flashing red lights of a police car and an ambulance flying down the road. Her heart stopped for a moment. She wished Felicia and Ben would drive up right now. She was so good about being home right on time. Surely they would be home shortly. She went over and leaned to kiss George awake.

"Time to go to bed, Sleepyhead."

"I've been in bed," he grinned as he stretched and pulled her down beside him.

"An ambulance and police car just went by," she said into his neck. He stiffened and brought his arm up to look at his watch.

"They'll be home soon," he assured her. But soon he rose and walked out on the porch. Eleven-fifteen by his watch. He was beginning to feel very uneasy. He rubbed his arms and went back inside.

"I'll make tea," Beth said.

"That's a good idea. If she isn't home soon, she's going to get a piece of my . . . Wait! Beth, there's a police car coming up the drive." Beth turned white as she followed him out on the porch to meet Officer Tim Meadows on the walk.

"George, your daughter has been in an accident." Tim had to fight to keep his voice even. This was the worst part of his job, especially when it involved people he knew, like his old classmates.

"How bad?" Beth clutched his coat.

"They've taken her to the hospital in Greenville. You might want to get your coats—I'll go ahead of you with my light on."

"Should we wake Granny and Angel?" She screamed as George ran back in the house.

"No, we'll call them from the hospital when we know something." He jerked their jackets from the closet while Beth shivered uncontrollably with fear in their car.

They followed Tim, who drove the long fifteen miles at high speed, red light flashing. Other cars moved off the road as they whizzed past. They drove in silence, each afraid to talk, afraid to lose control.

He took them up to the emergency room entrance and they dashed from the car.

"Felicia Daniel," George shouted at the nurse on the desk.

She rose and went through a door behind her desk, then returned and motioned to them to follow. Weak-kneed, they walked in her silent steps past empty beds until they came to a drawn curtain. The nurse pulled it aside where they saw the still body of their daughter. Two doctors were hovered over her trying to get her awake.

"Come on. Can you hear me?" A young doctor pushed up his glasses as he saw them behind the nurse.

Beth sobbed as she saw the bloody face. Tiny pieces of glass shone on the torn sleeves of her blouse that were speckled with dark red.

"Felicia. My baby, my baby." She pushed past the doctor, George right behind her. The doctors stepped back for a few seconds while Felicia's parents touched her face, her hands, urging her to wake up. Then one of the doctors asked them to step aside while they finished their examination. The nurse took them back to a waiting area and poured them both coffees.

"Try to relax. They'll have news for you just as soon as they're finished," she said as she went back toward her station.

"Wait!" George shouted. "What about the driver?"

"He's at the other end of the corridor."

They looked at each other and sat down. George looked into the black coffee and felt nauseous. Felicia looked so pale beneath the swelling and the blood crusting on her face. He began to pray silently as he held Beth's cold hand. After what seemed like an eternity, the doctor came toward them. They rose on shaky rubbery legs as he began to talk.

"She has a lot of cuts and bruises, a concussion, and a broken left arm. But she's come to and is talking. We're going to take her into x-ray to make sure nothing else is broken. Then we'll take her into surgery to set her arm and stitch up some of her deeper cuts. I think she's going to be okay, but we won't know for sure until we've finished our evaluation. We'll take her up to a room just as soon as we're finished, and you can go up and stay with her." The older, balding doctor shook their hands. "Try not to worry," he added, gently.

"What about the young man who was with her?" Beth asked anxiously. The doctor shook his head.

As they returned to the waiting area, they found an older couple huddled together. They looked up as Beth and George came in, arms around each other.

"Are you Ben's parents?" George asked, as he seated the trembling Beth. They nodded, and Mr. Utley stood up.

"We're so sorry about this," he began but choked on the catch in his throat.

"How's your son?" Beth reached out to the woman who raised her head, her face swollen with tears.

"Not good," she said, dully. "He was thrown from the car, they say. They can't tell us much." Beth took her hand, and they sat quietly until they were able to talk.

"Ben is our youngest son," his father explained. "Our surprise child. The other boys were almost grown when we had Ben. He's been a special joy to us. We think he's kept us young." He paused to compose himself and his wife continued.

"He's been such a good boy. I know we spoiled him, but he's never been any trouble. The doctor told us your daughter is in x-ray?" Ben's mother dried her eyes with her husband's big handkerchief.

"Yes. He thinks she'll be okay." Beth shut her eyes and hoped that it was true.

Tim returned from the squad car with a clipboard of reports in his hand and followed the young doctor with the crew cut as he took the Utleys to see their son, talking to them softly as they walked away. Beth and George heard them both cry out as the door shut silently behind them.

The funeral was long and sad. The little church was full with Ben's large family and classmates taking up most of the pews. A police car, driven by Tim Meadows, led the procession to the cemetery, and Ben was laid to rest beneath the beautiful fallen foliage of maples and dogwoods. The Utleys were inconsolable. Beth and George hugged them at the gravesite and promised to keep in touch, but their thoughts were at the hospital with their daughter. They drove from the cemetery, leaving the grief-stricken parents at the grave, alone.

Joan greeted them outside Felicia's room. "How did it go?"

Beth sighed. "As well as you could expect. I feel so sorry for them, and at the same time, so thankful that my child lived."

Joan nodded as she rubbed Beth's back for comfort. "She is still very quiet. Dr. Adams said she will come out of it when she feels better. He said she could go home tomorrow, but he wants her to see her face first so she won't be shocked later."

"Well, it must be done," George frowned. "This is reality, and she has to face it sometime. She knows she's lucky to be alive. She can handle it."

Beth shook her head. "To a teen-age girl, George, a messed up face is a real tragedy. It is to her mother, too."

"I know." He put his arm around her. "Let's go in. You okay?"

She smiled bravely and the three of them opened the door to Beth's room. She was lying with her head turned toward the window, her arm, in a cast, rested on a pillow at her side. When she looked at them, tears were coursing down her swollen stitch-covered cheeks. Her parents took turns hugging her, murmuring words of love.

"How are his parents?" Felicia asked as Beth handed her a tissue.

"They held up well," Beth lied. "Half the school was there."

"I wish I could have been."

"We'll take you to see them when you're up to it, Honey," Beth sat on the edge of the bed. "Where are Angel and Granny?"

"They went to the cafeteria for a bite," Joan said, pulling the blinds against the sun's glare. Looking at her granddaughter's face with its crisscross lines of stitches, she wondered if the once beautiful face would ever be the smiling happy face that she adored.

"It's partly my fault," Felicia repeated the mantra she voiced over and over.

"Honey, it wasn't your fault. You had no idea what pot would do to Ben." Joan brushed a strand of hair from Felicia's face, careful to avoid her stitches.

"But I should have refused to ride with him. Maybe then he would have gone home, and we'd both been safe."

"You're second guessing, Honey," George took her hand. "Who knows what could have happened. You've got to stop blaming yourself. Ben's the one who caused the accident. Now why don't you get up and walk a little. The doctor says your bruised hip will be better if you walk on it some."

"Just around the room. I don't want to go out in the hall."

George helped her up, and they walked around the room with her leaning heavily on him and wincing every time she put weight on her leg.

Beth slipped into George's place and guided her toward the bathroom.

"No, Mom. I don't want to look in the mirror."

"Honey, you have to look at yourself. We're going to take you home tomorrow, but you have to face yourself first." Firmly she steered her into the tiny bathroom and stood her before the mirror. Felicia kept her eyes closed for a few seconds, then slowly opened her eyes.

"Oh . . . it looks just like it feels," she cried, tears oozing from her eyes.

"Now that's not so bad. You can have a little plastic surgery and you'll be as good as new," Beth said, encouragingly.

"It doesn't matter," she said dully, and turned back to the door.

Once she was back in bed, Granny and Angelea returned from the cafeteria. They looked questioningly at George. He nodded. Angelea perched on the bed and reached for the water glass and held it to Felicia's lips. She shook her head and turned away.

They took her home the next day, and she began to heal, mentally and physically. The stitches came out, and she went back to school. It took weeks, but she slowly returned to her old self. But she refused to have plastic surgery on her face, instead covering up her scars with make-up. No amount of coaxing from her parents would change her mind. "I want to remember," she told them. "I see myself everyday in the mirror, and it's a reminder that I put myself in a dangerous position. I won't do it again."

"But you don't need a scarred face to remember that," her mother argued, but to no avail. Angelea tried to encourage her to have the surgery, but she was not successful either. Felicia seemed determined to punish herself.

Chapter Sixteen

Life returned to normal; Beth went back to writing,
George to farming. He was concentrating on beef cattle
now and less on crops, although Charlie and Wade still
farmed part of the land, and they shared profits and
losses on the crops they raised.

The holidays came and went. Felicia stayed close
to home. Her friends were very supportive at first, but
as time went on, she wasn't asked on very many dates.
And she seemed content to gather around the fire with
her family and play games or read. Beth loved her
company, but worried about her scanty social life. After
all, this was her senior year.

In the spring, the farm turned green and gold with
forsythia and daffodils. The budding trees were in every
shade of green, pink, and pale maroon, their delicate
pastel branches reaching for the sun. March was windy,
but unusually warm with no unexpected snow showers
like in so many years past. Granny was busy planning

her beloved flowerbeds, barely able to wait until she had the newest plants from the catalogue in the ground.

Beth had a book signing the end of the month, and George went with her, leaving Joan and Bill at the farm to keep tabs on the girls—and Granny.

"You don't have to stay here, you know," Granny told them, testily. "I'm perfectly capable of handling things here when Beth and George are gone."

"We feel like we're on vacation, Mother," Bill assured her. "The girls are so busy with school; we hardly get to see them anymore. It's a good time to see what they're up to. And I get to play farmer for a little while."

"Don't let him kid you, Granny. It's a good excuse to get some of your good cooking," Joan laughed. "He likes mine, but nobody's is quite as good as yours."

Beth and George returned to the farm on a sticky, humid afternoon. According to the weather reports on the radio, thunderstorms were expected, and the skies grew darker as they reached the house. After thanking his dad and Joan for staying and helping them carry their bag to their car, George immediately went to check the cattle and talk with Wade. Beth unpacked her overnight case and caught up with her daughters' activities of the day as they sat cross-legged on the bed.

In the kitchen, Granny kept going to the window and talking to herself as she waited for coffee to perk. "I don't like the looks of this weather. It's too hot for this time of year, and those clouds look threatening. I'm going to turn on the TV."

Beth followed the wonderful aroma of the brewed coffee to the kitchen, filled her cup, and went in the living room where Granny and the girls now sat glued to the weather report.

"There are tornado warnings now, Mom," Angelea said frowning.

"We'll be okay, Honey," Beth soothed, trying not to show her own alarm, even though her hand shook, and she spilled coffee on her blouse. All throughout the girls' childhood, she had tried to keep her own fear of storms to herself. Anxious, she, too, kept drifting over by the window to look out at the ominous clouds.

George rushed in with a worried look on his face. "It looks really bad out there. We'd better get ready to go to the cellar. No sense taking any chances."

Wade was close behind George. He'd seen enough storms in his life to recognize that the greenish colored clouds on the horizon meant trouble. As they lingered to look out the windows, the sky grew black as night. Hurriedly, they crowded together down in the dirt-floored cellar and held on to each other.

"I love you," Angelea said in tears to her sister, as she hugged her. The howling of the wind and the hail that followed drowned their words until they could only hear the beat of their hearts drumming in their ears.

As the noise lessened, Wade rose, pulling off his cap and rubbing his bald head. "It seems to be getting quiet. I'm going upstairs and look out and see what's going on."

He opened the cellar door and listened. The rain had slowed to drizzle and the wind stilled. It seemed to be very quiet all of a sudden. He went to the back door to look out just as the roar began, not a gradual sound, but a sudden violent roar like a train coming closer and closer. He ran back to the cellar, slamming the door shut behind him.

"Squat and cover your heads. I hear the tornado coming," he ordered as he pushed Granny to the floor and covered her with his body.

"Amazing Grace, how sweet the sound," Granny began to sing, but was drowned out by the awful roar and the screams of the two girls. George covered Beth and the girls as best he could and squeezed his eyes shut. Shutters banged, and then things crashed overhead in terrifying secession. Glass jars on the shelves near the door exploded sending bits of glass and fruit hurling through the cellar. Dust swirled around their huddled bodies, stinging their eyes when they tried to open them.

As suddenly as it came, the noise receded into the distance, and they slowly lifted their heads. The girls were shivering and crying as George kept assuring them they were all right now. Beth turned to Granny and screamed at the sight of a piece of glass protruding from Granny's head.

"Granny's hurt, George!" She jerked the piece of glass out without thinking, releasing a flow of blood down Granny's face.

"Oh, it's just a scratch," Granny protested, as she pushed George away, but she took the offered handkerchief and pressed it to her cut.

Slowly they climbed the stairs on wobbly knees and opened the door into the kitchen. For a few seconds, it looked as though nothing was out of place. Then they saw the water trickling across the floor where the rain was pouring through a gaping hole in the dining room ceiling. The living room was littered with limbs and trash, its front wall gone and furnishings scattered around the yard. The porch lay splintered against the big oak that was amazingly still standing.

"Stay back," George ordered. "It isn't safe. There's glass all over everything."

"Our rooms," Angelea cried. "All our things . . ."

"Things don't matter," her sister reminded her as she put her arms around her. Beth held them both as her brain whirled in disbelief. She took them back to the kitchen and sat them down. Granny followed in a stupor, holding her head to one side.

"Sit down, Granny, and let me look at your head," Beth said firmly, removing the handkerchief from the wound, her hands still trembling. It had stopped bleeding profusely, but the scalp was opened in a jagged scar.

"I told you it was just a scratch," Granny snapped. "I can't believe those jars burst like that. I'm thankful none of you were cut."

George and Wade surveyed the damage. Amazingly, the girls' rooms upstairs were intact except for a small tree through the window in Felicia's room. From another upstairs window, they could see curtains and pieces of furniture strewn as far as the road.

They walked out back, stepping carefully over debris, expecting to see dead cattle everywhere. But the wild-eyed cattle gathered bawling around the remains of the barn, confused and frightened. The only dead cattle they found were two who were caught when a tree was pulled up by its roots and crushed them. To the left, the equipment shed stood, unscathed; it's equipment dusty, but undamaged.

"Could be worse," Wade mumbled, looking at a pale George. "We're alive, most of the herd's okay, just a house and a barn that can be replaced."

"You're right," George blinked back tears, unashamed. "Go home and check your place, Wade. Give me a few minutes to get the ladies packed up and into town and then we'll check on Charlie's place, too."

In the kitchen, Granny was gathering candles so they could see in the growing twilight. Beth was uselessly sweeping up glass and dirt. Both moved like zombies while the girls sat numbly and silently in kitchen chairs.

George placed his hands on their heads, then reached for Granny's hand. "You need to get stitches in that cut," he told her as he looked down at her bloodied head. "Beth, you and the girls gather up clothes, and we'll go into town. We need to leave things as they are until someone comes to appraise this damage. It's too dangerous to try and clean it up by ourselves."

"Is the upstairs okay?"

"It's safe for them to go up and get their things. Hurry, though. We don't know how our parents are, and we've got several people to check on.

"Oh, I haven't had time to wonder about Mom and Bill. Please let them be okay." Beth said, rushing the girls with her hands. "You heard your dad, girls. But be careful up there. And hurry so we can check on Mom and Bill and get Granny to Dr. Adams." She quickly packed clothes for herself, Granny, and George, and herded everyone to the car, muttering a prayer of thanks that their vehicles, though pock-marked from the hail, were not blown away.

The rag-tag band, dusty with cellar dirt, pulled away down the drive, pausing at the road to look back. As she saw the wreckage of her home from the road, Felicia began to cry softly.

"Hush, Filly," Angelea murmured, squeezing her hand. "We may be luckier than a lot of people. We're all still alive."

Driving through the countryside into town, they were relieved to find that the tornado had apparently done little damage elsewhere. There were tree branches and litter across the fields, but their neighbors' houses looked to be in good shape. And Joan and Bill's neighborhood was intact as well, much to their relief.

Joan grabbed and hugged each one with relief. "I was so afraid," she sobbed. "A friend passed by your place and called me. She didn't know if you were hurt or not, and I couldn't get an answer when I tried to call. I was terrified!"

"We're fine, Mom," Beth soothed her. "Just dirty and exhausted."

After a bite to eat and long baths, they fell into fresh beds. But none of them slept well that first night. Hearing Angelea cry out during the night, Beth got up to go to her daughter. She paused outside the door as she listened to Felicia murmuring words of comfort to her sister. Smiling for the first time in hours, Beth hurried back to bed and the warmth of George's tired body.

Chapter Seventeen

By the time Felicia was ready to graduate, the house was repaired and ready to move into. Granny suggested that they modernize the appearance of the old Victorian, but Beth wanted it put back just like it was, and Granny was secretly glad. They had much of the old furniture repaired that could be put back together and bought some new pieces. With new wallpaper and flooring in the living room and dining room, it did look brighter. They replaced the kitchen door with French doors going to the porch, and the once dark kitchen was light-filled without giving up the ambiance of the old house.

They decided to move back in after graduation night. George and Beth were so pleased that Felicia was the valedictorian of her class, and they didn't want anything to overshadow the special night with unpacking. Felicia was excited, but a little sad to be leaving her classmates.

The night of the event, she was pacing and going over her speech, fists clenched to her chest as in prayer.

"I'm so afraid I'll forget something," she sighed as she glanced at the notes on the table.

"Slip your notes up in your sleeve, then just slide them out when you reach the podium," George told her. "That's what I did and nobody ever knew. You'll feel more confident."

"Daddy, you're a genius. I'll do that." She hugged him, then asked, "Were you valedictorian of your class, too, Daddy?"

"Yeah. Where do you think you got those brains?"

"From Mom, of course," she teased.

"We have a little gift for you," Beth said, leading her to the window. There in the driveway was a blue Ford Pinto, shiny and new.

"Oh, Mom, Dad. Oh, thank you so much." She flew out the door and ran right into Henry, who came home for her graduation.

"Oh, Uncle Henry, look what I got for graduation." She threw her arms around him and thanked him, too.

"I didn't have anything to do with that," he laughed as he watched her running around and climbing in and out of her new car.

Henry was an engineer and still a bachelor. But lately, he had been talking about a teacher he met through friends. Joan wondered if he would ever bring her home for them to meet. As they watched Felicia touch every part of her new car, she asked, "Henry when are you going to introduce us to this girl?"

He grinned slyly. "She's driving down for graduation tonight. I thought we'd all go out for dinner before the ceremony."

"Great! I'll be glad to finally meet her. I was beginning to think she really didn't exist, that you just made her up." Joan cuffed him lightly on the shoulder.

The doorbell rang about five, and Henry opened it, taking the lovely blonde girl in his arms. She was dressed in a blue print dress and was as tall as he, her long pale hair a contrast to his deep auburn head as they embraced.

"Mom, Bill, this is Cynthia McClarty, my fiancée." Everybody offered their congratulations as he introduced Cynthia around to the rest of the family. Cynthia smiled and greeted them all with poise, all the while looking at Henry with her heart in her sparkling blue eyes.

"I told Henry that this was a bad time to make our announcement. This should be Felicia's night alone, but he insisted that I come and we share our news."

"Oh, I don't mind sharing," Felicia said, laughing. "This is such a relief. We were beginning to think Uncle Henry was going to stay a cranky old bachelor all his life."

Henry grabbed her around her neck and pretended to pound her on the head. "Dinner's on me. I've got reservations at the Blue Lantern. Even this knothead is invited, since it is in her honor." He gave her a quick kiss on the cheek.

The dinner was lovely. They all took to Cynthia immediately with her quiet manner and wit. Felicia had to leave before dessert to be at school early, but the rest had time to sit and discuss the upcoming wedding over coffee. It was to be a simple home wedding at Cynthia's parents' farm home. By the time they assembled at the auditorium, the whole family was enthralled with Cynthia McClarty.

Later, Beth sat through the opening march marveling that her firstborn was actually graduating from high school. She still looked small in her long flowing robe as she walked by with her classmates. Beth's palms were wet and sticky, waiting nervously for Felicia's speech to begin. Finally, after the chorus sang a hymn, Felicia rose, head high, and took her place at the podium. Only her father saw her slip her notes from her sleeve to the stand.

At the end of an excellent speech, she added some words not written in her notes.

"I want to take this time to personally thank all my teachers for their guidance and support. These men and women on this stage are the very best, caring teachers in the world. Sometimes they had to push and pull, but they got us all to the place where we are.

"My family is all sitting on the right, and they're feeling VERY relieved now that I didn't forget my speech." She paused for laughter. "I was blessed to have parents who raised me to be a good citizen and, I hope, a good person. I have a sister who has been my companion and confidant all my life. My grandparents have always been there for me and loved me, and my great grandmother, Granny, raised me from diapers to diploma. I just want to say thank you all, and I love you for being my family.

"To my classmates, onward and upward. We will go our own ways, and we will miss each other. But I want to declare right here and now, that we will be together again five years from this date to remember these years together. All in favor say 'aye,'"

"Aye!" Applause exploded among the students, and the whole crowd stood to applaud Felicia. Beth stopped trying to wipe her tears and let them stream down her face. George cleared his throat several times, swallowing back the lump that formed there. Granny and Joan dabbed at their eyes, and Bill, smiled in unabashed pride.

Later, while Felicia was out celebrating with some friends, they all sat around the table in Joan's kitchen.

"I'm so proud of that girl," Granny declared.

"You should be," Henry spoke up. "I knew when I was keeping her as a baby that she would make us all proud someday."

"I don't know how you were so sure," Beth retorted. "There were a few years that I would have given her away to the gypsies. But she's really grown up into quite a young lady. And guess what she told me tonight. She wants to have surgery on her face so she'll look good for your wedding in August, Henry."

George grinned. "Finally. We've hoped she would change her mind and get that done. I hope it's not too late for the surgeon to do a good job." He rose and stretched. "Well, I don't know about the rest of you, but I'm beat. Beth, Angelea, and I will go to the farm so you'll have more room," he added, looking at Cynthia.

"Oh, no," Cynthia rose quickly. I can stay at the motel. In fact, I left my things there, so I wouldn't be in the way. I'll be up and ready to help you all move in the morning."

"Are you sure?" Beth asked her. "We didn't want to initiate you into our family with dirty, hard work."

"My family moved just about every year until I was in high school. I know all about moving, and I do want to help."

The next day furniture came out of storage, out of the cabinetmaker's shop, and out of Bill's garage and back into the farmhouse. With all the help, things were back in place in record time and by seven o'clock that night, the moving crew was roasting hot dogs over a campfire of wood scraps gathered from the yard. Joan had picked up store-bought brownies and a package of marshmallows, and the tired group got a second wind after refueling.

Henry and Cynthia left right after the quick meal to drive back to the city. Bill and Joan helped unpack a few more boxes before giving in to fatigue and returning to their own place. By ten, beds were ready for the exhausted family.

"Oh my, but it does feel good to be back in my own bed again," Beth sighed, as she pulled the sheet over her aching body and stretched full length.

George groaned as he rolled over on his back. "I've never been as tired, or as glad to get back home. I'm grateful for Joan and Dad putting us up—and putting up with us—but there's no place like home."

"You said it," Beth murmured as she slipped into a deep sleep.

In her first of many dreams that night, she was playing with a dollhouse, moving the furniture around from room to room. "I want a house just like this one when I grow up," the child Beth in her dream said. Then the dollhouse turned into the farmhouse with snow on the roof and lights in the windows. Beth woke with a start, then smiled contentedly as she turned over and snuggled next to her husband. They were home again, at last.

Chapter Eighteen

Felicia did have two surgeries on her face that summer. The surgeon did an excellent job, and by the wedding date, only the palest of scars remained. It gave her a renewed confidence in herself as she made the rounds of showers for Cynthia and prepared for her own role as bridesmaid.

Angelea was also a bridesmaid, and Cynthia had chosen light blue print for their simple lawn dresses.

"We'll never wear these again," Angelea complained. "They are so old fashioned looking, like the gay nineties. All they lack is a bustle!" She tied the darker blue sash around her slim waist and turned before the long mirror.

"It fits you perfectly. And I think they're charming. Remember, this is an outside wedding in the country, not some big deal church wedding," Felicia scolded.

"Well, I'm going to have a big deal church wedding with the most expensive dress Mom and Dad can afford."

"If you can find somebody who'll have you," Felicia retorted as Beth came into the room.

"Oh, don't you look pretty," her mother exclaimed. "Granny did a wonderful job, didn't she? Poor thing. With her hands like they are, so sore and stiff, I was afraid she had bitten off more than she could chew making these dresses. Now take it off and we'll press it again, and we'll be ready to go next week. Was yours okay, Filly?"

"Mine fit fine. I tried it on for Granny earlier."

"I'll be glad when this wedding is over."

"Why, Angel? Weddings are so much fun."

"Ha! I'd rather be riding my horse. Unless, of course, we're talking about my wedding to Billy!" Angelea pulled the dress carelessly over her head, handed it to her mother, and wiggled into her jeans. "Gone riding," she added as she pulled on her old worn shirt and headed for the barn.

The day of the wedding dawned hot and sunny, but by noon clouds had begun to gather in the west. The McClarty farm was beautiful, and the house a new modern ranch. The large living room was beautifully decorated and there were folding chairs stacked in the closet just in case of rain. Mrs. McClarty seemed unfazed by the possibility, and Cynthia was so radiant that she didn't even notice the weather.

Beth saw where her almost sister-in-law got her beauty. Mrs. McClarty looked more like a sister than a mother, and she was as charming and sweet as her daughter.

At one forty-five, the sun peeked shyly out of the clouds as though Cynthia had ordered it to do so, and the wedding party gathered on the back porch to make their entrance into the garden where the vows would be pledged before a rose arbor afloat in tulle.

Earlier Beth had helped her dress. When the wedding dress came out of the closet, she smiled. Cynthia had chosen to wear her grandmother's dress and veil. The cotton lawn had aged to a creamy off-white, and Cynthia had added the pale blue trailing satin sash that perfectly matched her shoes.

"I knew I would love you when I saw your dress," Beth said as she buttoned the tiny buttons up the back. "I wore my mother's dress. I had longed for this special dress, a new dress, but I knew it would mean so much to my mother if I wore hers. And I was so glad that I did."

Cynthia turned and smiled, her blue eyes brimming with tears. "My grandmother died three years ago, and I promised myself then that if I ever got married, I would wear her dress so a part of her could be with me." They slipped the veil that fell from a coronet of tiny blue flowers on her blonde hair that had been fashioned into a mass of curls atop her head.

"You are breathtaking," Beth said as she hugged her.

By the time the vows were exchanged, the sun was out in full force, and the small company gratefully moved indoors for simple refreshments of beautiful salads, fruits, and cake. Then a radiant Cynthia and a beaming Henry left in a flurry of rice for their honeymoon at Niagara Falls. Joan and Bill stayed for awhile to clean up and visit with their new in-laws.

"Wasn't that a lovely wedding," Beth mused on the way home.

"It sure was," Angelea agreed. "I just loved her dress and the way ours were made to look just like hers."

"I thought you hated the dresses," Felicia reminded her.

"Did I say that? Well, they were perfect in that setting. Cynthia looked so pretty. Maybe I'll have an outdoor wedding at home."

Felicia shook her head and rolled her eyes.

When college classes began, Felicia became a full time student at the community college. Beth and George were happy that she chose to stay home and go there the first year, and hoped that she might go the three remaining years there as well. She had decided to go into teaching, and enjoyed all her classes and the campus activities.

As the year progressed, Granny began to tire more easily. She refused to give in and kept trying to do all the things that she normally did. Finally, when she dozed off at the supper table, George talked her into a check-up with Dr. Adams.

They checked in at the clinic two days later, and Dr. Adams put her through a battery of tests.

"These tests will kill you," Granny protested, as they rolled her away for yet another invasion of privacy. "I'm ready to go home where I can get some rest."

Dr. Adams called George in for a talk before he confronted Granny with the results of her tests.

"George, she's basically okay, except for her arthritis. She has that pretty much everywhere, and her blood pressure is higher than I would like. But mostly, she's just wearing out. She needs to stop pushing herself and rest more."

"Try and get her to do that," George replied. "She's stubborn as a mule. If you try and slow her down, she'll go that much harder."

Dr. Adams laughed, his brown eyes twinkling behind horned rimmed glasses. "Well, I'm going to give her something that will slow her down a little, make her relax. If Beth is too busy to take over all the chores, George, you might think about getting a housekeeper to help out. I know Beth writes a good part of the day."

"Well, she's slowed down some, but she still does workshops and has a book every two years to put out, so she's still quite busy. We'll talk about it."

"Housekeeper!! Not in my house!" Granny exclaimed later. "I'll not have someone else running my household. I've done it for sixty years, and I'll keep on doing it. Besides, Beth is here most of the time, and the girls are good cooks. We don't need anyone else."

Beth settled Granny in her chair and brought her a cup of tea. George put another log on the fire, and they both sat across from her.

"Granny," Beth began softly, rubbing the elder woman's frail hand. "Dr. Adams says you must slow down. You're blood pressure is too high, and you know yourself how your arthritis bothers you."

"Yep. And the best medicine for that is to keep moving."

"True to a point. But let's go back to Beth and the girls. Beth can't always be here, Granny, and the girls are busy. Felicia is gone most of the time now, and this is Angel's senior year. Would you have her give up her activities to stay home and do laundry and cook?"

"Wouldn't hurt her. Keep her out of trouble," she replied crossly. Then frowning, she shook her head and sighed. "I didn't mean that. I don't want those girls to give up what they're doing. If you want to hire some help, I'll go along with it. For a while anyway, until I'm feeling better."

Beth smiled. It had been much easier than she thought. She and George made eye contact and grinned.

The next day they interviewed some potential help. The first was a young girl. It would be her first job, and she explained that she helped raise a house full of kids and knew how to cook and keep house. But her sloppy appearance was a turn-off to Beth. The next lady looked almost as frail as Granny, and was so shy that they knew Granny would overpower her immediately.

The third woman was a Mrs. Nell Neeley. She sat as tall and stiff in her chair as her steel gray hair sprayed into a beehive coif.

"I've been the housekeeper for the mayor for thirteen years until they retired and moved to Florida.

They asked me to go with them, but I didn't want to leave my home, especially my gardens. I understand from my sister that your grandmother loves her flower gardens. I can help her there, too."

"Well, the gardens didn't get off to a good start last year, thanks to the tornado. There was so much else going on, she didn't have the time or energy to put into her gardens." But the clue to Granny's acceptance had been planted. Mrs. Neeley was hired.

The first morning, Mrs. Neeley was at the front door before Beth rolled out of bed.

"Good morning," she said as she pulled her robe around her and opened the door to the grim faced woman. "I didn't expect you quite so early. We haven't even started breakfast."

"That's my job now," Mrs. Neeley said as she breezed by, pulling off her sweater. "Show me where you keep things in the kitchen, and I'll get it going for you."

"Okay," Beth said, uneasily. Granny always cooked breakfast, and she wouldn't be expecting Mrs. Neeley to take over that chore right away.

Soon the smell of bacon frying brought Granny into the kitchen.

"I usually cook breakfast," she snapped, tying her robe with a jerk.

"Yes, Mrs. Daniel. But you have me now to do that for you so you can stay in bed a little longer and rest. Food will be ready in about ten minutes." She flipped the bacon and peeked in at the biscuits. After standing for a few seconds, Granny murmured a soft, "huh," and went to the cupboard for a cup.

"You don't mind, do you, Mrs. Neeley, if I get my first cup of coffee in my own house?"

"Indeed not," was the crisp reply as she took the pot and poured Granny's cup full.

"Thank you." Granny turned up her nose and went into the living room to watch the sun rise, grumbling to herself about the interloper in the kitchen.

Beth called George in, and they feasted on a breakfast of eggs, home fries, biscuits, bacon, and a blender mix of orange juice and banana.

"Wonderful breakfast, Mrs. Neeley," George said, casting an eye at Granny who sat quietly. Then he added, "Of course, we're used to big breakfasts like this with Granny. And I'm sure she'll be back at it when she's better."

"Huh!" Granny picked at her eggs peevishly.

The first day of her employ, Mrs. Neeley cooked three meals, did five loads of laundry, vacuumed, dusted, cleaned out the refrigerator and cleaned the oven. Granny went to her room, coming out only to see what the housekeeper was doing next, and then returning to her TV set. Mrs. Neeley left promptly at four o'clock with their dinner in the oven keeping until they were ready to eat. A fresh pie sat cooling on the counter.

Beth called George in for supper. As he was washing, she whispered in his ear, "George, I love this. I've done more on my book today that I've done for weeks. She does a crackerjack job."

"But is Granny happy?" he whispered back.

"Of course not," Beth grinned.

Granny refused to come out to eat at first, but after some coaxing from her great-granddaughters, she joined them at the table.

Beth lit candles, since Mrs. Neeley had set the table with the good china, and served the roast chicken and vegetables, cranberry sauce, and slaw. It was delicious.

"Chicken's too done," Granny said.

"Mine's good."

"Mine, too."

"Huh!"

"Not as good as yours, Granny, but passable," Angel said with a wink at her father. Granny brightened and wolfed down the rest of her meal.

"Well, we got through day one," Beth said to George later. "This is going to be interesting."

"Going to be? I've watched Granny all day, and she's not at all pleased. She may sabotage our efforts if she takes a mind to."

"Maybe they will become friends eventually," Beth said, hopefully.

"Don't count on it. But she'll have to get used to it."

"I'm going to check on her. I do want her to be happy with the arrangement."

Beth tiptoed into Granny's room and found her asleep, her head slumped over her Bible. Beth gently pulled out the book, eased Granny's head straight on her pillow and kissed her cheek as she turned out the light. She would just have to wait and talk to her tomorrow, out of Mrs. Neeley's hearing.

Chapter Nineteen

A few nights later, the weather turned cold bringing brisk winds and snow flurries. Granny was stiff and achy with her arthritis the next morning. Mrs. Neeley brought a breakfast tray into Granny's room with her medications on it plus a hardy oatmeal breakfast.

"Good morning, Mrs. Daniel. How are we this morning?"

"I don't know about you, but I'm fine. Sick and tired of this bed is all."

"That's nice," Mrs. Neeley said as she threw open the curtains. "Means you're getting better. Oops, you missed that yellow pill, must take them all, you know."

"Huh!" Granny obediently took her pills and ate the breakfast. Then she called George into her room.

"I want that woman out of my house!"

"Granny, you haven't given her a chance. And you have to admit that she is taking good care of all of us, including you."

"I'll be an invalid in a month if I don't get out of this bed and back to my business."

"You don't have to stay in bed all the time, Granny, and she doesn't care if you help her occasionally."

"Help her? Huh! She's too snippy."

"Keep her company while she works, and I'm sure you can learn to do things together."

"You're all against me." Turning her head away, she sighed hopelessly.

"No, Granny, we want you to get better. We want you to take it easy and do what the doctor says." He turned his head to hide his smile.

"Okay. I'll go along with this—for the time being," she agreed, reluctantly, raising her eyes to the ceiling and muttering under her breath.

Everyone else in the family grew to appreciate Mrs. Neeley's hard work. She was the perfect housekeeper. Her prickly personality was so much like Granny's that no one was bothered by her crispness. Except Granny. As she began to feel better, boredom sat in.

"I'm ready to take over now," she told George one sunny morning as he delivered her an extra cup of coffee.

"Granny, why can't you relax and let people help you? You already look so much better, not so tired like you were."

"Well, I'm not tired anymore. So I'm ready to get back to my job."

George sat on the bed and took her hand. "Listen, we can't just dismiss Mrs. Neeley for no reason. She needs the money. Did you know that she has a disabled son who lives with her? No? I didn't either until Angelea told me. You know Angel; she has a way of making people talk about themselves."

"Nosey, she is," Granny agreed with a sly grin. "So this is a benevolence matter, right?" She cocked her head to one side.

"You might say that," George went on. "But mostly we see you getting back to your old self, and we all feel so relieved. We were worried about you, you know. If you could just let her stay until you all have the gardens fixed . . ."

"She's a gardener?"

"Garden Club president, I think," George turned his head so she wouldn't detect the lie that slid effortlessly past his lips.

"Well, I guess I could use her help with the mess the garden has gotten into. My back isn't what it used to be, that's for sure."

George hugged her. "I knew you would agree."

She brushed him away and sat up in her bed. Reaching over to the end table she picked up one of her gardening magazines and began to browse through it.

She came into the kitchen in slacks and shirt that afternoon as Mrs. Neeley was peeling potatoes. Pulling open the drawer, she took a paring knife and began to help her peel. Mrs. Neeley managed a tight smile, but said nothing.

"George tells me that you like to garden."

"Oh, yes. Gardening is my first love. I'll take you over to see my gardens sometime; they're the talk of my neighborhood." Mrs. Neeley's face broke into a sunny smile.

"Really!"

"I guess I have just about every book on gardening that's been written. I just can't resist them at the bookstore."

"Well, last year we had that bad storm, you remember? Really tore up my garden spots, and rebuilding the house messed up my beds. I wondered—ah—if maybe you might want to help me get them back in shape? Of course, I would help you with the housework so you'd have the time."

Mrs. Neeley put down her knife and wiped her hands on her apron. "Why, I'd love to. Designing gardens is what I like to do best, and, of course, putting them together, too."

"Would you want to look at them now?" Granny asked hopefully. "It'll soon be time to get things planted, and I'd like to rearrange things so I would have more of an English garden look."

"Oh, I love to do English gardens. I did one for the mayor, and he just loved it." She took her sweater off the hook and the two of them went out into the early spring sun.

Beth and George were taking their customary afternoon coffee break when the two ladies came back in together, bubbling over with excitement.

"I saw you all walking around the yard as I came in," George said as he got down two more cups that

Beth filled with fresh coffee. "What do you think about the gardens, Mrs. Neeley? Do you think we can ever get them back in shape?"

"Oh, certainly. Mrs. Daniel—er—Felicia and I have been deciding what to plant where. You have so many nice perennials coming up that can be divided."

"Nell thinks we should move the irises to the back of the large bed and . . ."

"No, Felicia, I said to the front. We're putting the cleomes in the back among the foxgloves, remember?"

"But that was in the front bed, Nell. I'm talking about the back bed." Granny's voice rose a decibel.

"No, the front bed has the sun lovers, Dear. We talked about that . . ."

"But Nell, there's more sun in the back . . ."

As they went back and forth, Beth leaned over and whispered in George's ear. "We've created a monster here. Now what will we do with "Felicia and Nell"?"

He shrugged, and they left the table without being missed and retreated to the solitude of the back porch.

And so Nell Neeley was inducted into the household—and into the family.

Chapter Twenty

Angelea graduated from high school, not in the top ten of her class, but most popular. Her gaiety and warmth endeared her to all her teachers, even though she wasn't the student Felicia was. She had no idea what she wanted to do, other than to eventually marry Billy, who was taking college classes year around so they could marry when he graduated. So she joined her sister at the community college in the fall

It was the warmest autumn they had in years, with hot dry days and cool nights. Granny's—and Nell's— garden blazed with bright mums and asters, and the farm was like a picture postcard, bathed in reds and golds.

George's herd was now the biggest in the county and prizewinners at the state fair. He was recognized all over the state as a businessman farmer. For once, he was busier than Beth and gone as much. She was proud of him, but finally realized how lonely it was for him when she was gone. She finished her book three months ahead of schedule, thanks to the hiring of Nell, and it was off to the publishers. She was enjoying a rare time of leisure with a special time of quilting with Granny.

"It's good to see Mom out of her 'hideaway'," Felicia said to her sister in the college cafeteria as they sat opposite each other at a table.

"Well, she deserves a break," Angelea agreed, as she dipped her last French fry into a pool of catsup. "Do you ever stop and think how lucky we are? I mean, Mom's a successful writer and Dad's a successful farmer, and they both have made a good living for us. We haven't had to worry about anything, really."

There was a wistful tone in her voice that made Felicia ask, "So are you feeling guilty or something?"

"Sometimes I do. I think about all the people who are needy, and I have so much. It makes me sad."

"You know Mom and Dad give to church and so many other organizations that help people, don't you?"

"Yeah, I know that, but I think I want to do something with my life that would help others."

Felicia laughed. "I thought you just wanted to marry Billy and be a mommy."

"I want that, too. But I'm thinking about going into social work."

"Really? I think that's great. What made you decide that?"

Angelea twirled a lock of dark hair around her finger as she leaned forward and whispered, "Do you remember April Wilson? She was in my high school class. Anyway, one day she came to school with bruises and a black eye. She said she fell, but her best friend told me that her father was drunk and hit her, said it happens all the time. I never knew that. I always felt sorry for her because she came to school looking so haggard and ragged."

"And that made you decide to go into social work?" Felicia looked dubious.

"No, silly, I've been thinking about it for a long time. I just couldn't decide for sure until lately."

"Well, that's good. I've got something on my mind, too."

"What?" Angelea scooted her chair closer.

"Don't say anything to Mom, but I'm writing a story."

"Great! But why not tell Mom?"

"Because I think it can be made into a book, and I would love to co-author it with her. Think she would like to do that? After she has this little respite from writing, I mean."

"She'd love it. Two writers in the family. You can support me while I earn next to nothing doing good deeds."

"Excuse me, but do you mind if I sit here?" The owner of the voice was tall with blonde hair and bright blue eyes and a cocky smile. Both gaped and sputtered a surprised 'no' at the sight of the slim body as it slid into a chair.

"Whew! I feel like I've been through the wringer. I just had a session with my psych teacher, trying to get a second chance at a test I bombed." He eyed the hamburger before him and pushed it away.

"Hard time?" asked Felicia.

"Yeah, first test counts. Here I am so close to graduation, and I can't get through this class."

"You should have had that at least last year." Angelea pushed her chair back and started to pick up her tray.

"Right. But why don't we introduce ourselves. I'm Lance Smithers. And I already know that you are the Daniel sisters, but I don't know who is who."

"I'm Felicia, this is Angelea," Felicia said tugging at her sister's skirt to signal her to stay.

"Nice to meet you, but I've got to run. I've got one more paragraph to write before class." She ignored her sister's pleading eyes and pranced off with a "See you later" over her shoulder.

Felicia smiled uneasily. "I should go, too. I don't have another class until three, so I'm going home for awhile."

"Don't go. Keep me company while I eat this cold burger and tell me what I need to know about you." He took a bite and twisted his mouth into an irresistible crooked smile.

At the end of their chance meeting, Felicia knew that Lance was a Senior from Greenville who had four brothers and a father that was a pharmacist. His mother had passed away the year before. He divulged this information reluctantly, and she could hear the pain in his voice. She told him about her family, and found he knew her mother's books and had read some of them. And when they parted just in time for her next class, she had become his tutor in psychology.

At supper that night, Angelea teased her sister about their meeting with Lance.

"She was as nervous as a cat, Mom. I thought she would pull my skirt off trying to get me to sit back down." Her hazel eyes sparkled with laughter. "Now she's his tutor."

"Hush," Felicia said, crossly. "I just agreed to help him study for his next test. Then he's on his own." She smiled shyly. "He is cute though, don't you think?"

"Cute? He's a doll. Not as good looking as Billy, of course, but passable. Speaking of Billy, we have a date, so I'd better scoot. Good dinner, Mom."

"Thank Nell for that," Beth answered, shooting a look at Granny as she added, "Except for the dessert. You know that's Granny's good cobbler."

Angelea planted a kiss on her great-grandmother's gray hair and was gone. Beth turned to Felicia whose cheeks were pink from her teasing. She was glad to see her daughter interested in someone. She hadn't had a boyfriend since the accident.

"Well, Honey, tell me about this Lance."

They fell rapidly in love, the short, curly dark auburn haired girl and the tall, blonde boy. Together all the time, they despaired when they had to say goodnight, and rushed in to talk to each other on the phone until the wee hours.

George was skeptical about the romance. "I like him, Beth, but we don't really know him."

"What do we need to know, except that he's from a nice family? It's what Felicia thinks of him that matters."

George kept his counsel. There was something about Lance that he didn't like, and he just couldn't put his finger on it.

As Christmas came, warm and sunny, the family was gathered around the living room opening presents. The live tree was sparkling with lights, and Beth had decorated every nook and cranny of the house with holly and ivy. It looked like a Christmas card, minus snow.

They were examining their gifts among a sea of torn wrapping paper and drifts of ribbon when Lance knocked. Felicia sprang up and greeted him with a kiss. He was loaded with presents that he dispensed with a jocular air. There was a teapot for Granny, fancy dishtowels for Nell, and a book for her disabled son, Arthur, who chose to stay home by his own fire. Lance gave a big tin of homemade cookies that he and his brothers had made to Beth and George, and Beth was touched. To Angelea he gave a pair of leather gloves, and Joan and Bill received a box of candy. As Felicia waited for her gift, Lance whispered something to George who got up and followed him into the kitchen.

"Well!" Angelea said. "Guess you don't get a gift, Sis!"

Felicia smiled shyly. "Shall I dip the eggnog? I'm ready for some of Nell's nog and Granny's pound cake."

Before she had sliced the luscious pound cake and poured cups filled with the frothy drink, George and Lance came back in the room. Lance looked happy, and George looked stunned.

"Felicia, go for a walk with me?" Lance pulled her coat from the hall tree and helped her on with it. They walked from the cozy room into the sunshine. A cooler breeze had come up, signaling a cold front to follow.

"Look, the geraniums are still trying to bloom," Felicia said as they passed the patio with pots of flowers still adding some color.

"That won't last long," he said as he buttoned his coat. "Let's go sit in the gazebo."

Hand in hand they went up the steps and sat under the fancy Victorian scrollwork. He pulled her to him for a long kiss, and she snuggled her head into his chest.

"I have your gift," he said into her sweet smelling hair.

"What is it?"

"Look at me."

She pulled away and looked into his eyes as he reached into his pocket and brought out a tiny box. Her hand flew to her throat as he opened it and revealed the small diamond, sparkling in the sun.

"Oh, it's beautiful," she whispered.

"Will you marry me in the spring?"

"Oh, yes. Yes. Yes." She threw her arms around him. "I love you so much, Lance. I can't wait to be your wife."

"We could do it sooner. But I suppose you want a big wedding."

"No, not a big one, but a nice one. It's a once in a lifetime thing, Darling."

"I know. And I can wait. I don't think your dad is too happy about it though."

"Really? Is that what you talked about? What did he say?"

"He hopes we'll wait a year or two since we've only known each other three months."

"No chance," she whispered in his ear. "Now, let's go tell everyone. I'm about to burst, I'm so happy."

They ran back into the house, laughing with the sheer joy of their love. Felicia came in holding her hand out in front of her with dramatic flair. Angelea jumped up and hugged her sister.

"Oh, it's beautiful, Filly. Congratulations, you two," she threw her arms around Lance. Beth held her daughter's hand, admiring the ring and wiping her eyes with her other hand.

"Well, come show us," Granny said from her chair. "Nell and I are too tired to get up!" She shyly held out her left hand to them and to her grandparents. Joan and Bill hugged her, caught up in her excitement. Only George remained silent and still by the tree, arms folded and face grim. He managed a smile when Felicia held her small hand out for him to see.

"Very nice," as he slipped his arm around her waist and smiled at the anxious Lance.

"We want to get married in the spring, Daddy," she whispered, as she threw her arms around his neck.

He cleared his throat before he answered, "Well, that's between you and your mother. I don't handle those details." But he smiled, and she turned to Beth and Angelea, and the three of them went into the kitchen, giggling like schoolgirls as they prepared to plan Felicia's dream wedding.

"Welcome to the family," he held out his hand to Lance who grasped it firmly. He was glad when Granny and Nell busied Lance with eggnog and cake. He slipped quietly away and retreated to his study for a breather, closing the door against the excited laughter drifting from the kitchen.

Chapter Twenty-One

She pulled the car up to the curb in front of the old rambling manor that housed Lance's apartment. It had once been one of the mansions of the small town, but years before had been turned into apartments and neglected, it's grandeur lost in the chipped paint, the tacked on stairs, and the bevy of cars parked in the drive and on the lawn. Lance's car was not along them.

She took off her gloves and turned the ignition back on to keep the heat circulating against the cold March day. She was early; he wouldn't be here from his last class for a few minutes. She laid her head against the seat and tried to remember all the beautiful times they had together, all the lovely plans they had made when they first fell in love. It had been the most wonderful time in her life.

Then she thought back to the past month. It had been an unpleasant few weeks for her since they had begun to quarrel for the first time. His pleasant demeanor had turned cross, and he seemed jealous of her time with her family. If she didn't call at least once every night that they weren't together, he was angry. Then last night had been the worst of all. She laid her head back, remembering the awful fight.

It began with a long kiss in the car before she went in the house. He pulled away abruptly and put both hands on the wheel.

"What's the matter?' she asked anxiously.

"You know very well what's the matter. Don't act so innocent. If you really loved me, you'd go back to the apartment and spend the night with me."

"We've talked about that, Honey," she said in a soothing voice, rubbing his arm. "I want to wait until we're married. It's only six more weeks."

"Yeah, six more weeks," he rolled his eyes.

"Sweetheart, that's not too long, is it? And you'll be glad, I know you will. It will be something new, something wonderful for us, not something we've done before. Please try to understand. I wasn't brought up to believe that way, that it's okay to be intimate before marriage."

"Yeah, I know. My sweet little religious virgin," he said bitterly. He turned back to her with a sneer. "Do you know how hopelessly out of date you are? Nobody goes by those old rules anymore, especially people who are engaged. No, don't touch me. Maybe we'd better spend less time with each other until the wedding. So good night. Go on, get out and go in to your family. I'll call you." He sped off, tires spinning, leaving her standing in tears.

She shook her head to keep the tears from flowing again. Even after he called her this morning and apologized, she felt the hurt just as badly. He had asked her to come to the apartment after classes. "I'll fix supper for you. Come on, Honey. Let me make it up to you," he had pleaded.

So here she was, still hurting, but willing to make up. He was everything to her. They had been so happy, and she was sure they would be again. They would work it out. In a few weeks, all that desire would be satisfied. She felt a thrill down to her toes as she thought of what a very passionate wife she would be for him. He would be glad then. Now he was just a typical man, thinking below the belt.

She stretched to see herself in the rear view mirror to apply fresh powder and lipstick. There were circles under her eyes from the crying jag last night. She plastered on the powder to mask them and put on the bright pink lipstick he liked. As she finished, she saw his car pull up behind hers. Suddenly he was at her window with a bag of groceries and a big grin.

"Come into my abode, you gorgeous thing. I have two big steaks with our names on them."

She laughed and they walked, huddled together against the March wind, up the stairs to his apartment.

"Where's Buzz?" She inquired about his roommate as she took off coat and gloves.

From the tiny kitchen, he answered above the rattle of grocery bags. "He's got a date. Some new girl, I think.

You know Buzz, he doesn't tell me anything." He came into the small living room and caught her in his arms. She rested her head on his broad chest with a happy sigh. This would be okay, he did understand.

"Are you hungry? Or had you rather me fix you a cup of tea first?"

"Oh, that sounds heavenly. Hot tea would hit the spot."

She sat on the lumpy old sofa while he busied himself. The room was cheerless; a place where two guys just slept and ate. She thought about their own apartment that they planned to find and fix up soon. She could imagine just how it would look, like a doll's house, cheerful and bright.

"Your tea, Madam," he bowed as he handed her the warm cup and sat beside her with a soft drink in his hand. "Have you forgiven me for last night?"

She put down the tea on the wooden box that served as the coffee table. "Of course, I have. I know you didn't mean anything you said. You were just frustrated, and I can understand that."

"Frustrated is the word. Come here and cuddle with me," he said as he pulled her against him and ran his fingers through her hair. "You know I love you, don't you?"

"Yes, I know that."

"And you understand that I do need you badly. You drive me crazy when you're in my arms, and I can't make love to you."

She tried to sit up, but he held her close so she relaxed again.

"You know that works two ways. Don't you know that I want you, too? I have to fight myself sometimes."

"Then why is it such a big deal that we wait? We're going to be married soon, so what's the harm?"

"The harm," she said, as if to a child, "is that it will spoil the wedding night for us. There would be no surprises. And it's just the way it should be. You wait until marriage. It's better, that's all."

"That's silly." He slid her down deeper into the sofa. When she protested, he covered her mouth with a long kiss. "Oh, Darling, let me love you," he whispered.

She struggled halfway up and pushed him back. "No!" she said firmly. "This is the only thing I ask of you, Lance. Now let me up. If we're going to fight about this again, maybe I'd better just go home."

"No, Felicia. I'm not going to let you go," he said softly, as he pushed her down again. She squirmed against him, but he held her fast. "Stop it, you hear? Just be still, I'm not going to hurt you."

He was over her, his eyes glazed over, and she was suddenly very afraid. She pushed at him with all her might, but his weight was too much.

"Stop it, Lance!" she screamed as loudly as she could. He slapped her across the mouth with such force that her head bounced upward on the pillow.

"Shut up. Do you want to bring the landlord down on us?"

The sting of his slap brought tears to her eyes, and the metallic taste of blood in her mouth made her panic. She realized that she was about to be raped, and the nausea boiling up from her stomach brought bitter bile into her throat. His weight was crushing her; her breath came in gasps.

His blue eyes were dark with anger and she looked into them, realizing that she was seeing him as he really was. As he crushed his mouth on hers, she knew she had to get away somehow. She had to calm him, pretend to go along with him until she had a break.

"Okay, Sweetheart," she gasped, pushing his face away after the bruising kiss and caressing his mouth with trembling hands. "You're right. I've been silly and juvenile. It's my fault; forgive me. Just give me a minute, okay? This couch is too lumpy. Wouldn't your bed be a little more comfortable?"

He let go of her arms and raised up to sit on the edge of the couch. "Do you mean it?" he asked cautiously.

"I mean it. I don't want my first time to be on your sofa. Go and turn your bed down, and I'll go in the bathroom and get ready, okay?" She hoped her trembling voice wouldn't give her away as she sat up and smoothed down her clothes.

"The bed is ready," he whispered with a smile on his face. "But I'll be there waiting for you. Hurry. Hurry." He crossed to the bedroom, looking back at her with a satisfied grin, and Felicia turned toward the little bathroom that was unhandily placed off the kitchen. Seeing he was well inside the bedroom, she turned and tiptoed to the door, picking up only her purse. Opening it as quietly as she could, she heard his footsteps just before the door closed, and she ran, half falling, down the rickety stairs, tearing her hose.

She knew he was behind her, she could hear his voice begging her to stop, but the cold wind in her ears and the voice inside her pushed her on. She felt for her keys, plunging them into the ignition before she even slammed the car door. Taking off with a squeal of her tires, she drove down the next block, turning down an alley in case he had followed her. Then she headed home using a short cut. All the way, she took deep breaths to keep from shedding blinding tears. Only the memory of the past accident kept her from speeding wildly.

It seemed to take forever to reach the farm. When the lights of the farmhouse blazed into the darkening night, she allowed herself to give in and cry as she shot blindly up the driveway, ran up the walk and into the house. She slammed the door and leaned against it, sliding down to the floor. She was chilled to the bone, having left her coat behind, and her teeth chattered uncontrollably.

As moments passed and her sobbing ceased, she realized that no one heard her come in, so she wiped her eyes and called out, "Anybody home?" Her voice bounced off the wall; no one answered. She crossed the living room into the dining room where she saw the note on the table held down with a salt shaker. She reached for it, her hands shaking so hard she could hardly read the scrawl.

Filly, we're all at the hospital with Granny. Hurry!

She grabbed a coat from the closet, fresh adrenaline pumping through her veins, and ran back to her car. As she sped down the driveway, she met Lance's car moving at high speed. She didn't give as they headed toward each other, and at the last moment, he swerved over to the side to let her by. He didn't matter anymore. All that mattered was Granny.

Chapter Twenty-Two

Beth stood listening to the gurgle of the coffee perking in the big urn in the waiting room. It was the only sound in the silent room of straight green chairs and gray walls. The volunteer lady in a pink smock looked up from her desk and smiled. "I'll bring you some just as soon as it's done, Dear."

Beth nodded her thanks and turned back to George who sat with his head in his hands. She knelt in front of him and raised his face to hers.

"She'll get better, Honey. You know how determined Granny is."

He shook his head, grasped her hands, and pressed them to his lips, then slumped back in his chair. The doctor had just taken Granny in for a scan, having told them that she had suffered a stroke. Now it was just a matter of how much damage was done. It had all

happened so fast. He ran his fingers through his graying
sandy hair, remembering the past two hours.

Nell had just left for home when Granny turned to
them at the supper table with a confused look on her
face. She began to babble incoherently, and he and Beth
jumped up just as she sagged in her chair. He picked
her up like a child, and Beth covered her with a coat
and rode in the back seat with Granny's head in her lap
to the hospital, trying to comfort her. Her eyes sought
Beth's as though begging for an answer as to what was
happening to her.

Once there, hospital personnel took Granny to a
pod, and paged Dr. Adams. Fortunately, he was already
there, and he wheeled her off for tests, offering as much
comfort to Beth and George as he could. They stood in
the hall, choking back tears.

Suddenly there was Felicia, turning the corner in a
dead run with her arms reaching out to her parents,
worry etched into her face.

"What happened to Granny? How is she? Will she
be okay?"

Beth guided her to a chair. "She's had a stroke, Filly.
And we don't know how bad it is yet. Oh, you're
shivering and cold as ice." She rubbed the cold hands
between her own. "You sit here with your father while
I get us some coffee."

The tall elegant looking volunteer heard her and
motioned for her to sit back down, so Beth turned to
help Felicia out of her coat. She could feel her daughter's
trembling and put her arms around her.

"Honey, what happened to your lip? Your mouth is swollen."

"Oh, it's nothing; I'll tell you about it later. Right now tell me how it happened. And where is Angel?"

"She and Billy went to the movies. You did leave that note on the table, didn't you?" Felicia nodded and Beth went on to explain what had transpired with Granny. Before she had finished, Billy and Angelea had slipped in quietly. Angelea kissed them both, and then began to cry in Billy's arms.

"I'm so glad we decided not to go to that movie. We wouldn't have known for hours," Angelea sobbed as Billy guided her to a chair, pulling another one close to hers, and she rested her head on his shoulder, wiping her eyes with his handkerchief.

"Does Nell know?" Felicia asked.

"She had just left a few minutes before. I'll call her when we have definite news."

They took the coffee offered by the volunteer and sat quietly sipping its comforting warmth. Each was lost in their own particular thoughts of Granny and the possibility of life without her.

They sprang up in unison when Dr. Adams entered the room. His eyes had a cautious look as he began.

"She's holding her own. There is paralysis on her right side, and she's unconscious right now, but that's not bad. Her brain is resting from the attack. These next few hours are critical. At her age, it's hard to make predictions. But she is, as you know, a very stubborn determined woman, and that will be in her favor. I wish

I could tell you more, but for now, it's just wait and see. You may go in two at a time just as soon as we get her set up in intensive care." He gave the girls and Beth a brief hug, and shook George's hand and smiled as he walked away. "Keep good thoughts."

"I'm going to call Nell," Beth said, patting George's hand as she went outside to the phone by the door.

In a few minutes, they picked up coats and purses and went to the intensive care waiting room and took up their vigil. George and Felicia went in to see Granny first. Felicia gave a loud sob when she saw all the tubes connected to Granny's frail body. But George ignored them as he stood beside her and talked softly to her.

"You're going to be okay, Granny. You have to be because we just couldn't get along without you. You've been my mother, my farming partner, and a world of help raising my daughters. I'd be lost without you. So, you see, you've got to hang in there and get well again. We need you too much."

Felicia echoed her father's words on the other side of the bed. Then they quietly left so Beth and Angelea could go in.

Beth kissed the ashen cheek and brushed back a long gray hair. "When you're better, I'll fix your hair, Granny. It's a mess now. But we'll get you all dolled up, and I'll bring your bed jacket from home, you know, the one I gave you for your birthday. You like to read in that, don't you?"

"We love you, Granny," was all that Angelea could say as she kissed the moist forehead and slipped out into the hall where Billy waited to comfort her.

212

"Someone has to go home and try to get in touch with Dad and Joan," George said. "It will take them a day to get back from their vacation in Florida. I wish I had thought to grab the number they left us, but all I could think of then was getting to the hospital."

"You stay here, I'll go," Beth picked up her coat. "Felicia will go with me, and we'll bring back some hot tea. You'll be strung out if you drink very much of this strong coffee."

They braved the chilly wind as the big front doors closed behind them and ran to the car.

"We must be going to have a March snow," Beth said before she rested her head on the wheel and suddenly burst into tears.

"Oh, Mom." Felicia gently pulled up a dark strand of her mother's hair and tucked it tenderly into the bun at the nape of her neck.

"I'll be okay. I just held it back so long for your father. I wanted to be strong for him." She took a tissue from her daughter, blew her nose, and started the car. They drove silently through the darkened streets toward the farm.

"Now, why don't you tell me how you cut your lip? It sure is puffed up."

Felicia turned her head toward her window. "I'll tell you later, Mom. Please, I can't talk about it now."

Fear crept into Beth's heart. Something had happened to her daughter, and it wasn't an accident. It was an effort, but she said nothing else, hoping she would be told when the time was right.

Two days passed before there was a change in Granny's condition. Bill and Joan drove back home immediately after Beth's call, and Bill refused to leave the hospital, even to shave and shower. The second day Granny opened her eyes and tried to talk. It was somewhat scrambled and slurred at first, but by the fourth day, she was putting words and phrases together normally. Her first clear words were music to their ears.

"When can I go home?"

Dr. Adams was excited about her progress, but told the family that she would have to stay for at least another week and then be sent to the hospital in Nashville for rehabilitation.

The fourth night was the first time they had all gone home together, Joan and Bill to their own bed, and Beth, George and the girls to theirs. Relieved that Granny was so much better, they were all in a festive mood. Felicia smiled, but said little. Church members had brought a huge pot of soup, cakes, pies, and fruit salad. They sat at their own table that night and had a feast. Only the empty chair cast a pall over their meal.

As Beth, Angelea, and Billy cleared the table, George took Felicia's hand and led her out to the porch. The cold spell had given way to unseasonable warmth. The smell of spring was in the air, and in the dusk, they could see the sea of Granny's daffodils blooming golden in the garden in spite of the recent cold winds. They sat in the weathered wicker with the cozy faded, flowered pillows against their backs and inhaled the pungent air, heavy with earth and new grass.

"I haven't seen Lance around," George broke the silence. "Did you tell him about Granny?"

"No."

"Why not? Have you two had a spat or something?"

"Daddy, there is no 'Lance and I,'"

"Want to tell me why?"

"I found out that he isn't the person that I thought he was."

George drew a big breath. "Come on. Level with me, Filly. Your mother and I know something happened."

She rose and walked to the porch railing, pretending to watch Angel's horse as Wade brought him in for the night. After a moment, she dropped her head and spoke softly.

"He tried to—to force himself on me after I said 'no,'"

"Did he also give you that fat lip?" George's voice was brittle with anger.

"Yes."

"Do you want to press charges? I can assure you that I do—after I have a little time alone with him."

"Dad, please. Let me handle this. I took off the ring. I want nothing more to do with him. That's the end of it." She sat back down, imploring him with her eyes.

"Filly, I heard something from Charlie a few days ago that I never mentioned to you. Charlie's brother lives in Greenville close to the Smithers family, and he told Charlie that Mr. Smithers used to beat his wife before she became ill and died. So I asked everyone I knew from over that way if anyone else had heard it. No one knew anything about it, so I thought it might just be a rumor. But it has worried me ever since. I couldn't put my finger on why I never cared for Lance. But I have to tell you that I'm relieved that you aren't going to marry him."

"But I loved him so much, Daddy. I wanted to spend the rest of my life with him. My dress—Mom's dress—is hanging in the closet and the invitations are ready to mail. What will I do now?" She sobbed so loudly that Beth peered out the French doors, but George waved her back.

"I know," he whispered, as he motioned for her to sit in his lap. She rested her head on his shoulder, much like she did when she was a little girl, and bawled like a baby. She sat there, with her father rubbing her back, until she ran out of tears. Then, after mopping her face dry, she got up awkwardly and pulled him up by the hand.

"Go in with me, Daddy. I think it's time that I explained this all to Mom and Angel."

"Just one more thing," George said as he kissed her cheek. "I just want to say that I'm so proud of you, Baby."

Chapter Twenty-Three

Felicia took her mother and sister into the living room and explained why she and Lance were no longer engaged. She shied away from their attempts at comfort and went to her room. Taking the wedding dress from her closet, she smoothed a wrinkle lovingly from the skirt, then hung the dress back in the hall closet where she wouldn't have to look at it. Boxes of invitations were carried to the trash and dumped. Gifts from a recent kitchen shower were boxed and tagged to be returned to the givers. She cried as she performed these tasks, but she wouldn't let Beth or Angelea do it for her. It was part of her cleansing, and she needed to do it herself.

Beth and Angelea sat in the living room, hand in hand. Beth was in such pain for Felicia that she could hardly breathe. But she knew her daughter had to work it out.

"How can we help her, Mom?" Angelea's voice was tearful.

"Nothing. Just be here for her. It will take her some time to get over this, and we'll just have to be very understanding." Beth patted her younger daughter's hand as Felicia came into the room looking completely exhausted.

"That's done," she said flatly. "No more dress, no more gifts, no wedding, no Lance. All I want now is to finish school and get on with my life." She dropped on the couch beside her sister. Her eyes were red rimmed, the make-up streaked on her face.

"I love you, Filly," her sister pulled the dark head over on her own shoulder and smoothed her tangled hair.

"And I love you both," Beth whispered. The pain for her child was so intense that she couldn't say the words aloud.

At school the next day, Felicia found Lance waiting for her outside the door of her first class. He had dark circles under his bright blue eyes.

"Will you talk to me?" He asked softly, reaching for her hand.

She shook her head at his gesture. "There's nothing to say. We're finished."

"I'm so sorry, so sorry. If you will give me another chance, I promise you nothing like that will ever happen again. Please forgive me, Filly. I love you."

She took a deep breath, fighting the urge to throw her arms around him, to believe in him again. "I can't take that risk, Lance. You hurt me. That's not love, at least not the kind of love I want. I just hope you've learned something from this, that you'll never hurt another woman that way." She pulled the ring from her pocket and placed it in his hand. "Goodbye, Lance," she whispered. He stood looking at the shiny ring as she walked through the door and sat down at her desk. She thought there were tears in his eyes, but that didn't move her. Her tears were all dried up.

Granny continued to improve and after a month in rehab, she came home to a big family celebration. There was a huge supper of her favorite dishes and gifts passed out with dessert.

"It's not my birthday," she said, her eyes glittering. "You are all too sweet to me."

"We're so glad you're home," George kissed her withered cheek and tasted her tears. Beth had shopped for easy to fasten clothing for her since she still couldn't use her right hand very well. She was delighted to get into her new clothes and out of robes.

Her first night home, she asked about Lance, and they told her the story. She never mentioned him again, but she hugged Felicia every chance she got. She was mobile, but spent a lot of time in bed resting. Nell waited on her hand and foot, and spent time with her watching TV. Beth often went up to check, pausing outside the bedroom door at the sounds of their laughter, then turned away with a smile. Nell was the best person for Granny right now.

Gradually things became almost normal again, except for Felicia's moods, which they all accepted and did their best to help her cope.

Beth and Felicia took Granny in for a check-up one warm, sunny May afternoon, and were surprised to find a new doctor in Dr. Adams practice. As he introduced them to Dr. Jim Forrest, he told them he was getting ready to retire in a year, and Dr. Forrest would be taking over his practice.

"I wanted you to meet one of my favorite patients," he said to Dr. Forrest.

"One of your favorites? You told me I WAS your favorite," Granny teased, her words slightly slurring.

"I've heard a lot about you, Mrs. Daniel. I also heard that you sometimes bring cakes to the staff when you come in. I hope you won't abandon that practice when Dr. Adams goes off to Florida." He smiled broadly, knowing that she knew he was deliberately flattering her.

Granny looked the young doctor over from head to foot, taking in the dark good looks, the athletic medium build, and the absence of a wedding ring on his finger.

"Well," she said with a crooked smile, "why don't you join us for supper Friday night. I can't promise to make a cake yet, but our friend and housekeeper makes a mean strawberry dessert."

"Oh, I'd love to, Mrs. Daniel, but I'm moving this week-end. I found a small house out on Shady Creek road. It's just the kind of place I was looking for, quiet and remote."

"Well, what a coincidence! We live four miles out that road. It's the white house after you pass the new subdivision that's going in." Granny had all kinds of possibilities flowing through her mind.

"I'll take a rain check on that invitation, so ask me again. Now I want you to continue your exercises and your therapy here at the hospital, and I want to see you in a month. If you have any problems, call me, day or night. The answering service can get in touch with me. Okay? Any thing you want to add, Dr. Adams?"

Dr. Adams looked over his glasses and smiled in amusement. "No I think you've covered everything, Dr. Forrest."

Back in the car, Felicia jumped on Granny as soon as the car door closed.

"Granny, that was pretty obvious."

"Why, what do you mean?" she turned to her great-granddaughter, a study in innocence.

"Let me make one thing clear. I'm not interested in your new doctor, or anybody else, for that matter. If you invite him for dinner, I won't be there," she said firmly.

"Fine. I don't care if you are or not. I'm doing that for me. You know you have to coddle these doctors or they won't pay you any attention whatsoever. I want him to know me so I'll get a little notice if I need it, that's all."

Beth smiled. Granny was getting better. She was up to her old tricks.

The year passed and Granny got stronger. In the spring, she was out in the gardens again with Nell, though she tired more easily than before. Beth and George felt good enough to go on a trip and leave her with the girls and Nell.

They spent a whole week in New York and took time to do all the tours that they never had time for before.

The last night, they took a romantic night cruise of the harbor and had dinner on the deck. The lights of the Statue of Liberty glowed as they pulled back in port.

"Isn't that fantastic!" Beth laid her head on George's shoulder as they stood at the railing, a full moon above and city lights rippling on the waves below.

"Think of all the people who came here long ago to make a new life in this country. Millions of people passed through these portals, my ancestors and yours. Doesn't that make you proud that we live in this country?"

"Um," George kissed the top of her wind-blown dark hair. "It makes me feel proud, but I'm thinking about hurrying back to the hotel room right now."

"Are you tired?" she asked.

"No, not a bit," he said, grinning as he slipped his hand behind her head and kissed her.

They returned home rested and refreshed. Beth had a contract for a new book, and she had a notebook full of ideas jotted down before they got home. They found everyone okay and soon were back into the daily bustle of farm life.

Angelea had taken a renewed interest in caring for the cattle, especially the new calves. She and George were in the barn with a difficult birth one hot summer evening. The cow was tiring rapidly, and George was about to call the vet for help when Angelea surprised him by reaching into the birth canal and turning the calf. Soon the little fellow came out bawling, and the worn out mother perked up as she licked her newborn clean. George watched his daughter in amazement.

"Where did you learn to do that?" he asked as they washed up in the old tin sink.

"I helped Billy and his dad last week. My hands are smaller than yours, and Billy told me what to feel for. I couldn't have done it if he had been breech."

"You should be a vet. Have you ever thought about it?"

"Not really. But Billy has applied to State U. veterinary school, or have I told you?"

"You told me. Has he heard anything?"

"No, not yet. But his grades are excellent, so keep your fingers crossed."

As they walked to the house, he put his arm around her. "If you marry next May, won't that be a long haul for you two? That's a lot more years of school for Billy."

"We can do it. I'm already applying for jobs in social work even though I still have another year, and we can manage on my salary. We'll get through it okay, Dad."

"I know you will, Honey. Your Mother and I will help all we can."

She turned and walked backwards in front of George to gauge his reaction. "Not to change the subject, Dad, but Granny had the new doctor for supper while you and Mom were gone. It was so funny. Nell stayed to serve, and it was just Granny, Nell, Billy, and I. Felicia deliberately made other plans at the last minute and left before Jim got there. Granny was so mad at her." She chuckled as she recalled Granny's tirade after the doctor left.

George frowned. "Sometimes I think Granny should mind her own business."

"No, Dad. Jim was obviously disappointed that Felicia wasn't there. Leave Granny alone. She knows what she's doing. It's just going to take her awhile to make things go her way."

Chapter Twenty-Four

The year passed in a blur of activity, Felicia finishing up school, and Angelea preparing for her wedding. Felicia did her student teaching and fell more deeply in love with her chosen vocation. She and Beth were busy with showers for Angelea and the bustle of wedding plans.

In the midst of the whirlwind, she approached Beth about her ideas for them to do a book together. Beth was delighted that her daughter wanted to collaborate with her, and they put together an outline of the book, a mystery, which was something Beth had never tried. They put the research off until after Felicia's graduation and the wedding, making it a summer project.

Felicia graduated the middle of May with all her family present. Henry and Cynthia came with an announcement of Cynthia's pregnancy and a November date for the little one's arrival. Joan and Bill were beside themselves.

"We get to start all over again," she said, beaming. "One batch leaving and another arriving. That's the way to do it. A new baby is just what we all need." She hugged her daughter-in-law, joyfully. "I'm so glad Henry was a late bloomer."

"Better late than never," Henry retorted, smiling at his attractive mother, whose own happiness had taken years from her face. Her perfectly groomed hair and stylish clothing made her look like a young matron rather than the grandmother of two grown girls.

George and Beth watched as their daughter walked up to receive her diploma. She wore the gold scarf of an honor student, and they felt the enormous pride in her achievements as well as sadness, knowing that she would probably be leaving the nest. But she surprised them with her own announcement. She was going to teach first grade in Greenville, only a few miles away.

"Good," her father told her as they had their celebration at home. "You can drive that easily."

"No, Dad. I want to find a place to live closer to my work. One of the new teachers at Greenville Elementary has asked me to be her roommate, but I think I'd like to be by myself. I'm still thinking about it though."

Beth looked at George and smiled. He hated to give up his girls so badly. It was hard for him to realize that they were twenty-one and twenty-two and ready to go out on their own. She gave him a consoling hug as she laid out the plates of cake and cups of coffee.

Angelea's wedding day was May 30; an outdoor wedding was planned. Granny was in a tizzy working in the flowers, deadheading and pruning, trying to get the lawns looking just right.

"In a week, there will be a lot more blooms," she complained.

"Oh, Granny, the beds are lovely, and there will be plenty to decorate with," Angelea said, excitedly. "Besides Billy's mom has those blush roses in bloom and we're going to use a lot of those."

The day dawned warm and sunny, a perfect day for a lawn wedding. "I'm so relieved," Angelea said as her sister and mother put the finishing touches on the arch of tulle and roses. "I would have hated to have to move into the barn for the ceremony." She stepped back to approve the bank of flowers at the base of the arch, breathing deeply of the perfumed air, her heart aflutter with excitement.

"Well, the weather report says sunny for the next three days." Beth pulled her daughter toward the house. "Now let's don't dawdle. You need a good soaking bath to relax, and then we'll work on your fingernails and make-up."

After her toilette was completed, Angelea stood before them in the dress worn by Joan and Beth. The veil was new, having been dyed to match the creamy aged satin and fashioned in a pouf at the back of her head to sweep to the train of her dress.

Beth's eyes filled with happy tears. "Oh, you are so beautiful, Angel," she said as she fastened a ring of wild flowers around the puff of tulle atop the chignon of dark curls.

Felicia had to look away for a moment, as memories of her own wedding plans flooded her mind. Taking a deep breath, she grasped her sister's hand. "You are the most gorgeous bride I've ever seen. I'm going to get the photographer so he can start taking pictures." She paused outside the door to wipe away an unwanted tear.

The pictures of the three of them, Felicia in pale yellow, Beth in sky blue, were taken. Cynthia and Cassie, Angelea's bridesmaids, joined them for more. Then the photographer went off to catch the grandparents as they walked down the grassy aisle.

"Well, this is it," Felicia said nervously, as the string quartet began to play. They lifted skirts and veil and moved the bride to the porch where George waited to escort her down the aisle. As they draped and arranged train and veil, he closed his eyes and saw her as a baby lying on his chest on the old glider. He could almost smell her baby sweetness.

"Daddy?" She kissed his cheek, and he opened his eyes to his beautiful daughter in satin and tulle.

"I love you," they whispered to each other as Henry came to escort Beth to her seat. Then they followed Felicia down the steps toward Billy, who was nervously perspiring in his tuxedo.

After the vows, the guests moved into the tent where refreshments were served. Billy and Angelea led the dancing, Beth and George and Joan and Bill following. As other guests joined in, Felicia was amazed to see Jim Forrest leading Granny slowly across the floor. Her heart was touched by his thoughtfulness as Granny passed by, her delight in being included in the dancing shining in her smile.

Later he sought Felicia out and asked her for a turn around the floor. She accepted.

"Thank you for dancing with Granny. It meant a lot to her," she told him, as the music changed to a faster pace.

"It was my pleasure. I am becoming very attached to your great-grandmother; she's quite a lady. I don't think I've met an older person with as much gumption as she has." He swung her around and ducked under her arm.

She laughed, breathlessly. "I wish it was genetic, but I'm afraid she is one of a kind."

"Oh, I think it's in the genes. From what I've heard, you have plenty of gumption yourself." Feeling her stiffen, he realized his mistake and added, "That's what it takes to be a good teacher. Congratulations on your diploma."

"Thanks." She relaxed and enjoyed the rest of the dance. Then they drifted toward the buffet of fruits and finger foods. He carried her plate outside the noisy tent to one of the tables placed around the flowerbeds.

"This is just beautiful," he said as he pulled out her chair. "Does Mrs. Daniel do all this?"

"No, she and Nell work them together, and Mom helps, too, when she can. They argue about what to plant, where to plant it, what needs to be moved from here to there. But in the end they enjoy every minute of it, and this is the result." She smiled as her eyes swept the foxgloves and delphiniums, the vines climbing wildly up the side of the potting shed that was smaller version of the house.

"You are beautiful yourself," he said, casually. "That yellow is so lovely with your dark hair. Do you wear that color often?"

"It's my favorite color. My room is yellow and when I move, I'll probably paint my new rooms the same shade."

"You're moving?"

"Just to Greenville. I start teaching in the fall at the elementary school."

"Congratulations on finding a job so soon."

"I think they are getting ready to cut the cake. Let's go back in." They joined the family and guests at the punch and cake table.

Billy and Angelea cut the tall white cake with blush roses and lavender pansies, and drank a toast to each other, kissing every time a guest tapped on their glass. As the guests lined up for cake and punch, Jim's pager went off.

"I was afraid of that. I bet Mrs. Jergenson's baby has decided to arrive at last. Please excuse me, and if I don't make it back, I'll call you later." With a wave he was gone in a trot.

She blushed and stammered a goodbye, feeling flustered. She hadn't meant to dance with him, much less spend this much time with him. But the rosy glow that warmed her face told her that it was indeed pleasant.

Chapter Twenty-Four

"Line up, girls," Beth called out. "The bride is getting ready to toss her bouquet." Cassie, Felicia and a bevy of single friends clustered together as Angelea took her pose and tossed the bouquet over her shoulder. Cassie caught it with much squealing and laughing of the young women. Angelea grabbed her sister's hand.

"I wanted you to catch my bouquet."

"Well, Cassie was determined to catch it, she elbowed everyone else out of the way," Felicia laughed.

"I saw you and our doctor dancing. How was it?"

"He's a good dancer, and we had a pleasant conversation, Miss Nosey." Felicia pinched her sister's cheek. "Now you better get out of here; your bridegroom looks like he's had enough of this party stuff and not nearly enough of his bride. I love you, Angel." She hugged her sister tightly. "Have a wonderful honeymoon."

"We will. Bye, Filly. You're the best sister a girl ever had," she said, blowing a kiss, as she ran to her Billy and took his hand. The guests quickly lined up with their rice bags and pelted them as they ran to the house to change into traveling clothes.

Beth waved as the car drove away with her daughter and new son-in-law, knowing that this was a marriage that was meant to be. They had so much in common, so much to build on. She turned her attention to the last of the departing guests.

Later, she sat barefoot on the porch sipping iced tea with the family.

"Well, that's over," she said to George. "Now what will we do for excitement?"

231

"Nothing," Nell said wearily. "Nothing for a long time."

"Nell, I know you're worn out after all that cooking. I wish you had let the caterers do it all."

"No, I wanted Angel to have some of my best recipes at her wedding. She's such a darling girl."

"Yes, she is, and your little quiches were so delicious. The caterer asked me to get the recipe."

"Don't give it up, Nell," Granny piped in. "They'll just make a mint serving it at other weddings."

Felicia was stretched out on the chaise. She was exhausted from hiding her own feelings all day. A thread of jealousy kept trying to weave its way into the joy for her sister, and she was weary from fighting it off.

"I thought I would find you all back here," a chipper voice called, as Jim appeared from the corner of the house.

"Hey," George greeted him. "We're too pooped to get up. Grab yourself a chair and join us."

Felicia smiled and asked about his call.

"I was right, it was Mrs. Jergenson. But she had done most of the work for me; in fact, she barely made it to the hospital. She had another boy; that makes four, I think." He had changed into a sports shirt and slacks and looked as fresh as he did hours earlier. Accepting a glass of tea, he turned to Felicia.

"I thought if you aren't too tired, that we might drive over to the lodge for dinner."

"Don't mention food," she laughed. We've been around food all day."

"But you'll be hungry again by the time we get there; it's an hour's . . ."

"She needs to get away from here," cut in Granny. "She's worked hard on this wedding. It'll do her good to go somewhere and relax." She smiled at Felicia who was looking daggers back at her.

She surveyed the expectant faces around her—Joan and Bill, her parents, Nell and Granny, Henry and Cynthia—all with smiles urging her to go.

"Okay, sounds good," she said, finally. "Just give me time enough to get out of all these wedding duds."

Granny leaned back in her chair with a sigh. "Oh, Doc? Keep her out late, you hear? She's been such a homebody lately; we're all pretty tired of her." She winked at Jim who gave her a thumbs up.

Chapter Twenty-Five

Angelea wiped her hands on her dusty jeans. "Well, we're all packed and ready to roll," she said turning to her mother. "This is it. I'm going to miss you so much. We want you and Daddy to come up just as soon as we get settled in our quarters."

Beth pulled her daughter to her in a smothering hug. "We will. We're going to miss you, too. But time will fly by, and I hope you'll be back for visits every chance you get. Keep encouraging Billy to start his veterinary practice here."

"Oh, he's determined to do that. He wants us to build a house on his Dad's farm eventually. And I want to come back, too. This is home. We're part of this land."

"*The People of the Land*," Beth murmured, thinking of her best-selling book. "That's who we all are. It would take a lot to move us away from those rolling hills and peaceful valleys."

Felicia was saying her good-byes to Billy and Angelea. She had already moved to her apartment in Greenville, and was feeling the first pangs of homesickness along with the excitement of being on her own. She knew the feelings her sister was going through, except she had Billy to share it.

George stood back after loading the last box. The empty nest syndrome had bothered him the first few days after Filly had moved, but now he was resigned that it would just be he and Beth, Granny and Nell.

"Work hard, come back every chance you get. It's going to be boring around here without your popping in and out." Granny was taking this harder than she would admit.

George embraced his daughter and son-in-law and waved as their car headed down the driveway. Billy honked the horn until they turned down the highway and were lost from view.

Beth dropped her hand and turned to Felicia. "Can you stay for lunch? We can go over that last chapter. It needs some work."

"Can't, Mom. I want to go on to school and work on my classroom. I'm only half finished with the laminating and cutting. I want the kids to be awed by all the fun things I have on our wall."

Beth sighed. "Okay. We'll work on it the first weekend you're home."

"Which will be next weekend, Mom. Then I want you to come home with me and give me some ideas on decorating my little apartment."

"Oh, that'll be fun. Well, go on; I know you have things to do. We'll see you next weekend."

After kisses all around, she was gone.

Granny and Nell went back in the house, bound for a consoling cup of tea. George and Beth walked around to the gazebo and sat down under its vine-covered shade. The doves were cooing overhead, and a few leaves were beginning to fall, even though it was still August. The mums were budding out yellow and bronze, and summer flowers beginning to wilt in the heat.

"Another summer's end," Beth mused, as a bee circled too close to her head, and George swatted at it.

"Well, it's back to where we started out, just you and me," George put his arm around her and pulled her close.

"And Granny and Nell," she reminded him. "We've never been alone, totally alone. But you know, I wouldn't change a thing about our life together, not even one minute. Would you?"

"Well, I could have done without the tornado and a few upsets, but really everything that's happened brought us closer, made us appreciate life more."

"I think I'm in the mood to do some fall cleaning. If I'm busy, I won't miss my girls so much."

"Why don't you go see Sophie for a few days?" he suggested. Beth's old friend was married now with a ten-year-old son and was practicing law in the city.

"I didn't tell you, did I? We're going to get together for lunch next week. Her Seth will be back in school, and she's going to check on her parents. So I'll get to see her then. No, I think it's time to start a good fall cleaning. Nell will love me for this, I know." She sprang up with determination leaving George alone in the gazebo.

He knew he should get up. He had work to do, but he felt so tired. Believing his lethargy was due to the recent changes in his household, he fought the fatigue and walked lazily to the pasture to check on his herd.

Beth was in frenzy for a few days, washing windows and bedclothes, cleaning upholstery and rugs.

"You don't have to do all this yourself," Nell told her. "What I can't do, I can get that youngster of Wade's to do. He wants to work for extra money, and I promised him some jobs."

"We'll hire him to help George some. He's been down in the dumps lately. But I need to do this myself. Besides I'm almost finished." She smiled at Nell's serious stiff face.

Fall came in with a vengeance. Temperatures dropped before there was time to get out winter clothing. Then it settled into a beautiful warm Indian summer in October. The skies were a brilliant blue and the breeze, drifting over the fields, was balmy and lazy.

Beth was cutting back perennials with Granny and enjoying the sun on her face. As she straightened her back, she saw George limping to the house.

"What's wrong with you, Honey?" She dropped her shears and went to help him to the porch.

"I'm just tired," he said as he dropped into the wicker settee. "I don't know when I've felt so tired before. I can't seem to get anything done without sitting down every few minutes." Pulling off his cap, he ran his hands over his face that was damp with sweat.

Beth felt her stomach lurch and tighten. She had seen George when he was weary from long hours and hard work, but he had hardly done anything lately to tire him. She studied his rugged, still handsome face. He seemed to have lost his summer tan all of a sudden and was pale. She instantly knew that something was wrong, really wrong.

"We're going in to see Jim. I'm going to set you up an appointment right now." She rose to go to the phone, but he stopped her.

"I'll call him myself when I think it's necessary. All I need is a nap, and I'll be good as new. Don't go making a fuss."

He got up and went in leaving her standing.

"Wonder where he gets his stubbornness?" she thought as she followed him in, slamming the door. When she was sure he was lying down, she picked up the phone.

"May I speak with Dr. Forrest, please Ella? This is Beth Daniel . . . Oh, he's with a patient? No, it's not an emergency, but I'd appreciate it if he would call me back as soon as he can. Thanks." Before she could fix a pot of coffee for George to drink when he woke up, Jim was ringing back.

"Beth. It isn't Granny, is it?"

"No, Jim. I just wanted to talk to you about George. He's been really tired lately. I had to help him to the porch today, he was so exhausted. And he's not been doing any heavy work. I think he needs to see you."

"You sound serious, Beth. Look, I have a cancellation this afternoon. Bring him in around three, and Dr. Adams and I will both take a look at him, okay?"

"Thanks, Jim. Now if I can get him there without a fight."

"Sic Granny on him. That oughta do it!"

So she did. When George awoke, he smelled the coffee and came down for a cup. Beth and Granny were at the kitchen table, waiting.

"Ah, the coffee smells wonderful. I love to wake up to that smell. I'll just drink a fast cup and then head into town to pick up some supplies at the farm store," he said as he filled his cup and sat down beside Beth. She noticed the dark smudges under his eyes.

"I'm going with you," she said, taking his hand. "But we're going by Jim's office first. He wants to see you."

"You called? Beth, I told you it was nothing. I'm a grown man, and I don't need you to make decisions for me. When did you get to be so bossy?"

Granny jumped into the conversation. "And when did you get to be so stubborn, George Daniel? You've been looking peaked for awhile now. Oh, don't think I don't notice these things. You've drug around here like a whipped dog. Now if Beth says you need to see the doctor, then you need to see the doctor. And don't fuss at her; she's just trying to take care of you. Drink that coffee and get a shower. Your appointment is at three." She folded her arms on the table with a thump, her mouth set in determination.

George looked from one to the other and knew he had lost the battle. Grumbling, he slammed down his cup and went into the bedroom. When they heard water running, they looked at each other with satisfied grins.

"Thanks," Beth reached across the table and patted Granny's hand.

"Anytime."

The drive into town was quiet. George was nursing his wounds at being outdone by the two women. When they went in to see Jim, his expression was serious as George told him about the fatigue that had plagued him for several weeks. Beth went into the waiting room as Jim examined George. Thumbing through a magazine, she found she couldn't concentrate, so she put it down and walked to the window. Jim had put out bird feeders, and she watched the little wrens holding their own against the bigger birds as they fed noisily. How peaceful her world had seemed this morning in the warm October sun as she tidied up flowerbeds.

Jim broke her thoughts as he called her back to his office where George was sitting, buttoning his shirt.

"Well, Beth, I'm glad you brought him in because he probably wouldn't have come on his own for too long. As I told George, I need to do some tests."

"You've already taken a quart of blood," George fussed.

"Yes, but we need to do more than that. I'll set it up for Thursday, if that's okay and they can work it in at the hospital. We'll just keep you a couple of days and check everything out, just to be safe." He smiled at them both.

Beth looked into Jim's dark eyes and saw alarm there, even as he made light of the tests. "We'll be there

Thursday," she said, nervously twisting her wedding ring on her finger.

Chapter Twenty-Six

A tired George complained from his bed. "They really put you through the wringer here. I'm as weak as a kitten from all those tests."

"Well, they're over now," Beth murmured, soothingly, as she plumped up his pillow and kissed him.

"Hmm. Do that again," George said with a wink, and she obliged him, jerking away before he could pull her in the bed with him.

"Behave! And why didn't you eat your lunch? You didn't eat much breakfast either."

"Not hungry. I'll eat as soon as I get home to Nell's good cooking."

"Well, that won't be long now. Jim said he'd be in before lunch, and it's almost two. I'd hoped we could take you home this afternoon."

Just then the two doctors filed into the room. Beth felt a chill as she looked into their solemn faces.

"Well, George, we got all the results back from the blood work and the tests." Dr. Adams pulled up a chair, as Jim walked to the window and looked out. He went over the tests, one by one. "I know that doesn't mean much to you, George, but they aren't good. We suspect that you have something very serious."

"How serious?" George sat up in bed. "Just come out with it, Doc."

Dr. Adams drew a deep breath. "George, you have cancer. The CAT scan was pretty definite. We know where it is, but we don't know how far it's spread. It will take more tests and possibly surgery to determine that."

"Cancer?" Beth shook her head in disbelief. She felt faint and swallowed back the nausea that rose in her throat.

"But I haven't been sick. Nothing hurts. I've been unusually tired, that's all.'

"Sometimes that's the only symptom, George. But as you think back, you may remember when things didn't seem right, when you felt sick but just kept going."

"When can you do the surgery?" George's face was even paler and his hand shook as he reached for hers.

"We can do it here, or we can send you to Houston. I would recommend that you go there. They are doing things that are remarkable, and I'd like to see you get the very latest treatments. We just can't offer as much here. I can set it up for you, but don't wait too long before you decide."

"Just how bad is it? I mean . . . is it terminal?"

"I think you have a lot of hope, George. But you need to get whatever treatment the doctors there deem the best for your type of cancer."

"I'm still young, Doc. I have a lot of living I want to do. And I sure don't want to leave Beth and the girls. I'll do whatever you think I should do." He paused, swallowing back hot tears. "So go ahead and make the arrangements for me. We'll be ready to go as soon as you say."

"Good. Now, you get ready and go on home. Talk to your family; try to get some rest. I'll set up everything and be back in touch in the next couple of days. And try not to worry. Cancer isn't necessarily a death sentence anymore."

He shook George's hand, hugged Beth, and nodded to Jim.

"I just couldn't tell you," Jim said from the window. Turning, he came to the bed and sat on it, taking George's hand. "I'm so sorry. But please keep your spirits up. They really are on top of things down in Texas. I have a patient who went down there, and he came back as good as new. They got it all, and he'll soon be back at work. So keep that in mind. You came in early, and that's a good sign."

"Thanks, Jim. We'll try to remember that. It's just that it's a shock . . . didn't expect this." He squeezed Beth's hand. "We'll get through it, won't we, Honey?"

"Absolutely." She put on a smile. "Will you check us out, Jim? I think he needs to go home as quickly as you can get us out of here."

He took Beth's arm and propelled her outside the room.

"Are you okay?"

"I think so, just a bit shaken."

"I'll do anything I can, you know that. Will you be calling Felicia?"

"Yes. We'll call both the children tonight."

"Tell her I'll call her. If she comes home before you leave, tell her to call me. And Beth, keep up his spirits. And yours, too."

She kissed him on the cheek and went in to help George get dressed to go back to the farm. They collected their things, and the chair came to take him to the car. The sound of the rubber wheels, the click of her shoes, the hum of the elevator all seemed unusually loud. Everyone seemed to move in slow motion, each step heavy and plodding.

They tried to get George back in bed, but he insisted on checking on the cows. Wearily, he walked to the barn to talk to Wade. Beth watched them talking from the window. She sobbed as she saw Wade put his arms around George. They had been friends longer than they had worked together, friends since George was a little boy.

She felt arms go around her, and leaned back against Nell.

"I can bring Arthur here for awhile and stay with Felicia as long as you have to be gone."

She turned and hugged her. "No, Nell. Arthur likes his own home, and you need to take care of your son. We appreciate the thought, but Mom and Bill can stay here. You need to be in your own home. Thank you so much for being so good to us."

"I'll help in any way I can," Nell said, as she took her purse from atop the refrigerator. "You'll need me tomorrow?"

"Oh, yes. We may not go for several days. Be careful, Nell." She kissed her on her cheek and went to find Granny. She found her in the living room, quietly rocking in her chair. Beth sat on the couch across from her, kicking off her shoes and drawing her feet up under her. Nothing was said for a long time.

Finally, "I never dreamed George would have something like this. Why couldn't it have been me? My life is almost over, and he's in the prime of his."

"Granny, don't say that, he wouldn't want you to talk like that. Besides we can't choose. If we could, we'd all live to be at least one hundred and die making love. Let's just encourage him and pray . . . lots of praying . . ."

Granny smiled at the small joke. "You're right. It's not doom and gloom. It's about hope, faith, and Daniel determination. Right?"

"Right. Now let's call him in and feed him this good supper Nell left. He needs building up physically, too."

"You're a good girl, Beth," Granny said, as she rose painfully from her chair. "I can't imagine having been blessed any more than I have with you and George."

Beth put her arms around the bony shoulders and thought, "Please dear God, please let her live longer. We need her so." To Granny, she said simply, "I love you."

George ate like he was famished. Beth was afraid he would make himself sick, he ate so much. Then he took his hot tea into the living room and called them in after they had cleaned up.

"I have a few things to say before we call the girls and tell them. First, I want to make an appointment with Harold Sharp to make out my will. I've been meaning to do that."

"George, honey, that can wait until you recover."

"No, I want to do it as soon as possible. I'm not afraid that I'll die before I get another chance. It's just on my mind, and I'd like to take care of it. Second, I say that we don't tell the girls the whole truth. They are at such important times in their lives . . ."

"Sweetheart," Beth interrupted. "They're adults now. Of course, we'll have to tell them everything we know. They wouldn't forgive us if we glossed over things. They are strong, just like their father. Got it from Granny." She winked, and he smiled.

"Got it from their mother, too, I'd say. You're right though. Let's go call them and get it over with."

Felicia and Angelea were distraught, and both wanted to come right home. But Beth talked them into waiting until they had some news as to when they would go to Houston. It took long conversations to convince them that was the best thing to do. Once that was done, George seemed tired and ready to call it a night.

Though she wasn't sleepy, Beth went to bed with him, and they held each other in the dark. He started to reminisce, starting at the beginning, when they were neighbors and students, and he had a crush on her. They laughed as they recalled those days, then their wedding, and then the births of their babies. He talked about the irony of his mother dying of cancer, and his own battle ahead.

"You've always taken care of yourself, Sweetheart. You have a better chance than your mother did. Don't compare your cancer to hers."

"That's true, I'm being morbid. Hold me tight, Mrs. Daniel. I need to go to sleep with your arms around me."

She held him until he was asleep, whispering assurances against his cheek, her arms numb where he laid on them. Slowly she slipped them from under him, but stayed close to his body. Her mind was whirling with thoughts of the days ahead. She wished for a glass of water for her dry mouth, but would not move, lest she disturb him. So she lay awake and counted the strikes of the clock until four. Sleep mercifully claimed her tired mind and swept her away into a few hours of peace, the peace that had been erased that day by just one word.

Chapter Twenty-Seven

*B*oth girls took off from school to accompany their parents to the airport for the flight to Houston. They were chipper and bright, keeping George laughing with Felicia's tales of her new first graders, and Angelea's descriptions of her professors. As the plane took off into the deep blue sky, they dropped their pleasant demeanors and became teary-eyed as the plane rose out of sight.

"Please, God," Angelea said aloud.

"Bring him back well," Felicia finished for her.

When they arrived at the hospital five hours later, George and Beth were amazed at the size of the institution. It seemed to cover acres and acres, spreading this way and that with wings for every kind of medicine.

The nurses were cheerful and had George settled into his room with a minimum of paperwork and fuss.

The room itself was cheery with soft blue walls and tranquil paintings, much unlike a regular hospital room.

"Welcome to your little home away from home," a nurse named Kelly said with a grin on her freckled face. "I'm here until 7:00, so if you need anything, you call for me. You'll get to meet your doctors around six tonight, which is just a couple of hours from now, and your dinner will be here in an hour. Since you weren't here to order your meal, it will be potluck, but you'll be able to order what you want whenever you aren't having tests. Do you have any questions? Okay, I'll be in and out to look after you, but if you need me, ring." She was gone with a swish of her skirt.

"I like her," Beth said as she hung up her coat and put things in a drawer.

"Hey, I'm glad they let you wear your own pajamas here instead of those skimpy little numbers," George said, happily.

"I hate to burst your bubble, but I imagine they will have you in those 'skimpy little things' things part of the time. Come look out the window, Honey. Did you ever see as many cars and people coming and going? I wonder how many patients they treat here in a day?"

"There's no telling. I'm sure the doctors will have a rough idea. I'm only concerned with the one that just checked in." His face grew grim.

She smiled. "The trip tired you, didn't it? Climb in bed and rest until your meal gets here."

He lay down and began to question what was ahead for him, but she hushed him with her fingers, and he closed his eyes until the dinner tray arrived. The meal was light, and he was disappointed when he saw the soup and Jell-O.

"Uh oh, they have plans for me tomorrow," he grumbled. "Oh, well, I'm hungry. Honey, you didn't have any lunch. Go on down to the cafeteria and get something nourishing; you need it."

"I'm afraid I'll miss the doctors."

"Oh, you've got plenty of time," Kelly said as she came in to check on them. "They come around late, so go on. They won't leave without talking to you." She gave Beth directions to the cafeteria, and Beth gave in to her hunger pangs.

She ate at a table by herself, and found that she didn't want what she chose, but she forced herself to finish the salad and pudding. Still afraid she might not be there when the doctors came in, she didn't tarry.

Turning right as she left the cafeteria, she walked to the elevator and went up to the fourth floor. When she got off and looked around, nothing seemed the same. Was this the wrong floor? She looked for someone to ask, but the nurse's station was empty. She found the room number, but it seemed to be on the wrong side of the hall. She peeked inside, and a toothless elderly lady smiled at her from the bed.

"Hello, Dearie. Come on in and sit a spell. Do I know you?"

"I'm sorry. I . . . I . . . have the wrong room," she stammered as she fled.

She went back down and tried to find the information desk, but it wasn't where she had been before. She began to panic. She sat down on a bench in the hallway to get her bearings. In spite of her gritted teeth, tears of frustration slid down her face.

A young doctor passed by, glanced at her, then stopped.

"Can I help you, Ma'am?"

"I think I'm lost. I thought I was on the right floor, but . . ." she told him with trembling voice where she wanted to go.

"Somehow you got in the wrong wing. It's okay; I'll take you to the right elevator." He smiled and held out his hand and, taking her elbow, he walked her to the correct elevator that seemed a mile away. She thanked him profusely as the doors closed, thinking how much like Jim Forrest he looked, young, eager, kind.

"Did you have any trouble finding your way?" George asked when she returned.

"No trouble," she answered, hiding her anxiety. Later, she would tell him about the toothless woman, and they would laugh.

Dr. Raminsky was George's principal doctor, and Dr. Ammett worked with him. Both were congenial and had good bedside manners and George liked them immediately, which was good because they did many of the tests again before they came to them two days later with their diagnosis. Dr. Ammett discussed the test results, and then left to attend another patient.

"Here's what we have," Dr. Raminsky said, perching on the edge of the only chair rubbing his five o'clock shadow. "We think that your cancer in localized, but we can't be sure until we operate."

"When will that be?" Beth said, nervously.

"We have him scheduled for tomorrow at eight. So no food after supper and no water after midnight. And don't worry, it's a simple operation in itself, and afterward, we'll know for sure what we're dealing with. Any questions, George?"

"No, I guess you've covered everything. Just one thing."

"What's that?"

"Go on home and get a good night's sleep."

He laughed. "Don't worry. I'll be in tiptop shape. And we'll give you something for sleep so you can have a good night's rest, too."

"How about me?" Beth joked.

"You should go over to the family quarters and get some sleep," he suggested softly. "Tomorrow will be a busy day."

"I can't. I want to stay with George."

He patted her arm. "I figured as much. I'll have the nurse bring in a cot for you. See you both in the morning."

In spite of the pill, George only dozed, waking up every few minutes. Beth slept in spurts, with her head on the side of George's bed and her hand on his arm.

By the time they arrived to prepare George for surgery early in the morning, they both felt the night had been a week long.

After following his gurney down to surgery, she was directed to the surgery waiting room. Time seemed to drag. The silver-haired volunteer kept refilling her coffee cup until she could no longer bear the taste. She struck up a conversation with a pretty blonde woman in her fifties named Mary. Her husband was being operated for a tumor as well. As people will in those circumstances, they confided in each other their individual fears, and Beth was grateful for her company. They were exchanging stories about their families when the volunteer lady interrupted their conversation.

"Mrs. Daniel? Dr. Raminsky will see you over here." She led Beth to an adjoining room, and she sat down to wait, her heart in her throat. Her palms were sweaty as she fidgeted impatiently.

"Mrs. Daniel," he smiled as he sailed in, the medicinal odor filling the tiny room. "Good news. We believe we got it all. Everything went better than we thought."

Beth drew a deep breath of relief. "Thank God. Are you sure? How long will his recovery be, do you think?"

"He'll need chemo; we'll start him on that before you leave, then you'll be able to fly back and forth for successive treatments. It had not spread to the lymph nodes, but we want to be sure that we get any cells that might be in question. It will be the minimum amount just as a precaution, and he should be good as new."

"Oh, thank you, thank you. I was so afraid."

"Everyone is. And you do know what to expect with the chemo?"

"Yes, Dr. Ammett told us. We can get through that if we know he's going to be okay."

"George is an upbeat person, the kind of patient we want to have. He'll be fine. By the way, I've enjoyed your books, read most of them. I'm originally from that part of the country, myself."

Beth couldn't resist giving him a hug. "I knew there was something about you that I liked," she laughed.

She stayed in the room with George the first three nights. By then, he was feeling better and was up and around, but still weak. The fourth night, he sent her to the family quarters for a good night's sleep. She fell across the bed in her clothes and slept for nine hours. She had a long shower and a good breakfast before going back to his room. She felt like a new person when she walked in as he was talking to Granny. He held out the phone.

"Here, she doesn't believe that I've been chasing nurses all over this hospital. You talk to her."

"Hi, Granny. Yes, he really is doing great. No, I don't know when we'll have the first chemo. We talked to both girls yesterday. We'll be home after the first two chemo treatments, that's all I know. Are you okay? Yes, we love you, too."

As soon as George had his strength back, and his blood work was normal, he had his first chemo. He felt a little nauseous but wasn't really sick until the second one. Beth held his head over the commode and wiped his sweaty face, reminding him that it would be worth it to be sure the cancer didn't return. He agreed even as he moaned with dry heaves.

Each of those days seemed like an eternity. When he wasn't sick at his stomach, he slept. She never left the room except to get a quick bite. He lost fifteen pounds and Beth lost ten while he was in the hospital. But at last he began to feel better, and the doctors pronounced them ready to leave.

The day of departure dawned cool and rainy. After saying goodbye to the doctors and nurses and packing up their belongings, they were taken down to the cab by Kelly, whose freckled face and carrot red hair had become dear to them. They hugged goodbye and promised to see her again when they came back for treatments.

On the plane, sailing above the rain clouds, George looked over at Beth.

"Thanks for sticking with me, Bethie. I can't do this without you."

"You don't have to," she said as she laid her head on his shoulder. "We're a team, remember? Whatever happens."

The flight attendant came by with cold drinks. "Newlyweds?" She asked with a knowing wink.

"Not quite," George answered. "But better, much better than that. We're a team."

Chapter Twenty-Eight

They flew back and forth for George's treatments. He still got sick each time, but recovered faster after each one, and the last trip he hardly was sick at all. Dr. Raminsky was happy with his progress, and the last CAT scan showed no signs of cancer in his body. He was bald with just a little peach fuzz on his head when they left for home the last time. Although still terribly thin, he was slowly regaining strength and weight.

It was a cheerful trip home. They found something to laugh about in the most minute things; a child's antics on the plane, the way the man across the aisle snored, the lady who came from the restroom with the back of her dress tucked into her panty hose. Beth was laughing when they turned into their driveway, but her laughter turned to awed silence as the house came into view.

"What a beautiful home we have, George. It's like leaving the rest of the world behind to drive down this tree-lined lane and see that glorious old house beckoning to us. I'm forgetting Houston already." Her eyes widened. "Hey, look at all the cars. I believe we're about to have a homecoming celebration. Are you too tired for a party?"

"Tired? I feel like I could fly if I tried. How sweet of them to give us a big welcome. There's Dad's car . . ."

"And Sophie's . . . she just bought it before you got sick. I see Filly's and Billy and Angelea's, and Nell's . . . Oh, hurry, George. We can get the luggage out later."

"SURPRISE!" The group chorused as they opened the door. The house was ablaze with candles and crepe paper streamers. The smell of cinnamon filled the air.

"Son." Bill grabbed him in a bear hug, unable to say anything else.

"You're home at last," Joan said, blinking back tears as she threw her arms around them both.

"Welcome home," Granny slowly came to them with a big hug for each. Then everyone—Nell, Joan and Bill, Billy and Angelea, Henry, Cynthia and their little son, Josh, Felicia, Jim Forrest, Wade and his wife, Lucy, Charlie, and Sophie—moved in. It was chaotic, with everyone talking at once, but wonderful to embrace family and friends.

"This is great. Thanks, everybody," George said, a daughter clinging on each arm. "I can't tell you how glad we are to get home and how blessed we feel to be here to stay. No more Houston!"

A cheer went up, and after the applause, the group settled into chairs, the girls claiming the sofa where they questioned their father about the recent visit.

George was relaxed and happy as he told them about the good-byes to Kelly and the nurses and Drs. Raminsky and Ammett. "We felt like we were leaving family there. There's no way I can tell you how kind they all were. Except this one nurse, Miss Waddley, who did waddle when she walked, and had no sense of humor."

"That's because you tormented her with your teasing. She shot you with the biggest, thickest needle she had to pay you back," Beth laughed as she handed young Josh back to his mother and went into the kitchen for a private chat with Sophie.

Nell had baked a huge cake with 'Welcome Home' iced in pink and green.

"Underneath, it's his favorite—carrot cake," she said proudly. "But you get out of here and go back to your family. You're tired, and your Granny and I have everything under control."

"I'm doing steaks on the grill," Billy called to George. "Are you ready for me to put them on?"

"Do it! I'm starved," George answered.

Beth and Sophie slipped away to the bedroom. Sophie was radiant in a red sweater and slacks, her blonde curls perfectly coifed close to her head.

"You look wonderful," Beth told her. "Thank you so much for driving up to welcome us home."

Sophie hugged her tightly. "You don't know how many times I've thought of you and George while you were gone. I would have gone with you if my slate hadn't been so full."

"I know you would, but we made it just fine. Thanks for all your notes. You don't know how much they helped."

"You know I'm always here, even if I'm seventy miles away, I can be here in an hour."

"Yeah, with a speeding ticket in your pocket. Even lawyers get them, you know. No, I hope all that is behind us. It's so good to be home. And I'm coming down and have lunch with you just as soon as George gets stronger." Beth made a mental note to see more of her old friend. She had come to realize how short time could be.

The party broke up about nine. Henry, Cynthia and Josh went home with Bill and Joan to spend the night. Granny retired to her room, Nell and the others went home. And George excused himself from his family to crawl into his own bed. He was in a deep sleep in five minutes. Beth kissed his forehead and lightly rubbed his fuzzy head. She was too wired up to go to sleep, so she donned a sweater and joined the young people on the porch.

It was an unseasonably warm early March night, and already the air was thick with the earthy smell of damp earth and budding trees. There were no city odors, no factory exhausts, no endless sounds of traffic, just a farm awakening to the season of new life. *Home*, thought Beth, as she breathed deeply of the familiar smells.

Jim and Felicia, Billy and Angelea were deep in conversation about George. "Are you sure he's going to be okay now, Mom?" Angelea scooted over in the swing to make room for her mother.

"Yes, Darling. Dr. Raminsky was positive. He just needs to gain his strength back, and he's doing well there. There's nothing for you girls to worry about. Jim, I just want to thank you for checking on Granny so often, and for looking in on George between trips. You made it so much easier for us."

"You've made me feel like family." Jim tightened his arm around Felicia. "It's no trouble to take care of people you care for so much."

Felicia kissed him on the cheek, taking him by surprise, and leaned into his muscular shoulder. Beth smiled broadly. Things must have been heating up a bit while they were gone.

That would be icing on the cake, she thought as she leaned her head on the chain of the swing. After the past few months of wondering if this night would be theirs to enjoy, she was overcome with emotion.

"Mom, you're crying," Angelea murmured, as she put her arms around Beth.

"Yes, Honey. Joyous tears. I haven't had a good cry in a long time, so if you'll excuse me, I think I'll go and indulge myself. Then I'm going to shower and get in my own bed. I'll see you in the morning." She kissed each of them on the cheek and went inside where she let go of all the tears that were pent up, all the while saying a prayer of thanks for this blessed night.

Two months later, it was impossible to believe George had been sick. He was up early, brimming with energy for the day's work ahead. In the evenings he was tired, but it was a good tired. Beth teased him about his hair; it was coming in curly.

"Now you'll see what I go through with my naturally curly hair. It has a mind of its own," she said, as she tried to make his short curls lay down one Sunday morning.

"That's one thing that I'll thank God for this morning," he quipped. "I don't care how curly it is, I'm happy just to have some again."

The days became full. Felicia came home on weekends, and she and Beth worked on their novel. By June, Beth decided that it was ready to edit for the last time. They were working late one Saturday night when Beth summoned the courage to ask her daughter about her relationship with Jim.

"We've been seeing each other regularly."

"What does that mean?"

"Just that. I think a lot of him, Mom, but I don't think I'm ready to get really serious."

"Why not, Filly? He obviously adores you, or he wouldn't put up with your arm's length approach to the relationship."

"He loves me, Mom. And I think I love him. I don't know what holds me back. He's not anything like Lance was—the opposite, in fact—but I just can't seem to let myself . . ."

"You're afraid of getting hurt?"

"No, I don't think he would hurt me for the world. I don't know why I'm being so skittish." Felicia bit her lip as she laid the pages down on the desk.

"Well, you'll know when the time is right. I'm glad you're seeing him so much. He's such a fine man. And not that much older that you."

Felicia laughed. "Mom, you're such a romantic, you should be a romance writer. You could churn them out two or three times a year and make a mint. That's all anyone reads anymore."

"Changing the subject? Okay, I'll hush. Now let's go over chapter twenty again, I'm not satisfied with that ending. It doesn't grab me."

The book was sent to the publishers in early summer, and went to press in the fall. The publisher was thrilled with it. Even though Beth's previous books had been successful, he sensed that this one would be a real moneymaker. By November it was being shipped out to bookstores for the Christmas season.

Felicia became a celebrity at her school. The other teachers made a big thing of it, and she was both flattered and embarrassed. After all, Beth had gone quietly through life writing without a lot of hoopla, and she expected to do the same. But she was happy and nervous on the first book signing with her mother. She had been to many as a child, but never as an author— and equal.

"Mom," she said excitedly, as they drove home after the third signing. "I think it's going to be a best seller. Can you believe that? And it's because of your name on the front. Who would publish a book by an unknown like me?"

"Don't sell yourself short. And by the way, you're on your own. It's not my genre, but you are good at that kind of book. You should jump in and write a sequel, now that you have your foot in the door."

"You think so?" She rode in silence the rest of the way home, plots and murders running through her brain. Beth glanced at her repeatedly, knowing just what was going through her mind. She had been there herself.

As they drove up the driveway, Angelea ran out to meet them, bubbling over with excitement.

"How was it?" she asked her sister.

"Great! I know now why Mom gets so high over a book. It's like a baby you've given birth to."

Angelea burst into uncontrollable giggles. Felicia and Beth looked at each other, puzzled. Then it dawned on Beth.

"Angel, you're pregnant, aren't you?"

"Yes! Yes! I'm almost two months. I could hardly stand not telling you sooner, but Billy wanted us to wait. We're so happy."

"A baby! Oh, my sweet girl, you're making me a grandmother! How wonderful! Where's Billy?"

"He's inside helping Granny pin together a quilt top. We've told everybody else. Daddy's feet haven't touched the floor since we told him."

Felicia hugged her sister. "I'm so happy for you two. What will you do about your job?"

"Well, that's the good thing about being in social work. I can give over my cases to someone else and take a nice long maternity leave. Oh, come on. Billy can't wait to be congratulated, and Nell is putting together a feast for tonight." She locked arms with them and urged them into the house.

It was another happy celebration.

"It seems like we've been given so many things to be grateful for," George said, as they sat around the table after dinner. "This new child coming to our family is the best blessing of all. It'll be hard to wait seven more months."

"We can't wait either, Daddy," Angelea bubbled. "But we'd better scoot over to Grandma's and Grandpa's and tell them. They will be mad as hornets if they hear it from anyone else."

"Yes, indeed they will. Must you go back tonight? It's such a long drive, why don't you spend the night?" George said with a frown.

"I have a class." Billy helped Angelea on with her coat. "Otherwise, we'd just stay. But we'll be home for the weekend in two weeks. Granny will probably have a baby quilt put together by then."

"Great-great Granny," Granny laughed. "Now how about that! I never thought that I'd see the day. If Filly wasn't so slow, I'd have more than one to look forward to."

Everyone laughed except Felicia.

Chapter Twenty-Nine

Angelea groaned as she stooped down to pick up the spoon that she dropped on the kitchen floor of their tiny apartment. She was in her eighth month, and bending and stooping were almost impossible due to the weight she had gained. Most of her pregnancy had gone well, but she hadn't felt good the past few days. Hoping that it wasn't a bad sign, she picked up her purse and called to Billy.

"Honey, are you ready to take me to the doctor? My appointment is at ten, you know."

Billy came out of the bedroom where he had been studying for an exam.

"Sorry, Angel. I got engrossed in my reading. I'll pull the car around front and help you down the steps. You just sit here and wait."

Two hours later, he was on the phone to Beth and George, frantically explaining that he had Angelea in the hospital.

"Toxemia?" exclaimed Beth. "Oh, my goodness. We'll be there as soon as we can get there. Try and be calm, Billy, so you can keep her relaxed. Have you called your parents? Oh, they're in California, I forgot. Okay, we're on our way."

"What's wrong?" Granny looked up from the newspaper with a worried look.

"Angel has developed toxemia, and they've put her in the hospital. Would you get Nell to go for George, he's out on the tractor? I'm going to throw together a few things."

In less than an hour, they were on the road, anxious and worried. The drive seemed longer that usual and there was no stopping for coffee as they often did. Beth felt a little scared with George's driving; he usually kept to the speed limit religiously. Today he was flying.

When they arrived at the hospital, they found a pale shaken Billy pacing in the lobby.

"How is she?" George grabbed his shoulder.

"She's gone into labor," Billy said running his hand through his red hair. "They've got her hooked up to all kinds of machines . . ."

"Take us to her. They will let us in, won't they?" Beth asked anxiously.

"Oh, yes, they will. Let's go." George sprinted toward the elevator.

Billy shook his head. "No, this way." They followed him down the hall to Angel's room. George stopped in the doorway when he saw how pale his daughter's face was. He felt his knees weaken at the sight of all the IV's hanging over her bed. Beth looked questioningly at the nurse who smiled and moved out into the hall.

"Hi, Baby. How are you feeling? Tell us what the doctor said. Billy told us . . ."

"Mom, Daddy. Looks like we're going to have this baby a little early," Angelea's voice was shaky, but her eyes were bright. Too bright, Beth thought as she felt her head. She had a temperature and her skin felt clammy.

A small stooped man came in, and Billy introduced Dr. Wisemann to her parents. "I'm on call for Dr. Wilson," he explained, "who was called out of town with a death in the family. Now if you'll excuse me, I'd like to look at this young lady and see how she's coming along." He smiled warmly, and, for some unknown reason, Beth felt a confidence in this little man.

George had to be pulled from the room, but Beth settled him in the waiting area with a cup of coffee. Billy went back in to stay with Angelea, and Beth took the opportunity to call Felicia.

"Oh, Mom, will she be alright? I'm coming right now. Tell her to hang in there."

"Why don't you call Jim? If he's not on call at the hospital, he'll come with you. We could use his advice. They aren't telling us much."

"I'll call him. If he's tied up, I'm coming by myself."

Beth hung up, feeling helpless. George was in a conversation with a nurse so she slipped back to the room.

Billy was holding his wife's hand, perspiring in the chilly room. Beth walked to the bedside where Angelea lay with eyes closed.

"She just had a long contraction," Billy murmured, patting her hand.

"Want me to sit awhile?'

Angelea opened her eyes. "Mom, please stay with me. Billy, honey, would you go out and keep Daddy company for awhile? Go on. Mom will come get you if I need you. I love you." She squeezed his hand and he reluctantly kissed her, leaving the room on shaky legs.

"He's so scared," Angelea whispered as she braced for another pain. "You know, some men just aren't good at these things. I need you, Mom." Tears formed in the corners of her eyes as she squeezed them against the pain.

"Well, I'm here, Honey. Hold on to my hand and tell me everything you're feeling. You know, when I had you . . ."

The night grew long as she struggled with her pains. Two nurses were helping her breath, push, and relax, but she wasn't making much progress. Finally, Beth caught the doctor in the hall.

"She's not getting anywhere, Doctor Wisemann. Can't you do something for her?"

"I'd rather she do it herself, if possible. Let's give her another hour. If she's not dilated more by then, we'll prepare for a caesarian section."

Felicia and Jim had arrived, and Jim agreed with Dr. Wisemann, so they settled down to wait. Everyone catnapped except Beth and Billy, who stayed by Angelea's side as much as possible.

At seven o'clock the next morning, a tired Angelea gave birth to a nine pound twelve ounce girl.

Billy held the red-faced squalling baby and cried tears of relief.

Felicia and Jim went straight to the nursery to be the first to see her, and Beth sagged against George's shoulder as they brought the baby into the nursery window for her first viewing. A long night of fear and anxiety vanished as she gazed at her granddaughter's squashed little face. She was a carbon copy of Angelea, Beth's biggest baby, with the same mop of dark hair.

"Well, little girl, you've caused quite a stir, just like your mother did. Good thing she had you before you got any bigger."

"I hope that's her last baby," George said, clutching her hand in excitement. "I don't believe I could take this again."

Beth laughed. "She's doing better than you are. You go on to the apartment and get some sleep. I'm going to stay with her until she's gotten some rest. Then I'll join you. I'm dead on my feet."

She remained at the window watching her new granddaughter. She was already in love with the child and had yet to hold her. Happily, she turned away to go back to tend to Angelea. With the last glance, she was almost sure that Elizabeth Anne winked at her as the nurse placed her in her crib.

With all the demands of new fatherhood, Billy still managed to graduate from The School of Veterinary Medicine. His family as well as Angelea's stood in the hot sun and proudly cheered as he received his degree with honors.

"You have a lot to be proud of, Claude," George said as he shook Mr. Prentiss' hand. "I can't tell you how proud of your son I am, and how glad I am that he's my son-in-law."

Doris Prentiss put her arm through her husband's. They looked like brother and sister with the same deep red hair as their son, the same hazel eyes. "We're proud of Angelea, too. He couldn't have gone through as fast if she wasn't such a help for him."

"I think we're both lucky families," Beth joined in as she took a sleeping Elizabeth from Angelea so she could join Billy for pictures.

Beth and George's gift was the services of a mover to pack up, load, and unpack their belongings in the little house in town that they were renting. Billy would be interning with Dr. Kirksey, and later they would build their own house on the Prentiss farm. They stayed at Beth and George's for a few days while getting their house in order.

Beth loved every minute of taking care of Elizabeth. She loved bathing her, singing to her, kissing the sweet spots on her neck and the bottoms of her feet. She was amazed at the depth of love that she felt toward this precious tiny baby.

Felicia was enthralled with her and followed Beth around saying, "It's my turn, Mom."

After giving her over to her aunt, Beth caught a conversation between the sisters as she was warming up supper.

"Felicia, I couldn't imagine how wonderful it would be to be a mother. I knew it would be fantastic, but it's just overwhelming sometimes. I just love her so much." Angelea twirled the stubborn dark red hair into a curl on top while the baby slept in Felicia's lap.

Felicia was quietly smiling at the faces the dozing child made. Looking at her sister, she said quietly, "I want one."

"Well, go for it. You have a man who's ready and willing. Of course, I'd recommend marriage first. Poor Jim just adores you, and you keep putting him off when he mentions marriage. What on earth are you waiting for?"

"I'm not waiting any longer," she snapped, her chin set in a determined pose. "Here, take your daughter. I'm going to call Jim and see if he's busy tonight."

Chapter Thirty

Jim drove up the Daniels' drive about seven
o'clock, tired and hungry after an extra busy day with
patients. He had left an elderly man at the hospital that
he was especially concerned about. During the evening,
he would call in and check on him. He hesitated about
saying 'yes' to Felicia's invitation to dinner. He needed
quiet, and with Billy, Angel, and the baby, there wasn't
a lot of that. Still it would be good to see them.

Felicia met him at the door in a gauzy blouse and
skirt, long hair up in curls atop her head.

"Wow! You look terrific." He stood back and gave
her a sweeping look.

"Thank you, sir. Shed your lab coat and tie and
follow me to the kitchen." She beckoned with crooked
finger, and he obeyed.

"Where is everyone?" he asked, bending to pick up
a stuffed lamb and drop it in Elizabeth's little basket
her grandmother kept on the table.

"We're alone. They've all gone out to dinner. It's a special treat for Nell and Granny. Even Nell's son, Arthur, is going along."

"That's good. He doesn't get out much, does he? Have we ever been alone in this house before?"

"Nope. I'm not sure I've ever been in this house alone. Maybe that's why I enjoy my apartment and am so ready to get back tomorrow."

He picked up a lid and sniffed. "Smells wonderful. Homemade soup?"

"Made it myself. Along with home baked bread and your favorite, Waldorf Salad."

"I'm impressed and very hungry." He put his arm around her while she stirred the pot and filled two bowls. She handed him the bread knife, and he sliced the bread, still warm from the oven, and they sat down to their meal.

"This is wonderful soup. Are you sure you made it?"

She threw her napkin at him. "Yes. Nell isn't the only one around here that cooks. I'll have you know that I'm a great cook—well, a fairly good cook, anyway."

He laughed. "You're so beautiful, it doesn't matter if you can cook or not."

They took their dessert, strawberry shortcake, and coffee on the porch. There was a gentle breeze blowing, rustling through the old oaks. The frogs were calling from the pond, and now and then a hoot owl called farewell to the setting sun from the barn roof.

"That was delicious," Jim told her as she gathered dishes and set them on the patio table. "I'm so glad you called me. I probably would have gone home and crashed, I was so tired. Now I feel like a new man."

"I called you because I needed to ask you something."

"Ask away." He put his arm around her and pulled her down beside him on the glider. She wiggled around to face him, the fluttering in her chest so pronounced she felt he must surely feel it, too. She hesitated, not knowing how to start.

"It's a little hard to ask, but I've been giving it some thought lately. You've been so patient with me—why, I don't know—while I've been holding back about the way I feel about you."

"You love me, I know you do, and that's good enough for me. I don't ask you to say it every day; I know how you feel." He pulled her closer, but she drew away and turned his face to look at her.

"Don't defend me; I know I've been unfair to keep you on a string. I know you're tired of it, and so am I. So what I wanted to ask you is . . ." she took a deep breath, "will you marry me?"

"W-w-what?"

"Will you marry me, Jim Forrest? I love you very much, and I want to be your wife. I don't want to wait any longer. What do you say?"

He broke into laughter. "Oh, Felicia, Felicia. I've wanted to ask you that question for months, but I thought you just weren't ready, and I didn't want to drive you away."

"You haven't answered my question," she snapped, nervously.

"Yes. Yes. Yes. I'll marry you, Darling. I'll marry you tomorrow, or right now, for that matter. I love you so much."

He pulled her back and kissed her, a long lingering kiss that shook her down to her shoes.

"Well! I was half afraid that you'd say no."

"You know better. Don't you know how long I've wanted to marry you? The first time I ever saw you in the office with Granny, I knew you were the one I wanted."

"You're kidding!"

"No, I'm not. And if it hadn't been for Granny, I would have never had the courage to ask you out. You were really distant, and not at all cooperative. She used to call me and let me know when to ask you out. She'd say, 'Jim, she's in a good mood, and she has no plans for tonight. It would be a good time. Are you going to call her or do you want me to ask you to dinner?'"

"She didn't!"

"She sure did. Then she decided that I wasn't going to go away and could handle it on my own."

Felicia threw back her head and laughed. "That sneaky, wonderful old woman. It used to make me angry when she interfered, but I'm so glad she did." She snuggled deeper into his arms. "When do you want to have our wedding? Our wedding. Wow, that sounds so good to me."

"The sooner, the better. Will we have a big blowout, or small intimate chat with the judge?"

"How about a small home wedding? I'd like to marry here in the living room with just family. Does that sound okay with you?" She traced the outline of his lips with her fingertip.

"Great. I was afraid you'd want a big church wedding, which would've been okay, but I like that idea better. How about next week?"

"Oh, silly, we can't get it together that fast," she giggled. "How about next month? September the fifth. Would Dr. Adams come back in and relieve you long enough for us to have a honeymoon?"

"I wouldn't ask him to; they just got settled in Florida. No, I can get someone to cover for me for a week. That's not very long, but maybe we can have a long trip later on."

She nuzzled his neck. "That's fine. We can just go to the mountains or anywhere. I don't care just as long as . . ."

They heard the car doors slam, and the sound of Elizabeth crying.

"They're back," she groaned.

"Can we tell them?"

"Sure. But let me do it, okay?"

She pulled him up from the glider, and they went in to greet the family. From the pungent odor surrounding Elizabeth, it was obvious that she needed a change, so Angelea disappeared with her. Beth, George, and Granny greeted them in the living room.

"We had a wonderful dinner at Corny's. Hamburgers with all the trimmings. I can't remember when we last had a real hamburger, and it sure tasted good." George patted his belly that had rounded out some since his illness.

"Nell and Granny have you all spoiled," Jim said, as he sat down by Granny on the sofa.

"Well, a change is good sometimes although I don't believe those greasy things are good for you," she snapped, with a wink. "Did you all have a good dinner? I know Felicia was making soup. She said it was your favorite."

"It is, and we did," he said, nervously watching Felicia leave the room. Billy and Angelea returned with Elizabeth, hanging the baby swing in the doorway, and settled their daughter in it.

"Anyone for coffee?" Angelea inquired.

"Lovely," Beth murmured.

Angelea turned to go into the kitchen, but Felicia ducked around the dangling baby and pushed her backward into the room. She had the box that contained the wedding dress, wrapped in tissue paper.

"Could we get this dress out just one more time?" She dropped the box, and pulled out the dress, holding it in front of her, twirling and humming the Wedding March.

"Oh, Filly!" Angelea squealed as she grabbed her sister in a bear hug, swaying with her. Beth looked up in amazement, and George grinned from ear to ear.

Granny smiled at Jim. "Does this mean our girl has finally come to her senses?"

"We plan to marry on the fifth of September," he said, happily, as George rose and reached for his hand.

"Oh, there's no way we can get together a big . . ." Beth began.

"No, Mom. Just a little home wedding. But I do want to wear the dress, if it can take one more makeover."

Beth hugged her daughter. "Oh, Honey, that's wonderful. I'm so happy for you. Jim, welcome to the family, although we've thought of you as family for a long time." She hugged him in turn.

He knelt down in front of Granny. "This woman made it all possible. If she hadn't interceded for me, Felicia wouldn't have given me the time of day. So I'd like to thank you, Mrs. Daniel . . ."

"Granny."

". . . Granny, for helping me out." He gave her a kiss on the cheek, and she blushed, waving him off with her hand.

"Angelea," she said, with a big smile, "put on the coffee and slice up that pound cake. We've got a wedding to plan."

Chapter Thirty-One

The preparations for the wedding were well under way. The dress was altered slightly, the pearls having been replaced for Angelea's wedding. Felicia wanted to dispense with the long veil and wear her mother's hat with veiling attached to the back. Granny didn't feel like doing much so Joan and Beth did the alterations.

There were the usual rounds of showers and teas, all pulled together in a hurry with only weeks to spare. In a daze, Felicia sailed through them with so much joy and happiness that Beth could hardly get her to concentrate on the wedding details.

Felicia gave up her apartment and her job, deciding to move into Jim's home after the wedding and work on another book. Later, she hoped to get a teaching position in town, as she didn't want to give up teaching altogether.

A week before the wedding, all the plans were in place. Boxes were packed and ready to be moved into

Jim's house. Dresses were pressed and ready, fresh flowers ordered for the big day. They had a night to sit around and relax. Jim was on call, and Billy was taking care of Elizabeth. George and Bill retreated to his study to do some bookkeeping, so the ladies sat around and recalled other weddings.

"Mine was pretty simple," Granny said with a smile. "We were married in the parlor of my home, and we moved in here the next day. Oh, it didn't look like this back then. We added as we could afford it."

"You didn't have a honeymoon, Granny?" Angelea looked at her sadly.

"Oh, child, everyday with that man was a honeymoon. We took a short trip before I got pregnant with the twins. My sweet little twins, I wish they had lived." She brushed away a tear.

"But then I finally had Bill, and got to raise George, too. It was the best life here on this farm. I wouldn't have missed one day."

Beth patted her withered, liver-spotted hand. "It is the best place anywhere. And I'm glad you did all that because I was lucky enough to let George catch me."

Angelea laughed. "Yeah, like Billy caught me. And Filly caught Jim. I believe—and I know it's corny—that some people are destined to be together. Billy and I knew it from back when we were just kids." And look at Grandma and Grandpa. They found each other after years of being alone."

"Well, I think sometimes other people manipulate things to make them happen." Felicia gave Granny a knowing glance.

"Well, sometimes they have to when certain people are stubborn and don't know a good thing when they see it!" She said crisply as she rose painfully. "And with that I'm going to bed, I'm worn out."

"It's early for you, Granny," Beth protested. "You're usually our night owl."

"Not tonight," she said as she walked slowly toward her bedroom, her cane thumping on the hardwood floors. She turned and blew a kiss, a rather unusual thing for her to do.

The next morning Beth and Felicia had a long cup of coffee after George went out to the barn. Nell had baked fresh muffins, and they slathered butter and strawberry jam on the tender crumbly halves.

"I'll have to get Nell to give me her recipe for these muffins," Felicia said with her mouth full. "I think these would be the way to any man's heart. By the way, where's Granny? She's usually up before now."

Beth frowned. "Maybe I'd better go check on her. She's probably just sleeping in. Be back in a minute. Don't eat the last one, hear?"

Beth opened the door, calling softly. Granny was turned on her side, her long gray hair out of its bun and fanned across the pillow. She wore her worn flannel gown even though it had been a warm night.

Beth crossed to the window to let in a little sunlight, but stopped as she reached the bed. She felt her knees go weak as she touched the hand lying limply on the pillow. It was icy cold.

Quickly she plunged her hand under the sheet and felt for a heartbeat, frantically pressing the bony chest.

There was none. She patted the cheek that was cold and stiff, and then brought her hand up to her own face to stifle a cry. Her weak knees forced her down on the edge of the bed, and she laid her face into the pillow, pulling Granny's curled fingers to her lips.

"What will we do without you?" She sobbed into the tendrils of hair on the embroidered pillowcase. She wanted to curl up beside her and cry her heart out. If only she could wrap her body around Granny's and bring warmth and life back into the frail bones. But reality jolted her, and she sprang up and stumbled her way to the kitchen.

"Felicia, go get your father. Now!"

"What's wrong? What is it, Mom? Granny? Oh, Mom—oh, no! Oh, no!" She knocked over her chair as she ran out calling wildly for her father.

Beth called Jim, who was with a patient, but she had the secretary interrupt him with the message, and she reported back that he was on his way. As she hung up, George ran in and went to his grandmother's room, Felicia on his heels. Beth waited outside for them to have a moment alone with her, then grabbed them both as they came out of the room. They stood together, arms around each other, and wept.

Nell came in from the garden with a bouquet of flowers in her hand, and they gave her the news. She quietly put the flowers in a vase and placed them by Granny's bed, wiping her eyes on her apron.

"Goodbye, dear friend," she said softly. "I'll take care of our flowers, don't you worry."

After George called his father and Angelea, Jim arrived and pronounced Granny dead. He held a sobbing Felicia as Bill and Joan, Billy and Angelea arrived. Bill went in alone and sat by his mother's body until Joan came in and took his hand and led him back to the living room. When everyone had said their good-byes, Jim called the ambulance.

The arrangements were made, and news spread quickly among friends and neighbors. Soon the kitchen was full of food, the living room a constant interchange of friends offering their sympathies. The family moved in a daze, doing what was expected, accepting symbols of caring from their small community.

The wedding was forgotten as they lived through the next two days of visitation and finally, the funeral. The small church was overflowing, as the family followed the coffin as it was positioned at the altar. The minister gave a short talk, using old stories about Granny that brought chuckles and tears.

At Bill's request, Beth rose and read her early poem, **The Matriarch**. Her voice quivered as she repeated the familiar lines:

. . . With her hands, her heart, her voice
She guides and leads,
Leaving the imprint
On those whom she loves
Like the many hued quilts
With tiny but strong stitches
That warm and comfort them.
. . . Queen of her home

Bestower of all that is good
. . . And we rise up
And bless her,
Mother of the land
And it's people.

The procession threaded its way back to the farm where she was laid to rest beside her beloved husband in the small graveyard in the meadow. The family lingered after the Prentisses and close friends returned to the house to lay out the meal for the guests.

Felicia clung to the rusting iron fence that enclosed the plots and watched as Beth, holding Elizabeth in one arm, stooped to straighten a spray of flowers. Angelea and George stood in silence, and Joan clung to Bill's hand as he wiped away tears with his handkerchief. The clouds were forming overhead, and the smell of warm rain was blowing in the breeze as they said silent farewells to the woman who had raised, nurtured, and guided their steps for so many years.

Angelea turned away from the fresh mound of earth and came to her sister.

"Are you okay, Filly?" She asked as she threaded her arm through hers. Felicia nodded, numbly, and she continued. "No one has said anything about the wedding. What will you do, postpone it for awhile?"

"No," Felicia smiled. "If I did that, Granny would have a fit—if she were here. No, the wedding will go on as usual. It is what she would want. Don't you think so, Daddy?"

George enveloped his daughters with his arms. "Yes, that's exactly what she would want."

Beth passed little Elizabeth to George with a kiss on his cheek and followed them back across the meadow to the big house that was full of busy, caring people, yet seemed so unbearably empty.

Chapter Thirty-Two

George stood at the foot of the stairs and watched his daughters slowly descending to the music softly playing on the harp. Angelea's dark auburn hair shone against the simple aqua silk dress. The sweet odor of the gardenias in her bouquet filled the air as she approached the last steps and gave her father a broad smile.

"You sure are a handsome devil," she teased softly.

"Yeah." He grinned and rolled his eyes. But his heart stopped as he looked past her to Felicia, who had paused for a moment to adjust the veiled hat perched on her dark curls. She was the image of her mother in the creamy ivory satin gown. His mind darted back to Beth in that same dress and hat—his beautiful Beth so young and nervous on her wedding day. The smell of the candles burning took him back years, past so many years, and he could still feel the icy coldness of her hand in his as they turned to the minister.

But this was Felicia, a radiant laughing Felicia, who took his arm and gave him a kiss on the cheek as they turned into the living room where the family had gathered and where Jim waited anxiously with Billy by a bank of ferns to receive his bride.

The large room was filled with family and friends. Henry, Cynthia, and Josh were sitting next to Sophie and her family. Wade, Charlie and their wives, Nell and Arthur were seated in linen covered straight chairs in the center while Billy's parents occupied the large sofa. Elizabeth lay on Mrs. Prentiss's shoulder, lulled by the soft strains of the harp into contented sleep.

Bill, Joan and Beth sat on the front row. To the left of the minister was Granny's rocker, her afghan tossed over the back as though she had just gotten up for a moment and would return and wrap it around her legs. The fireplace mantel was covered with baskets of blooms, and green ferns hung in the windows and decorated the hearth.

As the bridal march rang from the harp, situated awkwardly in the dining room, Beth stood and the group turned to see the beautiful bride clinging to her father's arm. As he put Felicia's hand in Jim's, George felt a lump in his throat so that when the minister asked, "Who gives this woman to this man?" he could barely answer. He sat down beside Beth, and she laced her arm through his.

Jim and Felicia had chosen the familiar vows and the ceremony was brief. After the groom kissed the bride, the minister introduced Dr. and Mrs. Jim Forrest to the small audience. Applause rang out as everyone rose, and the couple stood in the dining room archway and hugged their guests.

"I didn't realize how much Felicia looks like you," Sophie said to Beth. "I could have sworn that it was you coming down those stairs."

"It took me back," George said with his arm around his wife. Turning to Sophie's husband, Len, he explained that Felicia wore the same dress that Angelea and Beth had worn and Joan before them.

Len smiled. "Well, I guess that beautiful granddaughter will be the next to wear it, huh?" By this time, Elizabeth was awake and captivating everyone with her antics and was highly displeased when Angelea came to take her away.

"Excuse me," Nell called loudly over the chatter. "There is food here on the table and on the back porch as well, and there are chairs in the yard, if you care to go out on the lawn. The fall flowers are especially beautiful out there."

The dining table was laden with canapés, fruits, and punch. A large table was set up on the tulle-draped porch with other goodies and the bride and groom's cakes. In the arbor, white linen-covered chairs were placed with small tables. The porch furniture, worn, but comfortable, was left as it was, and since the day was cool and sunny, almost everyone gravitated there or to the arbor.

"Finally," Jim said as he took his bride in his arms. "I didn't think this day would ever come."

"Well, it has, my husband. I'm all yours, now and forever," she whispered in his ear.

Beth touched Felicia lightly on the shoulder. "Sorry to interrupt, but it's about time to cut the cake."

"There's something we have to do first," Felicia whispered to her mother. "Now?" she asked Jim. He nodded, and she picked up her bouquet from the table.

"We'll be right back," she said, blowing a kiss to her father and Angelea, who knew where they were going.

They walked across the yard, Felicia holding up the hem of her dress, into the meadow where goldenrod bloomed in clumps among the waving wild grasses. Jim opened the creaking iron gate, and they walked, hand-in-hand to the foot of Granny's grave.

"We came to give you our flowers, Granny—," Felicia began, but a sob caught in her throat.

"And to thank you," Jim continued, "for getting us together. You'll always be the guiding angel in our lives." He unpinned his boutonniere and laid it gently on the grave.

"And, if we are lucky enough to have a girl, we'll carry on your name," Felicia said as she knelt and placed her bridal bouquet on the fresh mound of dirt. She rested in Jim's arms while the breeze ruffled her skirt, and a dove in the pine cooed softly above them.

"Was that her answer?" she asked Jim with a smile as she pulled back from his arms, looking up at the gray bird.

"No. She would have said, "Glad you're finally getting around to it," or "It's about time," he chuckled. She laughed and brought her fingertips lightly to her lips and touched the headstone, and they turned away, wet-eyed, from the grave back to the friends and family, who were all silently watching from the yard.

Beth was overcome with emotion, and took both of them in her arms, before finally releasing them to cut the cake. The photographer positioned them and caught their happiness with his shutter. Later, when they looked at that picture of the two of them feeding cake to each other, they detected the shiny wetness of their tears still on their cheeks.

Chapter Thirty-Three

In the clean up after the wedding, Granny's quilts and embroidered linens were divided among the family. Her clothes were removed and taken to a poor widow, but her room was left just as it was, her prize-winning quilt on the bed and her silver mirror and hairbrush in its place on the marble topped dresser.

"It's so hard," Beth told George as she put fresh linens on the bed. "She's been with us throughout our marriage. I feel like an arm is missing or something, and I know you do, too."

George nodded as he picked up the picture of his grandparents when they were younger, the way he remembered them as a little boy. Granny was a beautiful woman back then. In the snapshot, they were sitting on the steps, arms around each other. He set it down quickly before emotions took over. "By the way, Nell asked me if we would still need her this morning."

"Of course, we need her," Beth replied indignantly. "She's family, too. She does want to stay, doesn't she?"

"I think she does, and I told her we still want her with us, but she didn't answer."

Beth found Nell tidying up the remains of the fall flowers. She took her by the hand and led her to the swing.

"Nell, do you still want to stay? We want you and need you, but if you feel you need a change. ."

"Oh, no, not at all. I love working here, and I feel like family, not an employee. I just thought with Felicia gone . . ."

"Well, put your mind at rest. We want you to stay with us as long as you will. You keep it from being so lonely around here. Actually, we need you now more than ever."

"Well, good," she answered as she took Beth's hands. "I've been happier here than any place I've been. Thank you. Now I'd better get back to my garden work. There's so much cleaning up to do. Felicia wouldn't have wanted those beds to look messy, even in the fall." She drew a loose strand of gray hair and secured it back in her bun before she went back to her clipping.

Beth started another book when the long winter days set in. She was basing this one on Granny's life and experiences, and could hardly wait to get it finished. But it turned out to be the hardest book of all to write. She thought she knew Granny so well, but found there were so many things about her past that she had never heard, and she turned to Bill to fill in the gaps. Spring turned into summer before she produced the first ten chapters that suited her.

Felicia was also working on the sequel to her mystery, but she was hampered by her pregnancy. A few days short of their wedding anniversary, she gave birth by cesarean section to twins, Felicia Danielle and James George, quickly dubbed Dani and Jamie. A few months later, Angelea produced Ellen Lee, with a minimum of difficulty this time.

The old house came alive with babies coming and going. Baby beds were lining the spare room, and Beth decorated it in a circus theme with a tent-like ceiling and clowns of all descriptions in corners and on furniture.

When Ellen was two months old, Felicia and Angelea and their spouses took a cruise and left the children with their grandparents.

"Isn't this fun?' Beth asked George, as they each juggled a cranky twin, both of whom were cutting teeth and hard to get down at bedtime.

"Yeah. But I didn't know they'd be churning out babies like rabbits. These guys are wonderful, but I'm getting older. What do you say we keep them one or two at a time next go round," he said loudly over Dani's display of healthy lungs.

Elizabeth toddled up and grabbed Beth's skirt. "Ganny, Baby Ellen crying. Come get her."

Having Jamie quiet and almost asleep, Beth bedded him down and turned to Ellen, who needed a bottle. Warming the milk in the microwave, she tested it on her wrist, then settled down in Granny's rocker to feed the smallest one. She felt such peace as she rocked and sang to the blue eyed baby with the thatch of dark red hair.

Finally they were all in their cribs, except for Elizabeth, who, as the oldest rated a story before she went to sleep. George read **The Little Engine That Could** twice before her eyes got heavy. She pulled her stuffed bear into her arms and dropped off. He kissed her forehead, still damp from her bath, and tiptoed out.

"Quick!" George pulled Beth toward the bedroom. "Let's see if we can get a few hours sleep before one of them wakes up!"

When Felicia and Jim, Angelea and Billy came home, they found tired grandparents, who were delighted to hug and kiss each child goodbye.

"Whew," George collapsed into a chair. "That's a job."

"But aren't they sweet? How blessed we are to have them so close together. They'll grow up more like sisters and brothers than cousins."

"And you've become the new 'Granny'," he pulled her into his lap. "Although you still don't look or feel like a 'granny,'" He nuzzled his face in her dark hair, heavily threaded with gray, but she wiggled away, feeling more fatigued than amorous.

"Nobody could take Granny's place," Beth said shaking her head.

"Someone has to be the family matriarch, and Joan and Dad are heading to Florida to spend their retirement."

"They won't stay long, they'll miss these babies too much," Beth declared.

But they did stay, with many trips back and forth to encourage the families to visit in their new home by a lake. They found their retirement complex comfortable, and made a lot of friends to do things with.

Beth missed her mother terribly, and was on the phone constantly the first few months they were gone. She couldn't believe that Joan chose to live away from the children and grandchildren, but was satisfied that she and Bill were so contented.

The months flew by in a whirlwind of writing and babysitting. Beth's book about Granny's life went to press after Felicia's mystery, which was a bestseller immediately. Felicia refused to do as much traveling as her agent and publisher wanted her to because of the twins, and she got away with it because the book was making money. Beth's book was a moderate success and that was just fine with her. She no longer craved that kind of recognition, and was pleased that she had done what she thought was a good work.

Elizabeth grew into a beautiful little auburn-haired child who adored baby Ellen, but was sometimes jealous of the attention she received. Ellen wasn't as pretty, but she charmed everyone with her smile and pleasant ways. The twins, Dani and Jamie, resembled their dark handsome father. He and Felicia were rather strict parents, but spent every possible moment of their busy lives with their children.

The August of the twins fourth birthday, Beth decided to have a big family party. She and Nell planned the decorations and food enough for an army. Joan and Bill flew up from Florida for the occasion and an extended stay.

"You picked the hottest time of the year for this gathering," Joan complained as she iced cupcakes. The kitchen was warm from the oven, and the air from the ceiling fan just seemed to move the heat around.

"Most everyone has summer birthdays," Beth answered. "Besides, we hardly get together as a family unless it's something special. The kids don't mind, and if it's too hot, the adults can crank up the air conditioner and stay inside. You should be used to the heat, living down there."

Joan smiled. "Yeah, we're used to it, and really enjoyed our time down there. But now we're ready to come home."

"You mean it?" Beth joyfully flung her arms around her mother. "I'm so glad. I missed you so much—Bill, too."

"Well, the truth is that we miss seeing everyone and those babies are growing up without us. We miss home. Besides, we're getting older, and we worried about becoming ill so far away."

"Oh, Mom. You both look like you're in your prime. But I won't argue; I'm so glad you came to that decision. Are you going to move back in the old house?"

"For a little while. George has been talking to Bill about helping him here on the farm. Maybe you could sell us a few acres and we could build a little house here."

"Mom, I had no idea. That George, he never tells me anything. Oh, that's a marvelous idea. Henry will be so happy. He's really missed you. I knew you'd come home to roost someday."

The troops began arriving before noon, and soon children and their parents were in the new pool. Elizabeth skinned her knee and had to be doctored by Uncle Jim. Ellen screamed in fear of the water until her grandmother came and dried her off, and she fell asleep on a pallet in the grass.

Joan and Beth took their lemonade and sat under the shade of the big oak by the peaceful child and watched the fun from the lounge chairs. Joan held the wiggly Irish setter puppy that wanted to get down and wake Ellen to play.

"Why didn't Cynthia come? In all the confusion, I didn't hear Henry say why. Is she sick?" Beth was watching Josh swimming side by side with his father like a young fish.

Joan frowned. "I talked with Henry when he first arrived. Cynthia hasn't been well, Beth. She's suffering from depression. That's another reason we came home."

"Why didn't you tell me? Oh, I wish I'd known. I've been so busy with my own family."

"She wants a divorce, Beth. Henry is very upset about it."

"Divorce? But they're so crazy about each other," Beth said in disbelief.

"It's the depression, I'm sure. Her mother has taken her to a doctor in the city today. She didn't want Henry to go with her, and she didn't want Josh around. I just hope the doctor will be able to help her."

"Jim could have helped her if she had only told us."

"She's quite mixed up right now. Later on, Henry's going to call her mother and see what they found out. Try not to worry," Joan rose and pulled her daughter up by the hand.

"We've got a party table to finish setting. Looks like everyone is getting tired and hungry."

Beth followed her mother toward the house with a heavy heart. "Poor Henry. He must be going through such a rough time," she thought, as she caught his eye and waved.

Chapter Thirty-Four

Cynthia was hospitalized with a breakdown for several weeks. The whole family was shocked that their usually jovial and poised Cynthia was suffering from mental illness. Beth and Joan spent as much time at Henry's house as they could, doing little things, baking desserts—anything to cheer Henry and Josh.

Henry came home from his allowed visits to the hospital looking haggard. "She doesn't talk to me. She seems obsessed with getting a divorce. I just wish I knew what I've done to make her feel this way. Have I been such a jerk that I didn't see this coming? I always thought of myself as a sensitive man. Guess I could use a little counseling, too." He chastised himself that way with every visit.

Beth tried to reassure him, as did Cynthia's parents, that it was part of her illness, but he searched his memory for signs that he had been too busy to see. He was completely white headed now, taking after his paternal grandfather, and these days he looked much older than his forty-two years.

But as the weeks went by, Cynthia began to improve. Her outlook on life brightened, and she was ready to see family. Henry came in after a visit much more hopeful.

Beth had brought Josh home after a visit at their house with all the grandchildren. "How was she?" she asked as they sat down for coffee and a chat.

"Much better. She seemed more like her old self. They finally found the combination of drugs and therapy that's really helping." He managed a smile, and Beth saw traces of the old Henry again.

Josh came in, asking for a coke, and Henry assured him again that his mother was better and would be home soon. The freckled face lit up in a huge smile, and he grabbed his father around the neck before he took his coke and went out to play with his dog.

"How has he been?" Henry asked anxiously.

"Quiet, but otherwise okay, at least on the outside. He talked to George some about his mother, but he just kept hugging me and thanking me for having him over. He really had a good time with Elizabeth. They are close enough in age to be good buddies."

"It's been pretty dull around here for the little guy. I appreciate your having him."

"No trouble. Well, I must get home." She hugged her brother. "Give her time, Henry. When she's well, she'll think differently about this divorce."

He kissed her cheek. "I hope so. She does seem to be less concerned with it. By the way, she wants you to come and visit, and bring some of the children."

"Do you think that it's wise to take the children?"

"We meet outside unless it's raining, and then there's a nice meeting room. I don't think there would be anything to frighten them."

"We'll go then," she said firmly. She and George visited a few days later with Elizabeth in tow, and their visit took place on the cheery sun porch with its tropical décor. Pleased with the home-like atmosphere, they nevertheless were shocked at Cynthia's appearance. She had dressed carefully, but there were dark circles under her blue eyes, her usually shiny blonde hair was dry and listless. But she did seem happier and more like herself.

"It's the medicine," she explained as she noticed Beth looking at her hair and brushed a strand from her face. "Makes the skin and hair pretty dry. They are lowering the dosage, so it should get better. I feel pretty good now," she assured them. "I really want to get back to Josh now, and that's a good sign."

"Do you know when you can leave?" Beth asked as she sat holding her hand.

"Soon. I'm a little nervous about it. It's so safe here." Elizabeth sat down beside her, and Cynthia pulled her closer, fingering the long auburn curls that bounced on the child's shoulders.

"You'll feel safe when you get home. Henry loves you and misses you so much. We all do."

"I know. But I don't think I'm quite ready, so I'll let the doctors tell me when it's time. I'm still unsure about our marriage, Beth. But I'm willing to try and work things out. Believe me, it's more my fault than your brother's."

Elizabeth decided she wanted to spend the night with Auntie Cynthia, and couldn't understand why she had to go home. Leaving with an unhappy Elizabeth, Beth and George felt better about Cynthia and the chances of the family being together again.

And in a few weeks Cynthia came home. She and Henry preferred to be alone for the first few weeks, so everyone stayed away and hoped for the best. Henry called one morning and reported that the divorce was on the back burner for now, and he had high hopes that it would never take place.

Joan and Bill were overjoyed with her progress and spent some time with them later. Things seemed to be looking up for Henry and Cynthia at last.

As the autumn days went hurrying by, George decided it was time that he and Beth took a trip before the holidays came with all the hustle and bustle.

"Do you realize how long it's been since we had a vacation? We've been so busy with kids and Cynthia and everything else. Let's get out of here for awhile."

"We haven't been anywhere together since my last book tour. And that's been months. Where do you want to go, Honey?"

"How about the mountains? It's not far and we can stay until the middle of the week."

"And we won't be so far from the grandchildren, huh? Okay, I'll pack a bag, give Nell a few days off, and we'll head out."

The next day they were winding up the mountains above the small resort town. It was November and the streets were already brilliant with white Christmas lights.

"It looks like a fairy land," Beth said in awe, as the station wagon climbed the mountain to the small chalet they rented. Inside they found a fire already laid and complimentary chocolates and cheeses in the refrigerator.

It was too cold to hike, so they spent a lot of time in front of the fire, playing games and reading, going out nights to different restaurants. One of their days was fairly warm and sunny, and they hit the shops, buying Christmas gifts for the grandchildren. They were fascinated in one of the candle shops as they watched the amazing process of hand-dipping fancy candles. Beth bought five.

"You said one for Felicia, one for Angel, one for Joan, one for Nell . . ."

"And one for me, silly!"

"That's what I thought," he laughed.

On their last night there, they sat bundled in blankets on the porch overlooking the glittering lights as dusk on the mountains rapidly turned to deep darkness. Soon the stillness was broken by the rustling of raccoons at the trash barrels. Their glassy eyes shone in the darkness as they fought over the bread that Beth threw to them. Finally, the chill drove them into the hot tub and a warm bed.

"I could easily have stayed another day or two," Beth said the next day, as they drove out of the mountains and back into the foothills to their home.

"Me, too," George sighed. "Unfortunately, I've got so much to attend to right now. There's no end of it when you're raising cattle. Sometimes I think I'd like to sell them off and get into something else."

"Like what?"

"Oh, I don't know. Maybe back into crops where I'm not so tied down."

"That's what you said when you got into cattle— that you wouldn't be so tied down," Beth remarked.

The wind was cold as they unloaded the car, and by the time they got in the house, an icy rain had begun to fall.

"We got back just in time," Beth said as she set the suitcase down and pulled off her coat. "I'm for putting on some hot tea before we unpack and check in with children—and animals. Sound okay?"

"Yeah," George mumbled as he rifled through the stack of mail.

As they sat down with their tea, the phone rang. Beth reached across to the wall phone and answered.

"It's for you, Honey. Someone named Ed Childers."

George took the phone, and Beth drained her tea and went to the bedroom to put up clothes.

"Who is Ed Childers?" Beth called out, as she heard George slam the hall closet door.

"He's a real estate developer. He wants to come out tomorrow and talk to us." George put on his old heavy farm coat and added, "I'm going to check on the herd."

"Talk to us about what?" Beth appeared in the doorway.

"I don't know, but I get the feeling he's interested in our property."

Beth put her hands on her hips. "What do you mean; you think he's interested in our property? It's not for sale."

"Well, I couldn't tell him not to come out. I'm curious about what he has to say."

"I know what I have to say," Beth retorted. "This place will never be for sale. Ever."

Chapter Thirty-Five

The next morning, Ed Childers was there promptly on time with another man named Martin Kuzo, a lawyer. Beth and George watched from the window as the two men stood in the yard, pointing over the fields. When they finally knocked on the door, George took their coats and seated them in the living room.

After chatting about the political situation and the current dilemma of the family farmer, they came down to business.

"Mr. Daniel . . ."

"George, please."

Ed smiled and ran his hand over his sleek brown hair. "George, we're interested in building an industrial park just far enough from town to be convenient, but not too close to the new subdivisions. You know, we have a new factory who's interested in locating here, and there are several others who have expressed an interest in this area. We have to have a place where all these businesses could locate in one park that's handy to all routes, in and out of town. We've driven all over the county, and this area right here is the ideal place to lay out such a park."

"That'll be good for our town, Mr. Childers . . ."

"Ed."

"And Martin," Mr. Kuzo interjected, smiling.

". . . Ed—and Martin—but our place is not for sale. My father and mother-in-law are planning to build a house along the side road, and we join the Prentiss farm where our children will build a house soon. So you can see, we're firmly entrenched in this farm."

"We hadn't considered the Prentiss farm, George," Martin Kuzo spoke up. "You're the one with so much frontage and depth, too. Your farm alone would be involved."

George stood. "Gentlemen, I think I made it clear, we just aren't interested in selling. There must be other properties that would be as good whose owners would be happy to sell. Farming's a hard business these days."

"Precisely," Ed Childers remarked without moving from his chair. "That's why we're authorized to offer you a million dollars for your farm. We think it would be worth the money in getting these new industries here. Our town could benefit with jobs; the growth could be phenomenal. Maybe we could keep our children right here with good jobs instead of losing them to the city."

George coughed as he sat back down. "Could you give me that price again? I think I misunderstood."

"A million, George. Think of what you could do with that much money. You could buy property anywhere in the world, help your children and grandchildren, do anything you wanted to do with it."

Beth looked at the two men and back to George. He was silent, mulling over the unexpected price.

"But this is our home. George's family has owned this farm for decades. He practically grew up here; we came to this house after our honeymoon. We've got a lot of memories invested in this place. There's no way we would sell—at any price," Beth said firmly.

"Honey, why don't you get us some coffee and some of those delicious cinnamon rolls you made this morning?" George turned to Ed and Martin and bragged. "She makes the best pastries you've ever put in your mouth."

Fuming, Beth rose and went into the kitchen, angry at being dismissed in such a servile way. She put on fresh coffee, slapped rolls on a plate with napkins, and waited impatiently by the pot as it dripped slowly.

In the living room, Ed and Martin were explaining more about the proposed industrial park.

"It sounds like a wonderful thing for our area, but I'll have to agree with my wife. It would be awfully difficult to leave this farm. My family has been here for ages, you understand."

Martin nodded. "We do understand your situation. That's why we can go back to the development committee and explain to them that it might take a little more to change your mind. This is a very important project, and we want you to benefit as well."

"Well, that seems like a good idea, and it'll give me more time to consult with our family. Our parents and children have an interest in this place, too. We wouldn't want to do anything if they didn't approve."

Beth entered with the tray, and passed around cups and pastries, and the conversation turned to the prospects of the local basketball team making it to the state tournament.

After compliments to Beth for the refreshments (which she accepted with only a nod), they left, promising to get back in touch in a few days. George walked them out to the porch and came in with a smile on his face. Beth stood, firmly planted in front of him, hands on hips.

"I can't believe you would even entertain such an idea. To sell this property, at any price, is unthinkable!"

"Beth! Did you hear that figure? One million dollars. A million dollars. What do you think we'd get for this farm if we sold it outright? Nothing near that, I'll guarantee you."

"Some things can't be bought, George. Besides, what do you want that you don't have already?"

"Well, a summer home—maybe a winter home, money for four grandchildren to go to college without having loans, something to leave our children . . ."

". . . Who are living quite comfortably, as are we. I tell you what—just get on the phone. Call everyone and invite them to supper. We'll put this on the table, and I'm betting they'll think that you've completely lost your mind!" With that, she picked up the tray and breezed through the swinging door into the kitchen.

Chapter Thirty-Five

For once, the family was all available for supper and
very curious as to what George wanted to talk to them
about. Gathered around the table after a huge spaghetti
meal, he told them about the proposed offer. Bill's mouth
dropped open. "A million dollars? Sell, Son. You'd never
have another opportunity like this. A million dollars!
Wow!"

"And maybe more, if we take our time deciding,"
George grinned. "They seem to want it pretty badly. I
intend to hold out for more, if we decide to take the
offer."

"My millionaire father-in-law. Can you believe that?"
Billy laughed.

"Have you brought in your lawyer?" asked Jim.

"No, but I will, certainly. What are your thoughts,
girls?"

Felicia frowned. "I'd hate to see this house torn
down. I'd hoped that Jim and I would live here someday,
you know, when you all get old and need help. I love
this place so much. But I guess this is a once in a lifetime
opportunity, Dad."

"Maybe this is the time for you and Mom to pare
down. You don't really need this big house, much as I
love it. You could travel, and do so many things with
the money," Angelea looked thoughtfully at Beth.

Slamming her hand on the table, Beth exclaimed,
"Am I the only one here with any sense? I can't believe
any of you. This is more than a farm, it's been the place
you girls were born, where we had all our hopes and
dreams, George, and where you grew up, Bill. This is
Granny's home where she came after her marriage on

the land her parents gave her as a wedding present. To flatten it all for an industrial park? Never!"

"Sweetheart, what you say is true. But we can't let the past dictate our future and the future of our children and grandchildren. What doors we could open for them. A house is a house, land is land. We have to look at this with a clear head."

Joan reached across the table and grasped Beth's hand. "I understand where Beth is coming from, George. You're going to have to give her some time to get used to this idea, if you decide to go forward with it. She's bound up in her home; most women are. Don't let the temptation of big money cloud your decision before you've had plenty of time to think it over."

George smiled at his mother-in-law. "As always, Joan, you're right. Don't worry, I'll take my time, and Beth and I will come to an agreement before any decision is made."

Beth frowned. She could never come over to his side on this. She had never felt so estranged from George. All through their marriage, they had been in agreement on the important things. Now it looked as though George could let money come between them. She sighed as she listened to the family exchange views until she became too frustrated to sit there and escaped to the kitchen.

Chapter Thirty-Six

The discussion went on for days, George, lured by the once in a lifetime opportunity, and Beth, determined to keep the family farm in spite of giving up more money than they could ever earn. The hostility between them grew. Each thought the other stubborn and unbending. Soon there was no communication between them on any other subject, only an occasional 'good morning' or a 'good night,'

The next week, the duo of Childers and Kuzo made an appointment to come out and talk to them again. It was an unseasonably warm day as Beth and George waited for their arrival. They only spoke when they had to; the tension between them was so great. Beth wanted to make her presence felt even though she would not hang around to hear their conversation.

When the two men arrived, Beth excused herself after exchanging stiff pleasantries. She had said her piece; now it was up to George to decide. To her, it had become whether or not he loved her more than the money. From the porch, she watched the three men in deep discussion as they strolled toward the barn wishing with all her might that she had never seen Childers and Kuzo.

Ed, Martin, and George walked around the farm, George in his boots, and the others in their tasseled loafers. They sensed George's reluctance and quickly upped the offer to two million. George was bowled over by the increase. It would be unthinkable to turn down that much money. As they stood in the meadow, he looked over at the small family cemetery.

"I hadn't thought about that," he mused aloud. Turning to Ed, he added, "Our burial ground will have to be moved as well."

"I'm afraid so, George. But that's a small thing; you can easily locate it somewhere else. Does this mean that you'll accept our offer?"

"Haven't had enough time. As you know, my wife is dead set against it. It's really caused a rift between us. Can you give me just a little more space? I promise to decide as soon as possible."

"George, we don't want to push you," Ed said, looking at the mud caked on his once shiny shoes. "But a decision will have to made soon or we'll lose the interest on the part of these companies."

"I understand. But you surely didn't expect us to take the offer without giving us some time. This affects our whole family and our lifestyle, so please, give us a few days. Now I'm going inside, but you gentlemen are free to look around as long as you'd like."

"George, we've seen enough, plus we have aerial photos of your property. That's what sold us on your farm in the first place. So we'll go, but please stay in touch and give us an answer just as soon as you can."

George watched them drive away, and then turned toward the barn. He had rather do chores than return to the house and Beth, with her icy silence. But Bill had helped him just yesterday, and he was caught up for the most part, so he sat on the bench by the barn door. His thoughts were on the impasse that he and Beth had reached.

He reflected on their bank balance. It was healthy, and they lived comfortably. He made a good, if sometimes sporadic, living as a farmer, and Beth's books made money. Of course, they had given a lot of it away to church and charities, glad to share their wealth with others. But they could do so much more with these millions, more to help others. He wondered if Beth had really thought about that; she was such a giver.

Lured by the unusual balmy breeze, he walked to the upper pasture where his herd stood lazily in the warm sunshine or laid around the pond. He walked among them, checking a cut foreleg on one cow, an eye infection on another, slapping them on their red flanks lovingly.

As he made his rounds among the cows, the old bull watched him with hostility, rolling his watery eyes and pawing at the ground. George wisely edged toward the fence. He had had enough of that old bull's antics. The last time he had charged Bill, they had decided they ought to get rid of him. He climbed over the fence just as the bull made a half-hearted charge at him. As he jumped down, he stepped into a hole and twisted his ankle. The pain shot up his leg, and he collapsed on the ground, rubbing the aching foot.

When the pain lessened, he got up. Seeing a long stick in the brush, he used it to make his way toward the house. Beth watched him limping across the back yard, and met him on the porch.

"What happened?"

"Oh, that old bull decided to play games with me. I'm getting rid of that old fella tomorrow," he grumbled as he sat on the wicker settee, wincing as he took off his boot. The foot and ankle were already swelling.

"Come on in, and I'll get you some ice to put on it. Do you think it's broken? Maybe we'd better go see Jim." Her concerned voice made him reach out and touch her hand, and he realized it was the first time he had touched her in days.

"Naw, it's just a sprain. But I'll take that ice."

The next day, after a restless night, George awoke to a badly bruised foot and ankle. He managed to get to the breakfast table, but the pain took away his appetite for Beth's breakfast of hotcakes. He took the aspirin she offered and went into the living room to read. But there was no getting comfortable.

"I'm taking you in to see Jim," Beth said handing him his coat.

"Oh, it'll be okay in a day or so. Don't make a big deal out of it."

She stood firmly with his coat extended until he finally groaned and put it on, muttering every step that she helped him to the car. The trip into town was frosty in its silence.

Jim poked and twisted the ankle gently. "I think it's just a sprain, George, but I want to send you over to the hospital for a scan."

"Why not just an x-ray? Does this call for a scan?"

Jim smiled and reached for his father-in-law's arm. "George, when did you last have a check-up? Weren't you supposed to go every year for a complete going over?"

"Has it been a year? Time gets away from me."

"It's been two years, George. This is a perfectly good time to admit you for that check-up, since we have to check out your ankle anyway."

"But . . . oh, okay. Did you two plan this whole thing?" He asked with much irritation.

Two days later, Jim faced them both over his desk. He wished that he didn't have to be the one to tell them the news.

Both were laughing about something Elizabeth had said that was so funny, and he, aware of the tension that had been between them, waited until the laughter died down before he put on a serious face.

"Jim, you look worried. Did the test turn out okay?" Beth asked anxiously.

"Not exactly," Jim said, leaning forward to reach for their hands. "George, there is something on the scan at the site of the previous tumor. We don't know if it's some form of scar tissue or the tumor coming back. We need to go in and take a biopsy and see just what it is. It's been over five years and that's a good sign, but you know that cancer can always come back. You're never really home free."

"Will I have to go back to Houston?"

"No, we can do the biopsy right here, and then, if it's something we can't handle, of course I would want to send you back there. But let's don't jump to conclusions. It's possible that this is nothing to worry about."

"When do you want to do the biopsy?" Beth asked shakily.

"Let's set it up for tomorrow. Dr. Rhoades, the new surgeon, is really good. I highly recommend him."

"Whatever you say, Jim," George murmured. "It's hard to believe anything could be wrong. I feel fine, really."

"That's good. Go home. No food or drink after midnight, you know the drill. I'll see you here at six o'clock."

"You won't mention this to Felicia, will you?" George pleaded.

"George, you know I can't keep this from your daughter."

"Of course, you can't," Beth said, feeling heaviness in her heart as she stood up and reached for George's hand. They had been down this road before. And selling, or not selling, the farm was the last thing on their minds.

Chapter Thirty-Seven

She stirred and opened her eyes. For a moment she forgot where she was; her sleep had been so deep. He was looking at her; she could see that his eyes were open by the light from the hall. Reaching for his hand, bruised from the IV, she gently laid her face against it.

"Good morning."

"What time is it?" he asked

She brought her watch up to her eyes. "I think it's five o'clock; I'm not sure. My reading glasses are in my purse. Are you hungry? You'll get to eat a big breakfast this morning."

"And go home, I hope." George rolled his eyes up to the ceiling. As he watched the shadows from the rising daylight, he asked her. "We haven't talked about what we would do if the tests are positive. I'd like to do that now."

"No!" she said sharply. "We won't look at the bad side until we know. Until then, all we have to worry about is getting your ankle well."

He smiled. "Can't be in denial, Beth. We have to face it."

"And we will—if we have to," Beth said as she stood up and leaned over to kiss his forehead. "Now why don't you see if you can sleep a few more minutes before it gets so noisy around here. You tossed and turned most of the night."

Sighing, he nodded, knowing he was done with sleep, but he closed his eyes to please her.

"I'm going for coffee," she whispered as she closed the door behind her.

The floor was already coming alive. Nurses were beginning to check their patients before the shift changed, and the new crew was exchanging pleasantries and information. Beth slipped into the nurses' little kitchen and inhaled the wonderful fragrance of a fresh pot of coffee. Pouring herself a cup, she dosed it heavily with milk and walked down the hall to the small chapel for a few minutes of quiet.

When she opened the door, she saw the back of a familiar head. Surprised, her hand shook, and she spilled coffee down her slacks.

"Felicia! What are you doing here so early? And why didn't you come to our room?"

Felicia turned and patted the seat beside her. "Come sit, Mom." Her eyes were red-rimmed from crying.

"What is it, Filly? What's wrong?"

"Mom, we brought Dani in last night. She began running a fever and complained of a headache. Jim had been called back to the hospital about eight. He no sooner left than her fever shot up really high, and she started having seizures. I put her in the car and got her to the hospital as fast as I could. I wasn't even worried until then, I just thought it was a virus or something. But Jim took one look at her and knew."

"Knew what? You're scaring me."

"They believe she has encephalitis; they aren't sure what type it is."

Beth grabbed her daughter's hand, her mind reeling.

"Why didn't you come get me?" she asked, almost angrily.

"I did look in, but you were sleeping and so was Dad. And there was nothing you could do to help. I foolishly hoped that we would find out it was just a scare and nothing to worry about before I told you and Dad. You have so much to worry about right now."

"But, Honey. Dani—our baby girl."

"I'm sorry, Mom. I was on my way to tell you now, but just thought I would stop off and say a prayer first."

"Can I see her?" Beth asked, tears brimming in her eyes.

"Not yet, Mom. She's in isolation until they determine exactly what it is."

Beth's mind whirled. Their precious Dani of the dark hair and sparkling eyes. She could see her on the pony, riding the tractor with George, dusted with flour as she helped Beth bake cookies. Shaking those thoughts away, Beth pulled Felicia to her.

"Where is Jim?"

"He's with her now. He and Dr. Rogers. I'd better get back. Come with me, Mom. We'll tell Dad after he hears from Dr. Rhoades, okay?" She massaged the back of her neck and then rose, reaching for Beth's hand. She got up slowly, lacing her fingers with her daughter's, and they walked, leaning against each other, up to pediatrics. Felicia pulled ahead, and Beth followed her to the end of the hall where the isolation rooms were. She knocked on the curtained window, and Jim pulled the curtain back. He spoke to the nurse, stripped off his mask, and gloves, and paper covering and came out into the hall.

"Oh, Jim," Beth began as he slipped his arm around her waist and pulled her head against his shoulder. "Why didn't you tell us?"

"Beth, we didn't get her in here until almost eleven last night. If she had gotten worse, we would have come to your room. But her temperature is coming down a little, and we're running tests. Now all we can do is keep her comfortable until we hear from them. Try not to worry, Granny." He looked over Beth's head at his wife with love and concern.

"Mask up, Honey, and go in. She's restless. See if you can comfort her."

Felicia rushed in, pausing to suit up in the small entry of the room.

"Can I see her?'" Beth looked up into Jim's worried eyes.

"Just through the glass right now. Then you'd better get back to George. You'll need to tell him about Dani.

Dr. Rhoades should be in by seven to talk to you both. Can't tell about him though, he may be there earlier."

"Do you know what he will tell us?" Beth asked, anxiously.

"No. He didn't return my call yesterday; he got tied up in some emergency surgery, so I really don't know anything. If this hadn't happened to Dani, I would have pursued him about George's test, but . . ."

"You had other things to think about, Jim."

They looked through the curtain and saw Felicia wiping Dani's forehead with a cloth. Beth closed her eyes, remembering the horror she once felt at the possibility of losing a child, and cold shivers ran through her body.

"I must get to George," she said as she kissed Jim's cheek. "Let me know the moment you hear."

Her mind was in turmoil as she made her way down to the first floor. Last night she was afraid for George. All of a sudden her fears extended to a beloved grandchild who was gravely ill.

"What else can happen?" she murmured as she approached the room. George was sitting up on the side of the bed, and the nurse was taking his vitals. Beth walked around picking up newspapers and extra pillows until the nurse finished. Then she sat beside him on the bed and took his hand.

"George, Dani is here in the hospital. She's running a high fever, and they don't know for sure what's causing it."

He sat up straight. "How sick is she?"

"Pretty sick, right now. But they're running tests, and Jim said they should know something soon."

Before he could answer, Dr. Rhoades rapped sharply on the door before entering. There was a smile on his ruddy handsome face.

"Good news," he said as he plopped down into a chair. "Looks like scar tissue, George. We found no cancer cells anywhere. You're home free this time. But don't let another two years go by before you get a check-up. If that had been a return of the tumor, you'd be in big trouble."

"That's good news, Doctor. Thanks so much for all you've done. If our grandchild wasn't so sick, I'd be jumping up and down."

"Oh, I hadn't heard. Jim's child? One of the twins? I'm so sorry. Let me know if there is anything I can do to help." He patted George's shoulder and gave Beth's hand a squeeze as he left the room.

The joy of the moment was overshadowed by worry about Dani as Beth silently helped George dress, and they made their way to Dani's room. The curtains were opened and they stood outside watching Felicia with her head lying on the bed by her daughter's face. Tears coursed down both their cheeks.

"Mom? How's she doing?" Angelea had slipped quietly up beside them.

Startled, Beth turned and threw her arms around Angel. "I don't know, honey." She blotted her damp face with her sleeve.

Angel rubbed her mother's back gently. "I've been down talking to Jim; he's gone to the lab to hurry the tests. He's pretty worried, but being a doctor, he won't let on. I wish I knew what to do to help. We have Jamie; he's with Billy and our kids."

"Well, that's a big help, Angel. At least you're doing something. Your dad and I feel so helpless."

She turned to George, slipping her arm around his waist. "How are you, Daddy? Have you heard anything from your biopsy?"

"I'm fine, Angel. No cancer."

"Oh, Dad!" She threw her arms around his neck. "I'm so glad. I was so afraid for you. Does Filly know?"

"No, we just found out a few minutes ago. We'd be so happy if it weren't for this," Beth said sadly, looking through the window.

The day passed slowly. Joan and Bill brought up hot food. Nell came with thermoses of coffee. The minister stayed until another sick call took him away. Still the child was feverish and slept fitfully, and there were no definite answers from the tests. They paced from Dani's room to the waiting room while Felicia and Jim kept their vigil beside the bed.

George looked out the window at the darkening skyline. A thin pale moon slipped from behind the clouds and hung over the bare trees in the park across the street, changing them into eerie specters. Turning, he took Angel in his arms. "Go home to your children. We'll call just as soon as we hear something. Billy must be at his wits end by now."

"You need to go home, Daddy. You're still weak from your anesthesia." George shook his head. "Okay," she sighed. "I'm going to wave at Filly and Jim. I'll be back early in the morning, but call the minute there's any news."

They tried to send Joan and Bill home, but they refused to go, and Beth was glad. She dozed against her mother's shoulder in sheer exhaustion. Bill kept his son distracted as much as possible with farm talk in the empty cafeteria over machine coffee. George tried to ignore the weakness he felt from his own tests as the night drug on endlessly.

As the sun came up, they washed their faces and accepted juices from the helpful nurses. Angel appeared with donuts that no one really wanted, but they ate them anyway.

Around noon, Jim came down the hall in a trot, a smile spread across his handsome face.

"The specialists have determined that it is not encephalitis. It seems to be a virulent form of a virus. We found out that we were doing the right things for her, and now we know what to add to her regimen. And good news! She's awake now; her fever is going down slowly, so things are looking good. Her speech is a little slow, but if there is a little damage from the high fever, we can work with that."

They were jubilant, hugging each other and breathing sighs of relief. Beth stood aside, feeling her face grow cold, and her vision fading away. Jim caught her as she slid silently down the wall, and laid her flat on the tile floor, bending her knees and placing a cushion under her head.

"Beth! Beth!" He patted her face as she groaned and opened her eyes. "You fainted, Beth. Here sit up, slowly now, that's it. Angel has some water here. Drink a little, okay? You're just worn out and stressed out. Why don't you take George home and rest."

Beth nodded, feeling embarrassed. She had never fainted before in her life. "But first, I want to go in and see Dani."

When she was steady on her feet again, Jim took her and George into the room where Dani lay looking confused and pale. They hugged Felicia in relief, and cuddled the sick child in their arms.

"W-when can I-I go -home?" Dani managed a smile as Beth wiped the damp dark curls from her forehead.

"Soon, Sweetheart," Felicia assured her daughter with a happy smile. "Soon."

Chapter Thirty-Eight

George pulled a heavy sweatshirt from the hook and handed it to her. "Take a walk with me."

"It's supposed to start raining any minute," Beth protested.

"It won't take long," he said as he helped her on with the jacket and pulled the hood over her silver-threaded hair.

They walked across the meadow holding hands. It felt so good to Beth to feel his strong fingers entwined with hers, to feel close and connected again and to know there were no cancer cells in the muscular body she loved so well. She smiled up at George as they paused by the cemetery.

"Oh, look. Nell has put an evergreen wreath on the gate. How pretty! Wasn't that nice of her?"

"She didn't do it, I did."

"Really? That was thoughtful of you, George. It looks nice, and we can leave it up all winter . . . or until . . ."

her words drifted away on the chilly breeze that swirled dead leaves in their path.

They walked past the herd, their frosty breath rising in snorts and puffs in the cold air, and around to the upper field, where soon winter wheat would be planted and wave golden in the spring breezes. George led her to the woods where deer tracks were in abundance, up the hill to a bare spot, and set her down on a big mossy boulder.

"This is a beautiful view, isn't it?" he said, waving his hand over the scene unfolded on three sides of their view.

"Before you go any further, George, I want to tell you something. I've been thinking. When there was a chance of the cancer returning and Dani was so sick, I decided that this farm wasn't the important thing. I love it, its true, but it doesn't matter where we live, just as long as our family is together and well. So if you want to sign those papers, I'm behind you all the way."

He laughed, startling a small squirrel that hastily scampered up the tree overhead and peered down at them. "I've been having second thoughts, too. You were right, Beth, we can't leave this place. It's too much a part of us. As for the money, we have all we need and more. We've worked too hard to give up the family home for mere money. There are too many memories here. I've decided to turn down the offer."

"Oh, George!" She threw her arms around him and kissed him so hard that she pushed him backward on the rock.

"Whoa! This isn't the most comfortable place for this. I can think of a number of better ones," he said with a wink as their kisses became more urgent.

She pulled him up and whispered, "Let's go to a warm cozy place."

They walked, hand-in-hand back toward the house, laughing and talking, as they hadn't done in weeks. As they rounded the barn, they saw cars in the driveway and their children scurrying back and forth with boxes and sacks. Going to investigate, they were bombarded with all of their grandchildren as they rounded the corner of the house.

"Hi, Granny and Grandpa." Jamie greeted them both with quick hugs. "It's almost Christmas," he exclaimed with sparkling eyes. Beth smiled at him, puzzled. Christmas was almost four weeks away.

Ellen followed her cousin's example and wrapped her arms around Beth's knees, "It's a 'prize, Granny."

"A surprise? For me?" She bent and picked her up and received a sticky kiss on the side of her mouth.

"What's going on?" George shouted at Billy, who was standing in the back of his truck untying something from the rails.

"Well, we decided we'd have a decorating party," he grinned as he held up the large fir tree. "Hope you didn't have plans for the afternoon."

"Nothing that can't wait," George laughed.

Beth put Ellen down and went inside to find Felicia moving furniture around in the living room under Angelea's directions.

"If we put the sofa there and . . . oh, hi, Mom. Angel and I thought the tree would look good over in this corner. What do you think?"

"The corner is just fine," Beth replied as she pulled off her jacket. "What in the world made you decide to do this?"

Bill answered as he and Joan came in through the kitchen carrying a large wreath.

"We decided that, if this is going to be the last Christmas for this old house, she's going to be dressed up in style. Hello, Beth, darlin,'" He brushed his lips across her forehead.

Beth opened her mouth to reply, then closed it. She would let George address that issue later with them. She was sure there would be sighs of relief all around.

"Mother, that's the most beautiful wreath I've ever seen." She admired the huge silver wreath with gold and red ornaments on it, topped with a huge draping silver bow.

Joan smiled. "I made it myself. Took me a week. Do you really like it? Not too much is it?"

"It's beautiful. Hang it on the front door, right now." Joan beamed at the praise, took the hammer from Bill, and headed for the front door.

Angel dropped a roll of garland by the archway to the kitchen. "Mom, where are our old handmade ornaments that you use every year?"

"They're in the hall closet marked Christmas stuff," Beth said as she started toward the hall.

"No, I'll get them. You just go make us some hot chocolate. And make some cinnamon toast, too.

340

Remember when we were little, and you didn't have any cookies in the house? You'd make cinnamon toast for us to eat with our hot chocolate. Let's do that again."

Beth grinned. "I can do that," she said, throwing her hands up and stepping aside. Elizabeth and Ellen ran by after their new puppy, who didn't seem to want to be part of the celebration.

Dani ran up and grabbed her around the legs. "Granny,—I—m-made—the—s-star," she boasted, proudly holding up her slightly crooked construction paper star and looking up at her grandmother with a blissful expression.

George slipped up behind her and whirled her around. "You are the star, Miss Dani-Pani!" She squealed until he put her down to join her cousins and the puppy.

Beth escaped to the kitchen, overcome with happiness. How blessed she was to have such a wonderful family. All were whole and healthy. Tears of joy spilled from her eyes as she stood at the sink looking out toward the fields. A veil of rain hid all but the arbor and the patio where tubs of frostbitten flowers drooped over the sides. Maybe this winter there would be one or two good snows when the fields and woods would wear their pristine white robes, and they could walk in virgin snow up the hill to the rock to view their world. In no time it would be spring and the yard would be graced with grandchildren, toys and games strewn over the green grass. Would their children, and the children after them play in this yard, these fields, these woods? She wanted to think so.

The rain was to change into snow flurries later on in the evening, according to the weather report from Granny's old radio on the kitchen counter. "But it's cozy and warm here in our house," she murmured with her eyes closed. "Thank you, God." Then she turned to her assigned task with cocoa and cinnamon, and soon the aroma, blending with the noise and laughter of the children, rose like incense throughout the old Victorian farmhouse, aglow with gilt and glitter in the deepening twilight.

To order additional copies of

The People
of the Land

Have your credit card ready and call:

1-877-421-READ (7323)

or please visit our web site at
www.pleasantword.com

Also available at:
www.amazon.com
and
www.barnesandnoble.com.

20 pages=_____ / 7 _____points

30 pages=_____ / / _____points

Printed in the United States
63139LVS00002B/150